GYPSY WOMAN

Get Lost
in your
journey!

GYPSY WOMAN

LORENZO ALEXANDER CHAMBERS

ISBN: 9781697138214

I tell this tale
Not so much to tell my tale
But to tell the tale that is
The tale of all of us.

In loving memory of my brother Jamal.

INNOCENCE LOST

Gypsy woman told my mama
Before I was born
Gotta man child comin'
That boy gonna be a son of a gun

He gon' make pretty women
Scream and shout
What's it all about

Bitches
Fuck 'em and suck 'em
Rape 'em and kill 'em

Bitches

———

We weren't always a bunch of drunk teenage boys taking liberty with Muddy Waters classic *I'm Your Hoochie Coochie Man*—Bosida, Khahari, Darwin, Adisa, and me, Maximus—standing in Ryerson Park on Ryerson Avenue in Clinton Hill, Brooklyn, drinking forty-ounce bottles of Olde English, and singing misogynistic songs about women. But growing up and seeing the things we did at the ages we saw them—well, that can be enough to drive you insane.

I remember meeting Bosida, a.k.a. Bosi, when I was all of seven years old. Where I'm from, if you did not have a nickname, it meant that you had not distinguished yourself among your peers. Khahari was known as Kabo, named after the pimp from one of the seventies' blaxploitation flicks. Darwin was D-Knowledge, named because he had a brain like Dustin Hoffman in *Rain Man*. His dad, of all people, gave him that name. Hell, Darwin was one of the few of us whose dad lived in his home as part of an intact traditional nuclear family. Adisa was A-Mac, a combination of his first and last names. I, Maximus, was Box—the boy known as Black Bart named me that because he said my face was shaped like a box. Where I'm from, whatever your nickname was, you embraced it and made it hot.

We were among the first families to move into 369 Grand Avenue—or 369, as we called it. 369 was one of three buildings in my complex known as Grand Towers, built under the Mitchell-Lama Housing Program that provided affordable rentals and cooperative housing to moderate- and middle-income families. The program was sponsored by New York state senator MacNeil Mitchell and assemblyman Alfred Lama and was signed into law in 1955. Everyone we knew in the Grand Towers had city jobs. My mom was a teacher. Bosida's dad worked for the post office. Darwin's dad was a fireman. In the jungle of the ghetto in which we all lived, this is what made us better than the residents of the Academy Gardens Apartments across the street from us, separated by Clauson Avenue and guarded by the Eighty-Eighth Precinct. Some of their residents were welfare recipients, and our buildings had balconies. Their apartments did not.

Bosida was my first friend in the building. He lived on the fifth floor, and I lived on the nineteenth. His grandmother would babysit us and yell at us to stop making a ruckus as we played tackle football in the living room on our knees or basketball with a sock for a ball and a bent hanger creased in the seam of a doorway as the rim.

By the time we started singing "Gypsy Woman" as part of our drunken ritual as the last act of the night before we went home, all of us had had "manhood moments" while we were yet still boys. By fifteen, Bosida was six feet, two inches tall and a strapping 185 pounds of lean, rangy muscle. He was there when Midnight Mark was stabbed to death over a girl. He held Midnight Mark in his arms as he bled out from the knife wound. That experience will fuck a teenage boy up for life. Add humiliating girl troubles, and it is hard, if not damn near impossible, to recover.

BOSIDA

In my early twenties, I formed a flag football team, and all the guys from the neighborhood played on the Tribe. It was my way of getting us together on Sundays in the fall just to be together with our families and, of course, our ladies. I remember Bosida and I driving to a game.

"Yo, Box, my lady is coming to the game today," Bosida announced.

"My man, I did not even know you had a lady," I responded, startled. "When did this happen?"

"Just a few weeks ago. I met her at Cooker's, and we've been cool since."

"Looking forward to meeting her," I said cautiously.

"Check it out," Bosida offered.

Since we had dressed for the games before we left home, Bosida had on his wristbands, ready to play outside linebacker. Under his right wristband was tucked a picture of his first and only honey that I knew about, Lola. Bosida played that day in front of Lola like a madman—he was free in the moment, raging sideline to sideline, either making every play, or he was in on every play. And we won the game.

Bosida introduced me to Lola after the game. Born in Puerto Rico and raised in Brooklyn, Lola was older than us by a couple of years. She had miles on her, as we would say, taller than average, solid build with tits, ass, and a raspy smoker's voice. She was friendly—a bit too friendly for my taste and based on the expectations of the bro code. She hugged Bosida's friends a little too close, a little too long, and a little too tight, and all of us peeped it.

As usual after a game, twenty-something of us crammed into someone's one-bedroom apartment, ordered pizza and beers, and watched the game film after. As the night crept on, and the drink flow grew heavy, Lola became more boisterous with disrespectful taunts of Bosida's sexual prowess or lack thereof.

"He's okay, you know." She could be heard in drunken whispers to the girls who huddled around her.

I did not even know how the topic was broached. Probably by someone else's girl asking, "So how did y'all meet?" and "We did not know Bosi had a girlfriend" and "So, girl, how is it…you know, 'it.'"

For all within earshot, Lola blurted out, "He doesn't want to do as much as I do 'cause I'm horny all the time."

Crickets. As everyone looked at each other with the "Did you hear what I think I just heard?" face; the proverbial pregnant pause, which was all of three seconds tops, was broken only by someone shouting, "Drinks all around!"

Imagine Bosida's face as his newly introduced girlfriend regaled his friends with tales of his low testosterone and her nymphomaniac horny nature.

That was my trigger to leave. I was not going to stand around and listen to my first friend in the world get trashed.

"I'm out!" I announced as I gave everyone the obligatory pound and hug, and my girl gave everyone a hug and a kiss on the cheek. Bosida was the last person I saw that night. We made the knowing eye contact that from me said, "What the fuck?" and from him said, "I know, but I really like her." I did not address Lola before I left.

The next day was a Monday, and as was customary, we met at 200 Fifth Avenue Sports Bar to watch *Monday Night Football*. This was traditionally a guys' night, and that was important on this night because the previous night's ending, which I was not present to experience, had turned out to be a night for the ages. When I walked into the bar, Khahari was already there.

"My man!" began Khahari; the excitement in his voice could only mean that he wanted my undivided attention. "After you left, things got crazy at Cheeba Mo's crib."

"What happened?" I asked.

"So Bosi and Lola ended up getting into it 'cause that chick is psycho," he said.

"Good for Bosi," I cheered.

"Nah," Khahari chimed. "Not good at all."

I braced for impact.

"Bosi ended up leaving that chick behind. By night's end, it was an all-out feeding frenzy. Lola and a couple of heads went into the back room and shut the door. I left when the moans turned into screams. Next thing I knew, D-Knowledge is calling me to say that he heard that chick was so drunk, and cats were tired of hearing her dog Bosi that they ran a train on her—back door and the whole nine."

That was how cats got down where I'm from. (For those of you not familiar with the hip talk of jazz musicians from the 60's, "cats" is what they called cool people who rocked with the culture. Hence, cats). Straight raw dogs. Savages with a savage sense of honor among thieves. But you had better never let us hear you call us savages. And not because anyone else could either. But because we had no sense of being savages. There was no relative context to some of our actions. It was what we knew. At least for some of us.

"Damn!" I blurted out, stunned. "Does Bosi know?"

Just then, Bosida sauntered in with Adisa and Darwin.

"I don't think so," Khahari almost whispered.

The topic of conversation ended abruptly.

I did not learn if Bosida ever knew. I only knew that I was not going to be the one to tell him. I do not suppose anyone did, though I do suspect that he had some sense that something dramatic and tragic happened to Lola.

Bosida and Lola dated a few more months as she progressed with episodes of being blackout drunk at every social function they attended. She ended the relationship after one night ended with her being woken up in a cab by a police officer who had been notified by the driver after he could not wake her up to pay her fare. She blamed Bosida. It was an easy out for him. I imagine he was relieved.

That was Bosida's luck of the draw with women his entire life. Starting from thirteen on, Bosida was never known to have a girlfriend other than Lola. As a grown man, he was known to go to the Dominican Republic—or DR, as we called it—every now and then to pick up underage prostitutes.

KHAHARI

Khahari came to 369 because of his grandmother, who lived on the third floor. He was all of twelve years old, short and stocky for his age. All of us were dark-skinned black boys, but Khahari was among three of us who were dark-chocolate black. Handsome in the face, he had a slight chromosome deficiency in his appearance. It was only as adults in our midforties that we learned Khahari came to live with his grandmother because his mom was addicted to heroin. She was committed to the drug as evidenced by her having heroin parties in their apartment in the Pink House Projects and having sex with men while Khahari was propped in front of the television, expected to act as if he did not know what was happening as she periodically disappeared into the bedroom with random men.

Khahari never met his dad, but when he came to live with his grandmother, Khahari had the benefit of living with his grandfather as well. Though Pop-Pop was hardly around, he was still a male role model, which most of us never had.

I think Khahari resented women because of his relationship with his mom.

"Box," he would say to me, "she was never there for me. Bringing dudes in the crib and fucking them like I didn't know."

I could only sit and listen.

"She never did shit for me and never gave me anything. Never been to any of my baseball games."

What was I supposed to say?

"I can never forgive her, Box."

And so when he talked about fucking bitches, I understood that maybe he was trying to say "fuck you" to his mother. Sometimes that attitude falls outside the lines of the bro code.

I remember when Khahari hunted down Nicoli's girl. Nicoli also lived on the third floor, and he and Khahari grew close because at the end of any night of debauchery, the two of them were the last to see each other because they got off the elevator on the same floor.

Nicoli was all of four feet, nine inches and very characteristically associated with short man's syndrome. To add to that, he was one of the few light-skinned dudes who hung out with us. The recipe did not make a tasteful cake.

In our day, the dark-skinned "field-nigger" type ruled as the alpha male. To compensate for his height, Nicoli became an accurate thrower of rocks, meaning that if he did not like you, or if you got into a physical altercation with him, you probably would become the recipient of rock projectiles hurled at you from a distance that meant you could not grab, let alone touch, Nicoli.

Nicoli dated V, a fine-ass dark-skinned princess from the private houses in the neighborhood. While we grew up in cooperative housing in the Clinton Hill section of Brooklyn, which was better than the projects of Academy Gardens, the row houses a few blocks up on Washington Avenue were next level. V was from that part of town, and Nicoli got respect for dating the girl from the next level.

The relationship did not last long, and before I could finish a forty-ounce bottle of Olde English, Khahari was dating her.

"My man," I asked Khahari, "when did this happen?"

"It just happened, man," Khahari answered in his nonchalant manner.

"Shit doesn't just happen, bro," I retorted. "What did you do?"

"Nothing."

"Really?" I asked rhetorically. "Last I heard, she was with Nicoli."

"Me too," Khahari deadpanned.

"So you just took Nicoli's woman?"

"Nah, yo," Khahari defended himself. "I went to Nicoli and was like, 'Yo, I see you and V are in a chill space, and me and her have been kicking it, and I want to date her.'"

"And he said?"

"He said yes," Khahari answered.

"What else was he supposed to say?" I offered. "Did you fuck her?"

There was an awkward silence that screamed, "Yes!"

"Yes," Khahari finally confessed.

Then came the deadly stare I gave to say, "Wow, that's fucked up."

"But Nicoli never hit it, so she was not really his girl," Khahari stammered.

After pausing for thought, mentally reviewing the bro code, I finally concluded, "True dat."

Technically, he was right. No sex meant that she was not really your girl. But still, it was violation. With all the girls in the neighborhood, why did he have to fuck with her?

It was validation for Khahari to be able to say, "Despite my mom being fucked up, I am worthy of any woman I pursue," especially when it came to a next-level chick.

Where I'm from, we hunted as predators mainly for the conquest. And when our natural human instincts for love allowed us to pursue healthy relationships, we were met with failure that called us back to our default predator position.

DARWIN

Darwin was probably the most well-adjusted of us all—well adjusted being relative. Darwin was a first-generation Haitian-American born in Brooklyn. His parents met and married in Haiti before immigrating to New York in the late fifties. Darwin was nicknamed D-Knowledge because of his trap-like memory regarding all sports trivia. I do not mean just the traditional sports such as baseball, basketball, and football. Darwin also knew trivia for soccer, boxing—you name it.

We were sitting around Ryerson Park one summer night, passing around a few quarts of Ballantine Ale.

"D-Knowledge," Khahari introduced a conversation.

"What up, Kabo?" deadpanned Darwin. His monotone voice betrayed his standing heart rate, which never rose above that of a sleeping person, it seemed. It was hard to tell what got Darwin excited.

"I was watching the Ali fight the other day, and I thought of the iconic picture of him and some of the other black athletes of his day and how they stuck together. That shit doesn't happen anymore."

"Yeah, that was the Ali summit meeting," Darwin began. "When he was protesting his draft into the army."

"That was in the late seventies, right?" Khahari asked.

"Nah, it was 1967 in Cleveland," Darwin stated in a matter-of-fact way.

"Why'd they do it in Cleveland?" Adisa asked.

"I think because Jim Brown wanted to ask Ali why he was not willing to be drafted. And they all came to Cleveland because Jim Brown was the man."

"Yeah," interrupted Khahari. "Bill Russell was there too."

"I bet ain't nobody else showed up," Adisa guessed.

"Nah, all the heavy hitters were there, including Kareem, who was Lew Alcindor back then," Darwin offered. "Willie Davis from the Green Bay Packers was there too."

"How do you even know that?" I asked.

"I just—" began Darwin.

"Better yet," I interrupted, "*why* do you know that?"

"I just do," Darwin continued.

Unfortunately for Darwin, being intelligent and coming from a traditional family did not spare anyone from the heartaches and despair that we all suffered.

At face value, his parents were model spouses and parents. Darwin went to church with his parents every Sunday, followed by Sunday family dinner. I can remember many times when Darwin could not hang out due to family obligations.

But on Friday and Saturday nights, when we were coming in from a late night of drinking and carousing, we were often met at the front door of the building by his pops who was obviously inebriated.

As we tried to make ourselves invisible in plain sight, Darwin's dad would greet us with a hearty "Well, good night, young men!" He said it with exuberance as if he was greeting us to start the day versus ending it.

"Good evening, Mr. Barrington," we responded in chorus.

Oftentimes Darwin was with us as we were coming in! On those occasions, it was hilarious to see and hear Darwin, in his drunken stupor, greet his equally drunk dad. His dad was always excited to see him.

"Darwin Barrington!" he would shout in a heavy Haitian patois, obviously inebriated but never slurring. He was a happy drunk.

In the early years, Darwin's typical response was subdued.

"Hey, Pops," he'd answer in a solemn tone. His dad would wrap his arms around him in a genuine gesture of love.

As he got older, Darwin learned to appreciate his father in these moments, and he began to return the embrace. Sometimes he would initiate it.

"Pops!" he would begin with enthusiasm when he saw his dad first.

His dad would raise his head from his concentrated stare at the ground in an effort to put one foot in front of the other through the alcohol-induced haze.

"Darwin, my son," he would call out.

The two would stumble toward each other and fall into the other's arms. It was a beautiful sight to experience. The rest of us were envious of Darwin being able to share such a moment with his father.

Early on, out of earshot of Mr. Barrington, we asked Darwin, "Where is your pops coming from?"

"Where do you think he's coming from?" Darwin asked rhetorically.

Based on his response, we assumed that Mr. Barrington had a mistress, like all of our fathers. We never asked again.

Darwin ended up marrying his second girlfriend in his life and having two children, a boy and a girl. They moved into his wife's childhood home that was willed to her upon her parents' deaths. Out of all of us, Darwin and his wife have remained married to this day, though Darwin has the same proclivities as his father.

ADISA

Older than the rest of us by three years, Adisa was the youngest of five brothers. His oldest brother died trying to save a girl from being raped while away at college in Tuskegee, Alabama. Like all the men in his family, Adisa was gangly. And like all of them, he grew to be over six feet.

What was different about Adisa was that unlike the typical youngest sibling, Adisa was the family protector. I remember one time that this became evident at Ryerson Park, the neighborhood park where everyone went to play ball and show off for the girls.

Saucy Sam—named because he was drunk, or "sauced," most of the time—was Adisa's brother who was closest in age to him. Saucy kept fouling Big Merk from Academy Gardens. Saucy was not fouling him on purpose. It was just that Saucy was no match for Big Merk, and everyone knew it. On top of that, Big Merk kept clowning around him throughout the whole game.

"You can't guard me, sucker," Big Merk taunted him. "And if you keep fouling me, I'm going to fuck you up."

As Saucy's sense of self shrunk with every basket Big Merk made, his last retort was, "It is not like I'm trying to foul you on purpose. But you acting like nobody can touch you."

"Foul me one more time, and see what happens," threatened Big Merk.

The last foul came, and Big Merk commenced to whuppin' that ass. The first punch bounced Saucy off the chain-link fence.

"Yo, man," Saucy chirped. "Why you doing that?"

Another punch sent Saucy reeling on his heels, stumbling backward as he tried in vain to avoid the punches raining down on him.

"I told you," Big Merk hurled at Saucy with the same venom he hurled punches between each word, "not to foul me anymore."

The last punch to the mouth caused blood to spurt across the court.

Somehow word got to Adisa, who was not at the park that day. Nonetheless he made a grand entrance with pace and purpose. He spotted Big Merk, who stood up to meet the challenge. In what we called a fair one, Adisa did enough damage that sent a message to all in the park that day that said, "Do not fuck with the MacArthur brothers." He had earned the respect of the hood.

Contrary to his luck as a protector, his luck with the ladies was as unlucky as his mother's luck was with his father.

Mr. MacArthur was one of the playboys of the building. It was not as if most adults did not know it, but no one said anything about it. He was hiding in plain sight. It was not until we were young men in our early twenties that I learned that Mr. MacArthur used to date the mother of the girlfriend of one of our other friends.

That friend is the one who told us about it, saying, "Check it. I would be at my lady's crib, chillin' on the couch in the living room, watching the Knicks. The doorbell rings. My girl's mom rushes to the door like she knows who it is, and guess who strolls in?"

We all were looking at him with blank stares because we had no clue as to what he was about to say. We did not bother with a guess.

"Mr. MacArthur walks up in the spot," dude announced, "like he's a regular. He gave me the head nod like 'What up?' and sat next to me on the couch as my girl's mom handed him a beer. So I'm chillin' with Mr. MacArthur, watching the game."

We turned to Adisa as if to say, "Is that true?"

"True story," is all he could muster.

I had no idea how to react to that. Then Adisa told his own Mr. MacArthur story.

Mr. and Mrs. MacArthur were an old-school couple from the old-school South who came to Brooklyn during the great migration north during the late forties and fifties. Many married black couples in that time married more for practicality than for love. It was easier for two to make it out of the South than for one, especially when both had jobs.

Mr. MacArthur spit his boys out, as they would say in the South. His tall, lanky DNA was imprinted on all five of his sons. He worked for the city as a bus driver.

Mrs. MacArthur was a petite woman who found work as a social worker.

During the sixties and seventies, black households were either matriarchal or patriarchal. There was rarely a balance. Mr. MacArthur was definitely in charge of his household.

"I remember the time Mr. and Mrs. Dunston from the twentieth floor knocked on our door," Adisa began. "My mom opened it. She asked if everything was all right. Mr. Dunston asked, 'Is your husband home?' My mom said yes, and Mr. Dunston said he needed a word with him."

At this point, Adisa had our undivided attention. Captivated, we kept our mouths shut, and our eyes were wide, locked on his face.

"My mom offered for him to come in. She yelled to the back for my pops to come to the living room. She invited the Dunstons to sit as they could hear my pops almost stomping down the hall. 'What is it?' he said before he saw them sitting in his living room. He and Mrs. Dunston looked at each other, but my pops plays it off like he do not know her like that. 'Hey, Al,' my pops said to Mr. Dunston. 'Bobby,' returned Mr. Dunston sternly. Now everyone was sitting. My pops was lounging in his La-Z-Boy chair without a care in the world."

"Where are y'all?" Khahari interrupted, referring to Adisa and his brothers.

We all looked at him with the stare that said, "Shut the fuck up, and let A-Mac tell the story."

Khahari looked at us with the "What, I can't ask a question?" face.

"We were around the corner at the beginning of the hallway where they couldn't see us," Adisa answered. "So Mr. Dunston says to my pops, 'So, Bobby, I've suspected that you and Myrna have been seeing each other, and when I asked her, she said yes.' At a closer glance, Mrs. Dunston was quivering ever so slightly, and the left side of her face under her left eye had a slowly rising welt. My mother looked at my pops. He did not look at her. Instead, he looked dead at Mrs. Dunston and said, 'Myrna, have I been seeing you?' With her eyes lowered to the floor, she said…" Adisa paused and looked each one of us in the eyes, then said, "'No.' Then my pops said to Mr. Dunston,

'Al, I think you and Myrna need to have a conversation.' With that, my pops pushed himself out of his La-Z-Boy and sauntered back to his bedroom."

"Damn," Khahari broke the brief silence that followed. "That's some pimp shit."

I could tell by the expression on Adisa's face that he was thinking about how his mom had felt in that moment.

Adisa did not fare any better in his own relationships than his mom did in hers. As the youngest of five, he was a mama's boy, and if Mama was hurt, so was he.

MAXIMUS ALEXANDER TALISMAN

Within the Talisman clan, there were whispers of traces of fortune-tellers among us. The story went that the midwife who delivered me in the bathtub of our house was my mother's great-aunt who had delivered all of the Talisman children in her generation, just as her mom and grandmothers and those who came before them had done in their times. When it was my mother's time to give birth, Aunt Divine, the family midwife, told her the tale.

"Talisman," she began in a silky-smooth voice that echoed with ancient voices passing through her. "Our family name." She spoke in halting and haunting stops and starts.

She placed both hands on my mother's stomach before hovering them just inches from her belly as she stood over her niece. Aunt Divine was anywhere between 85 and 105. It was hard to tell. Her full head of gray flowing locks contrasted her dark skin, which had few wrinkles. At five feet, ten inches tall, Aunt Divine was statuesque with a dancer's physique. She only drank water and herbal tea, and she juiced fresh vegetables and fruit daily.

"My child," she continued. "In ancient times, our family name was derived from our roots as the keepers of the objects that have magic powers of good fortune. Since that time, we have evolved to represent that power within our very being. Now, we embody power and good fortune and are built to inspire the world with our remarkable abilities to influence human feelings and actions."

Aunt Divine paused and inhaled a deep yoga breath before continuing.

"The boy-child that you carry is very powerful. He will be a leader of men, but you must be careful how you raise him—from his environment to the people he comes in contact with. The power he possesses must be nurtured for good, for if not, he can easily be led to use his gifts for selfish reasons that will not benefit people. This child is a sensitive being. If he is wounded deeply, he will wound others."

With that, I was born on September 30, 1963, at 3:45 p.m. Fifteen years later, I would be singing "Gypsy Woman."

—

My father named me Maximus Alexander because as a world-traveling jazz musician, he'd fallen in love with all things Italian. At least once a year he'd fly to Milan and spend a month touring with a rogue band of musicians he'd assembled. They would go from Milan to Torino, Trieste, Parma, Venice, Rome and Naples, then back to Milan for the return flight home. There were rumors within the family that I had an Italian sister out there somewhere, a rumor that was probably the bane of his existence once my mom got wind of it.

He gave me two of the strongest Italian names: *Maximus* means "the greatest," and *Alexander* means "the defender of men." No pressure there.

—

My Mother, Ava Mae Crown was born in 1935 in Asheville, North Carolina, to her hairdresser mother, Irma Louise Crown who also birthed a son named Jeb. Irma had been overweight all her life and died a premature death due to kidney failure. My mom never knew her real dad and only knew that he was probably one of two men that Irma had dated. One man was from the country and owned a farm, and the other was from the town and worked as the book-keeper at the local high school. Irma named the townsman to be my mom's dad, but she often took my mom to visit the country farmer on weekends.

On one such visit, my mother fell off a barbwire fence and cut her brow down to the white meat. Ordinarily, a gash like that would require stitches, but my grandma told the doctor to "just patch it up."

"Now when you git home," Irma instructed my mom, "your dad won't be home yet. When he does git home, tell him that you were horsing 'round in the house and banged your head on the kitchen table."

When my mom told me that story as we made our way on a fourteen-hour drive to my aunt LouAnn's funeral, she spoke of it in two tones. One was very matter-of-fact—that was just the way it was. The second was a tone of comfort and privilege. She seemed to enjoy having two dads and the secrets that went along with that.

My dad was born in Laurinburg, North Carolina, before moving to Philadelphia, Pennsylvania, with his parents and seven siblings. My father, Robert Alexander, was the oldest among his siblings. He grew to be six feet three and 230 pounds. I've been told that he was a better-than-average football player. He played running back and had a punishing style, running with high knees. This was before he turned his attention to music.

I was told two defining stories about my dad. One, he was so determined about his musical studies, primarily the piano, that he trekked through a winter blizzard to his weekly piano lesson once. He was the only person to be seen on the streets that day. His piano instructor almost did not open the door for him because he couldn't believe that anyone would dare attempt to walk through such a winter storm.

The second story was of Robert the protector. His youngest brother, Albert, came home from school one day. Instead of his usual gregarious self who always came home and spoke to everyone in the house as was the custom, Albert made a beeline to his bedroom that he shared with Frank, the second-oldest sibling.

"What happened?" my dad demanded to know.

"What?" Albert feigned ignorance.

"Do not play with me," my dad responded. "Your ass usually comes in all cheery, and today you can barely speak."

"Nothing," Albert answered.

"I'm not going to ask you again," my dad threatened.

"These boys at school keep calling me *faggot*."

"Well, you are," my dad steamed. "But that doesn't give them the right to tease you."

The next day, my dad went up to the school and beat up three guys at the same time, but not before receiving a switchblade slice that would run the length of his forearm and scar him for life. And though my dad would call my uncle Albert a faggot on several occasions during family gatherings late in the evening when the weed and drinks were flowing, no one else in the family or out of it could call Uncle Albert a faggot.

—

My mom and dad were divorced by the time I was nine years old. Ava and Robert met in New York City at a jazz club. My dad was gigging, and my mom and her girlfriends were out on the town. She was a music teacher in elementary school, and he was a struggling musician in pursuit of the dream. He never achieved the status of full-time musician able to provide for his family. His attention to family eventually waned.

I distinctly remember one incident between my parents that probably defined their relationship. It was a Sunday evening around dinnertime in the Talisman household. The table was set, and as my mom and I sat down to eat sans my father, the front door shook with the rattling of keys. My dad was coming home for the first time since getting paid Friday. This was fast becoming a payday ritual.

"The prodigal father has returned," my mother announced.

"Woman," my father growled. "Do not start with me."

"Maximus." She turned to me. "Go to your room, please."

I'd heard that command before and moved without retort. This time I did not retreat all the way to my room. Rather, I was out of sight but within earshot. I could see them from around the corner wall that led to the bedrooms, but they could not see me.

"What makes you think that you can get paid on a Friday and not come home till Sunday?" my ma demanded to know.

"Because I can, damn it," my father bellowed back. "And do not ask me no more damn questions about where I be and when I get home."

"Then I guess you won't be living here," my ma snapped back.

Bam! My dad gave a straight right jab to my mother's left eye, staggering her to a near fall before the nearest wall caught her. Blood squirted, painting a dab that sharply contrasted with the lime-green wall paint. The gash required six stitches to close the wound.

I swore that day that when I got big enough, I was going to fuck him up.

He was gone the next day. Soon afterward, within the year, my mother started dating. From the time I was nine years old until I was thirteen, my mother dated four different men. To accommodate her newfound freedom, I began spending many weekends a year at Aunt LouAnn's and Aunt Beulah's homes.

My ten years with my mom without a man in the house were challenging, to say the least. My mom took on an extra job and went to school at night. She was a teacher's assistant during the day and worked on her master's degree at night to become an English teacher. On weekends, she cleaned the homes of Jewish families who lived in Section Eight Public Housing in the Williamsburg section of Brooklyn. Money was tight, and I was becoming a teenager who wanted to impress girls.

At fourteen, I applied for my working papers, and like all of my boys, I filled out applications for summer jobs. When it came to signing the papers, my mom refused to sign because she could not lie about the income requirement threshold, which she was above.

"But, Ma," I complained. "Bosida's, Adisa's, and everyone's moms have signed the papers, and they make too much money too."

All my mother would say is, "I'm not their mother."

"Fret not" is the saying that the old-timers would say when something did not go their way. I can hear my grandma saying, "When one door closes, another door opens."

No sooner had I left the apartment, dejected from my mother denying me a chance to earn some money, than I bumped into Adisa's mom in the lobby of our building. She was coming upstairs from grocery shopping.

"Hey, Mrs. McArthur," I called out to her. "Let me help you with some of those bags."

"Thank you so much, Maximus," she returned with gratitude in her voice.

On the elevator ride up to the sixteenth floor, Mrs. McArthur noticed my solemn mood.

"You okay, Maximus?" she asked.

"Yeah, I guess. My mom won't sign the summer youth application because she makes too much."

"That's just the way your mom is, Maximus. She means well."

"I know, but that means I can't work this summer."

"Not necessarily. I heard that Assemblyman Vann has a summer work program that doesn't require working papers, and it pays more than the city's summer program."

And just like that, I was working at fourteen years old and earning more than all of my boys. If there was one thing we all learned from the necessity to earn one's way, it was a strong work ethic.

—

With no one to teach us how to be men, the homies and I raised ourselves, abiding by a code of manhood derived from our imaginations and from the men in our neighborhood whom we thought were cool. My idea of manhood was not my mother's.

"You are just like your father!" she would say.

Without having earned any privileges, at seventeen I wanted to come and go as I pleased.

"If you do not want to follow my rules," my ma would rant. "You can get out!"

What was a teenage boy to do when confronted with such an ultimatum? I left without a clue where I would stay. I did not ask anyone from the building because I did not want anyone to know what had happened. I remembered a friend from the Bronx who was a teammate of mine from little league football. He was a few years older than me and had his own place.

I rode the six train for over an hour and a half before it let me off near Yankee Stadium. Rising out of the train station, the smell of the Bronx greeted me first. Fried tostones, plantains, and roasted pork wafted on the wind's wings. The music of salsa and merengue dancing met my ears, and the air was alive. The Bronx was different from Brooklyn in that the immigrant populations were different. Brooklyn was about African-Caribbeans who liked jerk chicken and oxtails as well as reggae, soca, and calypso music, while the Bronx was full of Latino-Caribbean people who liked rice and beans versus peas and rice, and they liked the music from places such as the Dominican Republic. In the end, I felt comfortable in both places because we were all brown people, and we were all economically oppressed.

Fernando stood over six feet tall with the slim build of a basketball player but with the muscularity of a wide receiver. He was just as black as me, but he spoke Spanish.

"Where are you from?" I had asked him when I'd first met him. Hardly anyone on the team had spoken to him—not because they did not like him, but because they could not readily categorize him into a convenient racial or cultural box.

"My family is from Cuba," he'd replied.

Early on in my life I had realized the myth of what black and Latino people were supposed to look like was untrue.

Fernando had proven to be a team player committed to winning, and he had always been reliable.

"Hola, *hermano*," Fernando greeted me at the entrance to his apartment door building.

"Bro!" I exclaimed. "Good to see you."

I followed him as we walked past the one elevator door.

"We're gonna have to hoof it, bro," he announced. "The elevator is broken again, as usual."

"No worries," I responded too quickly as we ended up walking up four flights of stairs.

When we entered the apartment, it took a minute for my eyes to adjust to the darkness. Fernando disappeared into the dark for a minute, as he had to cross the room to turn on the light. Clothes were thrown about the living room, plates and cups littered the dining room table, and the kitchen sink was full of dirty dishes.

"You want something to drink?" he offered as he opened the refrigerator door. "I have beer and water."

"I'll take a beer," I decided as I caught a glimpse of roaches skittering around the kitchen wall.

"You want a glass?" he asked.

"No," I quickly answered.

"So your mom kicked you out, huh?"

"Pretty much," I answered.

"Happens to the best of us. You can crash here for as long as you need to."

"Thanks," I responded. "I appreciate it," I continued sincerely.

In my mind, I was hoping that it wouldn't be long because the filth made my skin crawl.

"This is a one-bedroom crib," Fernando stated. "So the couch is yours, or you're welcome to the bedroom."

I did not quite know how to take that, so I said, "I'm good on the couch."

After three days, the walls were closing in. We did not do much of anything all day except watch television, eat pizza, and drink beer. Later that night I called Adisa to check on what was happening in the neighborhood.

"Yo," Adisa began. "Your moms is looking for you."

"For real?" I asked excitedly.

"Yeah. Where you at?"

"The Bronx."

"Oh, shit."

"Yeah. Tell me about it," I deadpanned.

"My mom said your moms was crying to her about you."

That news made my day because I was missing home and couldn't wait to get back. I went to sleep that night comforted in knowing that I was going home.

Somewhere between REM sleep and just being groggy, I recall Fernando coming to me in the middle of the night. He pulled the covers back and seemed to try to pull me up.

"Come in the bedroom," he coaxed.

I did not move, and I guess the deadweight of my sleeping body was too much for him to move. It seemed he was gone the next moment because when I did wake in the middle of the night to use the bathroom, I didn't know if that memory was real or a dream. No matter—I was out at daybreak without a goodbye.

As soon as I reached home and my mom heard the sound of my keys in the lock, she rushed to the door to open it before I could finish unlocking it. I did not have the chance to set my bag down before she embraced me as never before. It was tight and close like you would hug a long-lost loved one you had not seen for years. It felt warm, like love.

Over the years, long into the adulthood of my midthirties, my mom and I would engage in difficult conversations. I would go on to tell her that I had felt abandoned because she had taken better care of her boyfriends than me.

"Well," she'd begin. "I did not know any better 'cause that's how I was brought up," she'd defend herself.

She would go on to tell me how straight after college, her mom had passed away, and not knowing who her real dad was, she was left on her own.

"I had to make my own way. I went to school and worked. I shared an apartment with an old college friend in DC before moving north to New York to stay with your aunt Beulah. There was no one to rely on, so I saved my money and made my way," she'd say.

"But, Ma," I'd counter. "Wouldn't you want to treat your son the way you wish you had been treated?"

Until that conversation, the thought had never crossed her mind.

AUNT LOUANN AND UNCLE JEB

Aunt LouAnn was married to my uncle Jeb, who was my mother's oldest brother. Uncle Jeb was a big man with big forearms. He was what we called country strong. He managed a gas station, which covered for his number-running operation. He always smelled like gas when he came home, and his hands were black with soot and oil. But his pockets were always filled with coins.

Whenever I was at their apartment and Uncle Jeb came home, all of us would run to him because he gave out coins like candy. Whether I was first to get to him or not, he always let me be the first boy to get loose change, after his daughters.

"Move aside," he'd order his sons. "Let Max come through." Then he'd direct me, "Go ahead and grab as much as your hand can hold."

I'd dig deep into his pockets and grab as much as I could. Though I could tell that three of his five sons were jealous of me, the truth was that there was enough coins for all of us.

Aunt LouAnn was a saint. Like so many women, she sacrificed her ambition and body to bear her man eight children. She never recovered, and she accepted her plot in life with grace and dignity.

Aunt LouAnn and Uncle Jeb lived in a three-bedroom apartment in the Bedford-Stuyvesant section of Brooklyn—Bed-Stuy to those who lived there and to any black person from Brooklyn. Their home was where I spent summer vacations. I do not remember ever sleeping in the same bed two nights in a row at Aunt LouAnn's, and I never slept alone. You lay down to sleep wherever you could, depending on when you went to sleep relative to everyone else in the house save for Aunt LouAnn and Uncle Jeb because they had their own room. And that did not guarantee that you would stay where you were because the older cousins, depending on how they felt any given night, could kick you out of your spot.

I was young when I realized the inequity between my life and my cousins' lives at Aunt LouAnn's apartment. I grew up a single child in a two-bedroom apartment with my mom. I had my own room and my own toys. Since my pops was a bit of a "rolling stone", it turned out that I had other siblings by different mothers who I would come to know later in life. Conversely, my eight cousins shared everything and fought over most things, including when to take a shit.

The one thing that there was never a fight about was Aunt LouAnn's Pepsi. Amazingly, in a household of eight children and two adults, not to count the additional four to five people who could be there on any given day or night, there were times when the refrigerator would be bare save for a lone sixteen-ounce bottle of Pepsi in the freezer. No matter how hungry or thirsty you were, everyone knew not to mess with Aunt LouAnn's soda.

One night over the phone, my cousin Tank and his brother Wanky and I got into an argument. Tank and I were the same age, ten, and Wanky was a couple years older.

"You comin' over this weekend?" Tank asked.

"Nah," I answered. "I'm just going to stay home this weekend."

"Why?" interjected Wanky. "Do you not want to come and get some of Daddy's change when he gets home?"

"No. I just don't feel like it."

"Why?" Tank tag teamed me. "You think you're better than everybody else just 'cause your mom got a city job?"

"No," I defended myself. "Sometimes I do not feel like having to fight to find some place to sleep."

"See," Wanky responded. "I told you, Tank; he think he better than us. Fuck you, Max!"

"Fuck you, Wanky!" I shouted into the phone.

"You think you're better than us 'cause your mom is always trying to tell people what to do," Tank yelled back. "That's why nobody likes your ma. 'Cause she's a ho!"

"Fuck you, Tank," I replied angrily. "That's why your pops is always running the streets, fuckin' bitches while your mom stays home doin' nothing in your stinkin' roach-infested house."

The phone line went silent on both ends. Then…

"Wait till I see you," threatened Wanky.

I hung up the phone.

Two weeks later, my ma had another date.

"Max," she said. "I'm going out, so I'm taking you to spend the weekend at Uncle Jeb's."

"I do not want to go over there," I responded adamantly.

"Nonsense—you love being with your cousins."

What was I going to say to that? Mom, I do not want to go because Wanky, Tank, and I cursed each other out on the phone two weeks ago? That would have been too much to have to explain to my mother because somewhere in the translation, she would have found fault with me no matter how responsible Tank and Wanky were in the matter. "I'm not their mother," she would say.

The ride over to Bushwick Avenue was excruciating. The silence. Deafening. I stared out the window the whole time, dreading the first encounter.

It was a Friday night, approaching eight o'clock when we arrived at Aunt LouAnn and Uncle Jeb's apartment, which was packed with people as usual. In addition to the immediate family members, there were always other cousins and neighborhood folk coming in and out. The apartment door leading in and out to the third-floor walk-up apartment hallway was never locked and always slightly ajar.

"Hello," my ma announced as she pushed the door open for both of us to enter.

"Hey, Ava," my aunt LouAnn was the first to greet us, as she was standing in the kitchen, which was closest to the front door.

"Hello, Aunt Ava," chorused some of the kids sitting in the living room watching television or sitting at the kitchen table playing spades.

"Hi, Aunt LouAnn," I greeted my aunt while the scent of slow-burning greens with ham hocks wafted into my nose. I was careful not to get too close to the chicken frying in three-day-old grease from a used spaghetti jar.

"Hello to our favorite nephew." My aunt greeted me with her usual kiss on the lips. "Go on in the back. Wanky and Tank been asking 'bout you."

What were they asking about me for? rang in my head as I dragged myself to the farthest bedroom in the rear of the apartment.

"Cousin," Wanky greeted me with unexpected enthusiasm.

"Cousin," echoed Tank with more enthusiasm than his older brother as he grabbed me in a bear hug.

"What's up?" I responded with cautious optimism, my face fixed between a smile and an unknowing frown.

We were watching a preseason football game on TV when my ma came in to announce that she was leaving for her date and that she would be back the next day to get me.

Wanky, Tank, and I got along well enough to start a Monopoly game, though we did not finish. I was beginning to think that the mutually disrespectful phone call had been forgotten or at least forgiven.

"Yo, Tank," called Wanky. "Let's go hang out in the hallway."

"Bet," answered Tank.

"Max, you want to come?" invited Wanky.

"Mos' def," I answered.

We started out pitching pennies against the wall, then playing Cee-lo, our Brooklyn dice game, and then a little tag, though it was close quarters. Afterward we just sat on the stairs, resting in silence. I lowered my head to tie my shoelaces, and by the time I raised my head, Wanky was hanging dangerously over the wooden banister railing that was the only safeguard between him and a straight fall three flights to the lobby of the building.

"Dude," I said in an alarmed voice. "What are you doing?"

Hanging nearly upside down, Wanky responded, "I'm doing some daredevil shit. You scared?"

"I wouldn't say that," I answered, "but it is dangerous."

"Tank," Wanky called to his younger brother. "Show Mr. Intellectual how we get down."

Wanky pulled himself upright off the banister and was now standing. In nearly the same spot where Wanky had been, Tank slung himself headfirst over the banister while holding on to the individual posts.

"This is crazy fun!" he rejoiced.

After a few minutes, Wanky coaxed me with, "You are next, schoolboy."

Damn, I thought. *I do not want to do that crazy shit, but if I do not, then they'll think I'm a punk.*

In a split decision that seemed to take several minutes, I walked around to the banister where Tank had just pulled himself from hanging over the banister. I looked over the top of the waist-high banister and saw a clear path to the lobby floor. It looked like a descending rectangular ladder of wooden banisters. I slowly bent over the top banister, creasing myself in half at the waist, just as they had, bracing my weight with my arms.

This isn't so bad, I thought. My heart was racing with exhilaration at accepting the dare. The element of danger produced a rush of adrenaline.

Out of the corner of my eye, I saw Wanky nod to Tank in my direction. Tank moved toward me, and then…he pushed me over.

I do not remember much about the fall except that it seemed to happen in slow motion. I do not remember seeing anything in particular as I was falling. I remember landing in a heap in the lobby, just sheer body impact on a Sheetrock floor. I do remember not lying on the ground for long because Jeb Jr.—Aunt LouAnn and Uncle Jeb's eldest boy-child—and three of his friends were smoking weed in the lobby foyer. They must've heard the thud and came to see what happened.

"Oh, shit!" Jeb Jr. screamed. "What the fuck!"

Jeb Jr. and his friends circled around me, staring.

"Yo, man," began the tallest and skinniest of the boys. "Let's get him upstairs."

They carried me up the stairs and laid me down in Aunt LouAnn and Uncle Jeb's bed. That was how I knew it was serious. No one went in their bedroom.

Between bouts of groggy consciousness, I saw Uncle Jeb wearing Tank's and Wanky's asses out with the belt-buckle end of the belt. We learned to beat our children this way from the days of slavery when the ends of the whips that met our flesh were sown with metal and bones to maximize the pain inflicted by the slave master. You would have thought that we would have learned the unbearable consequences of our actions.

My mom arrived in the middle of the night, frustrated that her date had ended early but genuinely concerned about my welfare. She stormed through the apartment, not speaking to anyone and with no one speaking to her because no one knew what to say. She picked me up and carried me down the stairs and took me to the hospital. Miraculously, there was no serious damage as far as the doctors were concerned. But back then, they did not do CAT scans and concussion protocols as they do now. My eyesight, however, would be forever altered.

It would be years before the world would learn that I needed glasses for two reasons. First, we did not get regular eye exams when I was growing up. Second, I hid my deficiency by squinting in class in order to see well by stretching the side of my eye with my left index finger. And it worked for a time, until it did not. I found myself sitting in the back of a classroom one day, and at that point, my stopgap measures were bound to fail as all stopgap measures do eventually.

When I finally went for an eye exam, I could barely make out the gigantic *E* on the chart, which is the very first letter. I would go on to wear coke-bottle glasses with the black horned rims until my senior year in high school when my ma finally bought me a pair of contact lenses. Not only was my nickname Box, but I now had magnifying glasses as eyeglasses. How does one make it through to the other side past adversity?

To prove myself beyond any feelings of pity, I played rough tackle with no pads in the grassy area protected by a knee-high chain-link fence. What?

I did not visit Aunt LouAnn and Uncle Jeb's apartment for two years after that. My ma was still dating, in search of her next husband. She eventually got married two more times. The second one ended in divorce, and the third one ended when he had a stroke and, after a few years of existing in a VA hospital, died. But while she was dating, she needed a babysitter. Since Uncle Jeb's place was off limits, I spent a lot of time at Aunt Beulah's.

AUNT BEULAH

Aunt Beulah was my ma's mother's sister. That made Aunt Beulah my great-aunt, though I just called her Aunt B.

Aunt B was a boss lady before there were boss ladies. She was five feet seven and two hundred solid pounds. Her presence in any room commanded attention. She smoked, drank, and hosted card game parties every Friday night where she took a cut off the top because Aunt B was the house.

By 1958, she owned her own four-story brownstone in the Stuyvesant Heights section of Bed-Stuy. That was where black professionals lived before they could live in the integrated suburbs. She hosted bus rides to Atlantic City in the seventies and boat rides on the Hudson. Aunt B was a hustler. She gave me my first one hundred dollar bill when I was eleven years old.

"Aunt Beulah," my ma exclaimed. "Why'd you give him so much?"

"Hush, Ava," Aunt B commanded. "Leave the boy alone." Then she directed her attention to me. "A man ain't a man unless he got at least a hundred dollars in his pocket. Ain't no woman worth her salt gon' be with a man who ain't got at least that."

My ma looked at Aunt B as if she was about to say something, when Aunt B shot her a look that said, "Don't you dare." Aunt B was the only person I knew who could shut my ma up.

Aunt B's house was always full, until it was not. She raised seven children in that house. Not until I was in my midtwenties did I learn that only one, Teddy, came from Aunt B's womb but not of her husband's seed. Her husband, Uncle Hudley, was a mere fixture around the house. I cannot remember ever having a conversation with him that lasted more than two minutes. Her son Teddy never knew his biological father.

The other six children in the house were foster children for whom Aunt B received payment from New York City. Two of the children were siblings, another three were siblings, and one was on her own.

I learned early on not to get on Aunt B's bad side because she had a way of letting you know not to mess with her. If you were going to be mischievous in her house, you had better get your dodging skills up to par because Aunt B could be deadly with anything within arm's reach.

One time the girl from the sibling duo, Roxanne, plotted to sneak a few donuts from the refrigerator just before dinner. She put them in the front right pocket of her baggy sweatshirt. She turned her back toward Aunt B and casually made a beeline toward the staircase that led to the second-floor parlor area and master bedroom.

"Where you think you going?" Aunt B declared just as Roxanne passed by her while Aunt B poured leftover grease from the tin can on the stove into a black wrought iron frying pan to fry some chicken.

"Upstairs to wash for dinner," Roxanne replied.

"Not with those donuts, you not," Aunt B commanded.

Roxanne shuffled her feet back to the refrigerator, opened it, and replaced two of the three donuts. She quickly shut the refrigerator door and again made her way toward the stairs. Just a few paces from the first step, Aunt B called out.

"Did you put all of them back?" Aunt B questioned.

To the trained ear, the hesitation in Roxanne's response revealed the truth no matter what she said.

"Yes," Roxanne said, slightly above a whisper.

A serving fork whizzed by Roxanne's head, striking the doorframe near the dining room and ricocheting against two walls before clanging to the tiled floor.

"Do not lie to me, girl!" Aunt B exclaimed. She turned and stomped toward Roxanne.

Roxanne's next move was to the first step of the stairwell as Aunt B quickened her pace, swift for a middle-aged heavyset woman. Roxanne was bounding two steps at a time when Aunt B arrived at the foot of the stairs. Her right slipper had been flipped to her right hand, and she was cocked and loaded.

Aunt B released the slipper with careful aim and connected with the base of Roxanne's head, propelling her forward, sending her crashing to the floor, and crushing the donut.

"That's what you get!" Aunt B announced.

Like many of us growing up in the late sixties and early seventies, Roxanne had the misfortune of being born dark skinned, and to top it off, she was skinny and underdeveloped, with small breasts and hips that reminded you more of a boy than a girl. The lightening of black America was a phenomenon. She wanted to be liked and tried to be kind to others, but the world simply did not want to be kind back.

Roxanne and I got along well enough that I thought we respected each other and enjoyed each other's company on occasion. I remember laughter, jokes, and playfulness with Roxanne. She was older than I was and was expected to babysit me on several occasions.

Aunt B was the last person to leave the house on one fateful day. It was summertime, and she had chartered a bus to Atlantic City that would not be returning until the early morning hours. Her husband, Uncle Hudley, had a boys' night out. Aunt B's biological son, Teddy, was older than us, and he was staying at his girlfriend's house for the night. The other foster children went to their biological parents' homes for the weekend as children in foster care sometimes did when it was convenient for the biological parents.

Roxanne did not go with her brother to their biological parents' this weekend because her mom had decided that she couldn't handle two children, so she chose Roxanne's brother. My mom had an overnight date.

"Guess it is me, you, and the dog," Roxanne said, pleasant enough.

"That's cool, Roxanne," I returned. "What do you want to do?"

"Well, since my real mama did not want me to come home, and so I ain't getting no good cooked food, you gon' cook for me."

"I'm not old enough to cook," I announced.

"You gon' learn today," Roxanne informed me.

Roxanne got the pots out of the cabinets and the food out of the refrigerator.

"We're going to have some chicken, rice, and vegetables," she described the menu.

"First," she instructed me, "you are going to rinse off the vegetables, then set the rice to boil, and last clean the chicken, and season it for cooking."

I do not know if you have ever cleaned chicken before, but it is a totally different meat than when it is cooked. I liked chicken up until that point because all I had done was eat it.

It was slimy in my hands as it sloshed around the kitchen sink under the warm water from the faucet. The dead meat was rubbery to my touch as I imagined how the chicken must have died and the journey it had taken to get to my Aunt B's house.

As I was cleaning the last thigh, I felt whatever was in my stomach at the time churning its way back up my esophagus. This was my first experience with the proverbial vomit in one's mouth as I tried to hold it back, continuing to rinse off the chicken.

Uncontrollably, I simultaneously squeezed the last chicken thigh between my fingers and fumbled it onto the kitchen floor while turning my head to heave a projectile of vomit away from the sink and slightly toward and onto Roxanne.

Smack! came a backhanded left hand across my right cheek.

"Boy, are you fucking crazy?"

Stunned and staggering, I was speechless, trying to process how vomiting because of the sight and touch of uncooked dead meat and letting a chicken thigh fall on the floor resulted in being pimp smacked. And since it did not make sense to me, a yet-to-boil rage was slowly simmering inside of me.

"And don't you look at me like that," Roxanne commanded. "Now clean up that vomit, and finish cleaning the chicken while I go change my clothes."

Roxanne stomped out of the kitchen and up the stairs while Mercy barked from outside in the backyard. I reluctantly cleaned up the mess and carefully picked up the chicken so as to not let it fall again.

The sound of Roxanne's footsteps clumping down the stairs caused me to be anxious for the unknown to come. I finished cooking, and Roxanne commanded me to set the table for one.

I began to walk out of the kitchen in search of a quiet place, dreading the night to come, hoping that morning would come quickly. It did not come quickly enough.

"Where you think you goin'?" Roxanne asked rhetorically. "Sit your ass down."

I spent the next half hour watching Roxanne eat. Afterward she told me to wash the dishes, which I did. As I was washing the dishes, she let Mercy into the house from the backyard door that led directly into the kitchen.

Mercy ran into the kitchen, hunting the smell of food. I was startled when she jumped on me playfully. Roxanne fed her the scraps, and Mercy spread herself out, belly flat on the cool kitchen floor, for a feast.

Dishes done, I headed for the den that was adjoined to the kitchen.

"Ain't nobody told you to go nowhere," Roxanne commanded.

My rage was growing with every thought of what had occurred, beginning with the face slap.

"I'm going to watch TV," I stated.

I took a few more steps before Roxanne planted herself firmly in my path.

My rage and sense of wrong told me that though I was only ten years old and several inches shorter and at least ten pounds lighter than Roxanne, I would take my chances against her bony ass. I pushed by her, determined to get by.

"You ain't goin' nowhere," she said as she flung me back and into the wood-paneled dining room wall.

Roxanne was at least five years older than me. There was something about teenage strength versus preadolescent strength that one cannot account for in terms of height and weight. It was the same for what they called old-man strength versus young-man strength. It was not to be taken for granted.

"So you think you are a big man now, huh?" Roxanne teased. "Get your ass in that corner." She shoved me into a gap between a bookshelf and the wall with the dining table on the far side.

"Mercy," she shouted. "Come here, girl."

The dog sauntered over before being riled up by Roxanne's rhetoric of "Get him, girl" and "He tried to hurt me" and "You wouldn't let him hurt me, would you?"

Mercy responded to Roxanne as if she understood language. But it was Roxanne's tone that revealed an energy that caused Mercy to growl and bare her teeth at me.

Roxanne and Mercy hemmed me in the corner for what seemed like hours, literally terrorizing me with the threat of being bitten by a dog or whipped with the steel-linked dog chain.

When it was over, neither happened. No dog bites or bruises from a dog chain, and therefore no evidence with which to tell the night's tale. This story would have to travel with me awhile until I could figure out the lesson. In the short term, I was determined not to let something like this happen again.

And though that never happened again, memories of Roxanne conjured the sexual miscues, confusion, and ambiguities that occurred in the absence of adult supervision and guidance. You want to talk about unrealistic expectations? How could any adult guide us when they did not know what they did not know?

HOOD LOVE

Hood love started out just like love anywhere else. For me, it started in first grade when I had a crush on Nikki Fox because when we raced, she was the fastest girl in the class, and I was the fastest boy. Pure and simple. We went together until fifth grade. There was no thought of romance in the least, and until fifth grade we hadn't even considered kissing. Nonetheless, she was my girl. By then, Roxanne had taught me everything I needed to know, or so I thought. Why is it that some families leave older cousins to not only babysit younger ones but to also sleep together in the same bed, boy and girl?

"Come over here," Roxanne had coaxed me. I had maybe been nine, and she had been all of fourteen.

I'd inched toward her, not moving more than a foot, not close enough to touch.

"Come here, boy," she'd demanded.

With that, I had moved all at once, close enough to feel the warmth of her skin and breath. She had smelled shower fresh, and her breath had had the benefit of minty toothpaste.

"See, I'm not going to bite you," she'd offered before gnashing her teeth against thin air as in a biting motion toward my face. I had flinched instinctively.

"Kiss me," she'd directed.

I had stretched my neck in her direction, closed my eyes, and pouted my lips, embracing for impact.

"Not like that," Roxanne had responded. "Like this. Open your eyes."

I'd opened my eyes to see her face slowly closing in on mine until her lips had softly pressed against my lips.

"Now touch me." Her voice had been soft as she'd guided my hands between her legs, where I'd felt warmth and wetness.

It had not so bad, just as Roxanne had predicted. The actual physical act itself had not been so bad. The exception was that I had felt nothing, knowing not what to feel. The experience had been neutral, neither good nor bad. It had felt different and new and curious. I processed it on a mental level in the sense that I had an idea that what I was doing was for older people, even older than Roxanne, and yet I was experiencing it and handling it. *I must be a big boy now*, I thought to myself.

You know, in life you are told to do unto others as you would have them do unto you? Easier said than done, right? Most of the time, it seems we do unto others as others have done unto us.

After Roxanne, as I got older, after more challenging experiences and after watching and learning from the experiences of Bosida, Khahari, Darwin, and Adisa, it boiled down to one of two choices for me: become the prey, or become the predator.

When I was nineteen, The Garage was *the* dance club in New York City. If you were into disco and house music, this was the scene where you wanted to be. First, you did not go until after midnight, and you stayed until past dawn, and sometimes you went directly to work from the club. They did not serve alcohol, but drugs were abundant, and not just the common drugs of weed and blow. The Garage was home to psychedelic drugs such as meth and mushrooms and introduced Quaalude. I suspect that ecstasy was in the mix before the world knew about it.

Lisa from apartment 21M was a regular at The Garage. She was four years older than me, and she was a loner. Of Puerto Rican and Dominican descent, Lisa was all of five feet, five inches tall, and at 140 pounds she had ass, hips, and tits way before the other girls on the block. She swung her body proudly as she walked with her breasts bouncing braless under her skintight shirts and blouses.

Every guy in our neighborhood wanted Lisa, but none could have her until one eventful night at The Garage. Someone slipped her a roofie, and she was never the same again. After that, it seemed everyone got a chance to be with Lisa. In time it was my turn to try.

Under the misguided direction of Adisa's older brother Adama, I plotted to run a train on her because that was what dogs who ran in packs did. Adama was older than Adisa; he had been old enough to watch me when I was young while my mom was off on one of her dates. He had taught me behaviors befitting the savages we were becoming simply because no one had shown us a different way.

"Hey, Max," Adama had encouraged me one day while I had been staying at the MacArthurs' apartment across the hall from my mom's apartment for a few hours while my mom had stepped out. "The next time you see a bitch looking at you, but she do not want to speak, you grab your nuts like this and say, 'Kiss my nuts!'"

Since I had been under ten years old, and Adama had been nearly seventeen, I had gladly imitated him. I'd stood up and grabbed what sack I'd had, and before I could utter the words, Mrs. MacArthur had passed by the open door to Adama's bedroom.

"What in the hell!" she'd exclaimed.

"Adama made me do it," I'd confessed immediately.

"I know, Max," Mrs. MacArthur had comforted me. "Adama, get on outta this house now before I tell your father what you did."

"But, Ma—" Adama had attempted to stall.

"But, Ma, nothing. Be gone."

That was the same Adama whom I was still following almost ten years later.

I lured Lisa to my apartment when my mom was not home. Her dates now extended into weekend-long excursions.

Lisa and I made our way to my bedroom, where we began to kiss and touch each other. Awkwardly we fumbled in our attempts to take off each other's clothes before resigning to taking off our own. Down to our underwear, we were grinding on each other in my twin bed, careful not to tumble onto the floor. Just as Lisa was about to take me in her hand, Adama stumbled out of the nearby closet, crashing to the floor with his pants around his ankles.

"What the fuck?" Lisa shouted, jumping from the bed and covering herself with my shirt. "This is fucked up! Adama, what are you doing here?"

"What does it look like?" Adama answered without shame. "Waiting for you."

"Sick bastards," Lisa responded while throwing my shirt in my face before storming out of the apartment.

Like many others growing up, we spent our early adolescent days scheming to get laid any way we could, without regard for others' feelings and emotions. Conquest for the sake of conquest as a measure of a man.

A DIFFERENT
KIND OF BROKEN

Do you still wonder how real-life monsters are created? Our children have been alone too often to fend for themselves without proper supervision, direction, and instruction on how to conduct themselves. Our lives become a living testimony to the book *Lord of the Flies,* written by William Golding. The propensities of man reveal themselves through learned experiences and trauma.

I have lived through such traumatizing events, and I know how they suck the soul out of people. We are physically alive, existing, but our souls have been paralyzed within. You know it when you see people staring into the distance, not really there. Not present. The distant not-there look can appear the same as when someone is daydreaming or thinking about having a better life or being somewhere else or thinking about their to-do list. The look I'm talking about is a dead look. And when you ask the person with the dead look, "What are you thinking?" or "Where were you?" as you bring them back to reality, their reply is "Nothing" or "Nowhere." And we press them to tell us otherwise because we do not believe them. Believe them. Believe us.

It is that thing that happens when a woman or man is being raped, and they just give up and go numb. They go to places other than where they are, to the point that they may not feel the physical trauma in real time. Soul-paralyzing experiences are too painful to confront. Soul paralysis can lead to self-inflicted wounds such as cutting.

This is what I think the poet Langston Hughes meant in his epic poem "A Dream Deferred." This poem is so often quoted without the follow-up question that I often ponder.

"What do the explosions look like?"

I remember Tuma—Roxanne's older brother, which made him that much older than me. He also lived with Aunt B in the house that became a refuge for unwanted foster children who were cared for yet rightfully angered by abandonment. Tuma was a happy-go-lucky teenager who saw the best in everyone. He was an average student. At five feet six and less than a buck fifty, he was below average in stature. Tuma was not necessarily athletic. What he was, though, was quick witted and quick of foot. He was prone to say something slick and then dare you to try to catch him. And because of his lack of discernment in terms of whom to mouth off to and whom not to—regardless that his jest was rarely ill intended—some people in the neighborhood did not have the time or patience to figure out his intent.

Coming home late one day from a drum practice that Tuma hosted for kids at the neighborhood recreation center, Tuma and I were confronted by five boys who were a year or two older than Tuma. We were on Aunt B's block, within eyesight of the house. The boys surrounded us as a pack would circle its prey.

"What's up, Mr. Always-Got-Something-Slick-To-Say with your comedian ass?" the smallest of the five began. "What did you say about my mother the other day?"

"What's up, Tyrell?" Tuma responded. "Don't be mad at me because my 'yo mama' jokes are funnier than yours."

"That's exactly what I'm talking about," Tyrell snapped back.

"Listen, bruh. It is late as hell right now, and I'm just trying to get my little cousin home before his moms busts my ass." Tuma used me as reason enough to let us pass.

"Do not include little man in this," Tyrell countered.

As if by telepathic communication, two of the five boys surrounding us parted to allow me to walk out of the circle. I looked to Tuma for direction. He nodded his approval for me to leave the lion's den.

"So for having such a big mouth, Tuma," began Tyrell, "here's something to fill it."

Two of the biggest guys rushed to restrain Tuma by his arms while a third one handed something to Tyrell from a canvas bag. When Tyrell turned within view, I could see that the something was alive, and it looked like a rat as Tyrell dangled it from its tail.

"Let's see if you can handle this, Mr. Talk-Shit."

Tuma squirmed in the arms of the two older boys as his eyes bulged in his head.

"What, the cat's got your tongue? Ain't got nothing to say now, huh?" Tyrell taunted Tuma. "Better yet, the rat's got your tongue."

Tuma shook his head violently from side to side and up and down, all the while keeping his mouth shut. That ended when Tyrell punched Tuma in the stomach.

"Stay your ass still, motherfucker, 'fore I have to really fuck you up."

Tuma gasped for air from the savage blow to his gut; the fifth boy holding him by his head and neck forced his head up and back.

Tyrell started lowering the rat into Tuma's gagging throat. As the rat slowly disappeared, I could not turn away from the proverbial car wreck that was happening before me. With half the rat's body in Tuma's mouth, Tyrell suddenly stopped.

"You had enough?" Tyrell asked rhetorically.

Tuma mumbled something that meant "Yes, and please stop."

Tyrell slowly removed the dangling rat and tossed it in the street.

"Don't you ever let me hear you say a goddamn word about me or my mama ever again!" demanded Tyrell. "Ever!" Tuma vomited a projectile of whatever he'd digested from his last meal.

Tuma nodded in agreement and staggered toward me.

"Come on, Max," he said to me, his breath reeking of fresh vomit.

We never spoke a word of that night.

LOVE IS WHAT THEY CALL IT

I remember that December when I came home for Christmas recess during my tenth grade year of boarding school.

"Ma," I began. "I do not want to go back there."

"Why, pray tell?" my mother responded.

"Because they make it difficult for no good reason. I had a great year in football, and I was one of the top students in my class. I do not need the extra disciplinary stuff."

"That may be so," my mother went on to advise me. "However, if that is the case, then it should come easy for you to adhere to the rules that are the same for everyone."

"They should consider individual performance as they apply the rules," I answered.

"I tell you what," my mom began to negotiate. "Finish out the school year, and then if you do not want to go back you do not have to."

The place I did not want to return to was Saint Michael's Military Academy in the Ozark Mountain region of Missouri. My attending Saint Michael's was a perfect confluence of events. First, my mother had always prayed that she wanted me to attend school out of New York City proper— and out of Brooklyn, specifically—because teenage black boys were being murdered at an alarming rate in the midseventies. Imagine your thirteen-year-old son leaving the house daily, and you spend the rest of your day worried whether he will make it home that evening. That thought, coupled with the idea of having more free time for dates, was enough to motivate my mom's prayer submission to God. Second, I had the talent and work ethic to be an elite football player at the tender age of twelve. The trifecta was completed with Mr. Gates, who was my eighth-grade math teacher by day and a basketball coach and prep school recruiter by night.

From first to eighth grade, I attended Brooklyn Leadership Academy. Mr. Gates's family had founded the school in the late sixties to educate black boys and girls. It was a private school that charged a modest tuition for working-class black folk. We wore uniforms and sung, "God is great, and God is good, and we thank him for our food—amen" before lunch was served. Almost sight unseen, Mr. Gates heard about my exploits on the football field and extended a scholarship for me to attend Saint Michael's. My mom was ecstatic with praise and shouts of hallelujah, and I was proud that someone thought enough of my athletic talent that they would pay for me to attend their school.

Within three months of conversations about attending Saint Michael's, I was on a plane alone, at thirteen, going to Missouri to be met at the airport by a football coach I had never met.

I remember two events from my first year at school that haunted me enough to make me not want to go back—and one pivotal experience that ultimately made me stay.

The natural order in a military school is hierarchical, in that cadets who have seniority outrank new-boys, as first-year cadets are called. So even as a thirteen-year-old rising sophomore, I was under the command of other cadets who were sophomores as well, but they outranked me because they had been at the school a year or more than me.

As a kid growing up on the streets of Brooklyn, I'd learned that if you let your peers boss you around, you become a mark. So you can imagine what happened when a short skinny white boy weighing less than a buck twenty-five with sergeant stripes got in my face.

"Fall in!" shouted the company commander.

It was dinnertime, and the weather was inclement as a tornado with hail passed through. We lined up in formation before every meal to account for all cadets present and to enter the dining hall as a company.

Company B was, as was all companies, divided into two units called platoons. Each platoon had a lieutenant in command who reported to the captain of the company. Each platoon consisted of three squads of ten boys, and each squad was commanded by a staff sergeant. I was a first-year new-boy, not even a private yet, standing at the end of the second squad.

Staff Sergeant Melvin Melbourne from Racine, Wisconsin, was inspecting the squad, walking down the line, stopping in front of each cadet, looking him up and down, starting from the floor. His eyes met each cadet with laser focus. He got to me and eyeballed me from my recently shined shoes to my shiny brass belt buckle to my tightly tied tie, and when his eyes expected to meet mine, I stared straight into the distance, thinking about the upcoming homecoming football game.

"New-Boy Talisman," Sergeant Melbourne began.

I did not respond.

"Did you hear me, new-boy?" Melbourne said, his voice raised an octave. He took a step closer, and his face came that much closer to mine.

"I heard you," I answered.

"Then say something," Melbourne gritted through his teeth.

"I did not know that saying my name required a response."

"Well, it does, so the next time I address you…" Sergeant Melbourne was loud enough for the entire platoon to hear. He began to walk away.

"And what would you like to me say?" I asked.

"What did you say?" he said as he spun on his heels and made a beeline back into my face.

"I asked you—" I began.

"I know what you asked," Sergeant Melbourne interrupted me. "You speak when I address you, and you shut up when I dismiss you!" he shouted with hysterics.

Sergeant Melbourne was mere inches from my face when he spewed these words, so I could feel the warmth of his breath on my chin.

"Do you hear me, boy?" he ended as he poked me in the chest.

In an instinctive automatic response, purely on a physical level, with no thought given, I slapped him hard enough to cause him to stumble back a few steps and almost fall down, if not for the wall he hit to hold him up.

"Who you callin' *boy*?" I asked rhetorically as I stood over him.

My challenge was greeted by silence as Sergeant Melbourne held his left hand to his now red left cheek. Everyone else in the platoon stared and stood paralyzed in shock. There was no protocol response for what had just happened.

"Lieutenants," ordered the captain. "Ready your platoons to move out to the mess hall."

Staff Sergeant Melbourne did not get a chance to retaliate in the moment, but he would eventually get his pound of flesh. December—before winter recess, when we got a chance to go home—was the traditional time for the ceremony where new-boys received their first stripes as privates first class. The day before the awarding of stripes, and three days before I would fly back to Brooklyn, the commandant called me into his office.

Command Sergeant Major Abbott Shelby had been born and raised in Clay, Kentucky, which was the poorest county in the state with a population under thirty thousand people and an average annual household income of less than $10,000. Abbott Shelby was desperate to get out. And like many poor boys—white, black, Asian, or Latino—growing up in a rural or urban environment in 1910, joining the military was a viable option to escape poverty.

Sergeant Major Shelby had joined the marines at eighteen, just as World War I was ending. It would be some twenty-some-odd years later that he would find himself as an officer in World War II. What he learned over his years as a marine, fighting alongside black boys and men from New York, Chicago, and Los Angeles, coupled with his upbringing as a poor country boy, was that it did not matter the color of the human being when your life depended on that other human being.

"Mr. Talisman," he began his preamble. "Please have a seat."

He waved his hand in the direction of one of two leather chairs on the opposite side of the mahogany desk that he sat behind.

"Thank you, sir," I replied.

"You have a bright future ahead of you, son. Not only are you a hell of a football player, but you have demonstrated academic ability and fortitude that will serve you longer than football ever could. I do not want to see you throw that away with stupid decisions."

There was a break in his delivery, filled with silence because I did not get the idea that it was my turn to talk.

"Do you understand me?" he asked.

"Yes sir," I answered, not really knowing what specifically he was referring to.

"I cannot have the hotshot football player and gold star academic-award winner—the student with the highest GPA in the school for the fall semester—who happens to be a new-boy, slapping around my staff sergeants. Do I make myself clear?"

"Yes sir," I responded.

"As such," he continued, "you will not attend the pinning ceremony for new-boys becoming privates because you have not earned your stripes and will not earn them until after the Christmas recess. Do you understand?"

"Yes sir."

Sergeant Major Shelby stood up, and I stood up too. He saluted and said, "Dismissed!"

I saluted in return, turned on my heels with military precision, and exited his office.

My emotions were conflicted. On the one hand, I was super pissed that I was singled out to not receive my stripes, and as such I wanted to punch Marvin Melbourne in the face. I was surprised that I cared so much when I professed to not care. Lastly, though, Sergeant Major Shelby had sternly scolded me; I sensed that he was supportive and that he wanted to see me succeed. Ultimately, I was a little inspired. But still pissed.

The second incident that made me tell my ma that I did not want to return to Saint Michael's was a betrayal of friendship, or at least what I thought was friendship.

Svenson Gustafsson was assigned as my roommate my first year at Saint Michael's. Sven, as he wanted to be called, was born in Sheboygan, Wisconsin, the same year I was born in Brooklyn. His family was of Swedish descent, and they looked every bit the part. Sven was all of six feet three at thirteen years old, with a muscular frame of 210 pounds chiseled from spending time outdoors in all seasons, whether hunting bears or deer or ice fishing, skiing, or swimming in a lake. Sven's athletic gifts were rooted in sheer size and brute strength versus speed, agility, and coordination. He was a prototype goon save for his general good nature.

In late October of our first year together, Sven invited me to his home for a weekend getaway. We were going to attend a Green Bay Packers game that Sunday before heading back to school. When we arrived at his home Friday evening, he introduced me to his family. Sven's parents looked like they could have been brother and sister. Both of them had blondish hair and blue eyes, were tall in stature, and had sunburned skin and builds that evidenced athletic backgrounds in their youths, though they now had a layer of middle-aged fat over muscular frames.

"Max," Sven introduced me, "this is my dad and mom, Mr. and Mrs. Gustafsson."

"Hello, Mr. and Mrs. Gustafsson," I answered.

"Welcome, Max," Mr. Gustafsson bellowed from his gut, extending his right hand for a handshake while his left hand patted me on the back with enough force to cause me to stumble toward him a step.

"Welcome to our home," Mrs. Gustafsson offered as she extended her hand to shake mine. "Sven has told us so much about you."

Her grip was weak as she barely put her fingers in my hand, and our palms did not touch. I did not take offense because it reminded me of an incident after the first football game at Saint Michael's. A little white girl who could have been eight years old and her brother, who may have been twelve, had come up to me to ask for my autograph. As I had been signing my name on the program from the game, the little girl had innocently brushed her hand against my forearm to touch my skin.

The boy had then asked, "May I touch your skin too?"

"Sure," I had responded, equally as amazed and curious that they had never touched the skin of a black person as they were to touch my skin.

Then I'd thought, *Wow, in 1979, there are still white people in America who have never come in contact with black people.*

This was the same sensation I got when Mrs. Gustafsson extended her fingers for me to shake limply. Except she was an adult with the skeptical mind of an adult but with enough social grace to attempt to offer some kind of greeting. She'd probably never touched a black person before either.

As we stood in the foyer of the open-style wood-framed house from which you could see the living room and dining room on opposite sides of the entrance with a view to the roof of the house capped with a skylight opening, Sven's sister appeared at the top of the staircase. She gracefully took her time walking down the stairs. She looked at me the whole way down, and I returned the gaze until just before she reached the landing because I was aware that her parents may have been watching me stare at their daughter.

"And this is my little sister, Deirdre," Sven introduced her, upon which I returned my eyes to meet hers.

Deirdre was nothing like the other three blond-haired, blue-eyed members of her family. She had fiery-red hair and green eyes. And there was nothing little about her. At sixteen years old, she was stacked with natural 36D breasts and proportionate hips and ass to go on her five-foot, seven-inch frame. It was her eyes and lips that captivated me. Her full lips captured my undivided attention as they formed words.

"Pleasure to meet you," I offered, extending my hand to shake hers.

"Finally," she began. "The great Maximus," she calmly exclaimed, bypassing me to give me a full embrace.

I gently hugged her back before quickly disengaging the embrace.

"Let me show you to your room." Deirdre took the initiative while grabbing my leather duffle-style bag by the straps. "Follow me."

She turned and headed up the stairs. I turned to look at Sven, who shrugged his shoulders and rolled his eyes.

"Come back down for dinner once you get settled," he directed me.

Deirdre told me her story while she waited for me to unpack my things, when I asked her, "So where'd you get such an interesting name?"

"The story of Deirdre—she's known as 'Deirdre of the Sorrows' in Irish mythology. Basically, she was to marry some king to whom she was promised at birth. Imagine that! Of course she did not want to and instead ran off with her warrior stud boyfriend and his two brothers, who swore to protect them. Wherever they went, the tyrant king of each kingdom I guess wanted to marry her, so she, her boyfriend, and his brothers eventually went into hiding. The king to whom she was promised tracked her down and killed her lover and his two brothers. She eventually died, brokenhearted. The end. So you see—I am destined not to be with my one true love."

"Maximus!" I heard Sven's booming voice call to me.

"We'd better get downstairs," Deirdre began. "We do not want Sven to get jealous of me hanging out with his friend."

That weekend was a much-needed break from the military rigor of Saint Michael's. Sven's dad let us have a beer or two with him, which I though was respectful. "Teenagers are going to drink, so why not teach them to drink responsibly?" was his motto. That Saturday we went on their pontoon on the lake and cooked outdoors on the backyard deck under the stars, with a campfire to keep us warm. The Gustafssons did everything as a family, so Dierdre was always around. Though we kept our distance that weekend, we always managed enough nonsuspicious eye contact to let the other know we were thinking about the other. After the game Sunday at Lambeau Field, Sven and I hopped in his pickup truck to start the ten-hour drive back to campus.

I would see Deirdre a few more times during the football season when she came to campus with her parents to see Sven. We wrote letters in between her visits to campus. Mostly we talked about life stuff—college, current events, traveling. We were growing as friends.

After the last game that season, Deirdre and I were able to steal away from everyone else and take a walk down by the school's golf course. The only light was the half-moon shining in a cloudless sky. Before we started back, we stared into each other's eyes and moved beyond any uncomfortable moments to settle into that rare air of acceptance of your feelings. We embraced and kissed deeply.

As we slowly pulled our lips apart, but our bodies were still close, I heard a rustling in the dead leaves on the ground just feet away from us.

Instinctively, I jumped back in defense. Deirdre laughed.

"It is probably a fox. Do not worry; it won't bite," Deirdre teased.

I sensed it was something much more than a fox—something that did not want to be seen.

That night would be the last time I would see Deirdre until February at the Midwinter Ball, and we would never be alone again. I wrote to her over the winter recess while I was in New York like we had promised. There was no reply. When I got back to campus, I called, but there was no response. Sven had been conveniently transferred to another company that January. When I asked him about his sister, he just shrugged his shoulders and said, "Hell if I know. I do not understand women at all."

Since I did not have a date for the annual Midwinter Ball, I decided to DJ the party with another cadet who did not have a date. Before we started playing music, there was the traditional playing of the bagpipes for cadets and their dates to enter the transformed gymnasium under an arch of swords presented by underclassmen officers.

After about ten couples, I began to lose interest in watching the processional and almost turned my eye away, when I caught a glimpse of fiery-red hair.

"And now, please welcome Company D captain in his senior year, Daniel O'Rourke," the announcer began to shout over the microphone as he had done for every couple that evening, "...and his date, Deirdre Gustafsson!"

I almost passed the fuck out! My knees buckled, but I quickly regained composure. Deirdre was eyeing the room with a broad smile and sparkling eyes from being happy in the moment until her eyes met mine. The sadness we felt permeated the space and distance between us.

We did not speak at the dance, as I played music and she danced. Later that night, there was an after-party for seniors and their dates at the local hotel in town. A few of the wealthier seniors had rented out the only suite in the hotel. I managed to get a ride and be invited in because I was the stud football player from New York, though I would always say I was from Brooklyn.

I managed to borrow some of Deirdre's time, away from everyone yet in plain sight of all.

"Max," Captain O'Rourke called me over to where he and Deirdre were standing.

I walked with purpose to join them.

"Max," Captain O'Rourke continued, "have you met my hot date, Deirdre?"

"Have we met, Deirdre?" I directed the question to Deirdre with as much discretion and playfulness that I could muster.

"Actually," Deirdre began stammering, "we met when my brother brought him home for a Packers game."

"What a coincidence." Captain O'Rourke appeared surprised. "Sven never mentioned that to me. Hmm."

Captain O'Rourke was stuck in thought for a few seconds, pondering the idea that Deirdre and I already knew each other and what it meant.

"Well." He came back to the moment. "Then it shouldn't be awkward if I leave you two alone to talk while I go get us some drinks?"

"Not at all," I quickly replied.

Captain O'Rourke turned away and blended into the crowd. Once he was out of eyesight, I turned squarely to face Deirdre. She faced me, and our eyes met once again. This time, mine were undoubtedly filled with sadness, anger, and confusion, while hers were filled with shame.

"What happened, Deirdre?" I demanded.

"My brother was the fox in the woods that night, Max," Deirdre started. "Once he told my parents, I was forbidden to see you."

"Because I'm black," I concluded, asking as much as stating it to her.

"Max, it would be too hard for us as a couple." She lowered her head and gazed at the floor. Moments later, she lifted up her head to see me again. She continued, "Besides, it is not like we were going to get married and have babies."

"What are you talking about, Deirdre? Married and babies? We're in high school, and I'm trying to be friends first."

"Well, that's how people think out here. People marry their high school sweethearts who come from where they come from, and they marry people who look like them."

I saw it clearly now. Deirdre was living the mythical life of her namesake. Like most of us, she was trapped in the narrative that had been sold to her by adults who had lost hope. It was what she knew, and it was comfortable.

"I hear you. I do not come from that place, Deirdre. In Brooklyn, in high school, you date a girl you like. You may date a few girls. You fool around to learn how to really fool around as you get older. I forgot where I was. I really wanted us to be cool."

"I'm so sorry, Max." Deirdre was teary eyed.

"So am I. Listen—two things. We're kindred spirits from another lifetime, so I'll see you in another lifetime. And"—I paused for effect—"we would've made beautiful babies."

We rushed to each other to embrace.

"Whoa, whoa, whoa here," Captain O'Rourke interrupted. "Is there something I missed here?"

"No," Deirdre responded. "We were having a philosophical discussion about the idea of kindred spirits. It made me emotional."

"Well, darling," Captain O'Rourke interjected, "I plan on some emotions later on." He laughed and put on a wry smile. "Come on, my queen," he feigned.

Deirdre and her date walked away. I watched as they disappeared into the crowd.

—

So what made me stay at Saint Michael's, you ask? Commitment to the purpose for being there. Despite the abuse of perceived positional power that some cadets had over others or the racism that was being passed from parents to children, I was thriving at Saint Michael's. The football season ended with me leading the conference in rushing yards and touchdowns. Academically, I was at the top of my class. In the scheme of life, I knew that I was winning. The rewards were worth the risks and sacrifices. I remained thankful to Saint Michael's because I learned discipline along the way.

—

I agreed to my mother's proposal to finish out the school year and then re-evaluate my decision to leave, thinking that it was fair because at some point I had a choice to make. It would be my decision.

The next May, when school ended, I flew back to Brooklyn and took a taxi home, and my mom greeted me at the door, arms wide open, smiling ear to ear, with her upper middle-teeth gap on full display.

"So do you want to go back or stay here?"

Within the rhythm of her question, I stayed in time, responding, "I definitely want to go back."

It would be years later that I would find the wisdom in my mother's subtle proposal.

My ma taught me perseverance through adversity without me even knowing. The indirect and subtle lessons that I was taught through life experiences became the lessons that lingered with me long after that day. By the time that May of the school year came around, the adversity had passed, and I had made it through to the other side, where effort and perseverance were rewarded. Not only did I excel at athletics and academics, but I was learning the invaluable skill set of leadership.

◼

Sade was never wrong when she sang "Never as Good as the First Time." Love's name was Catherine Aliah Caverton.

Catherine—never Cathy, but sometimes Cat—and I met the summer preceding my senior year in high school. I had just received my first pair of contact lenses! She had graduated that June and was heading to Harvard in September. I was preparing for my final season of high school football in hopes of earning a scholarship to college. Sidebar—going away to school saved my life. It gave me a purpose in my life. Nonetheless, black boys in Brooklyn shouldn't have to go away to school for their lives to be saved. I always knew that one day I would choose to return home to make a contribution—to contribute a verse to the poem of life.

A friend of mine from Brooklyn, Conrad, was dating Catherine's best friend, Kim. I knew Conrad through Bosida. The two of them were first cousins. Conrad introduced me to Catherine. Conrad and I were astrological brothers, in that we were both Libras. Conrad stood at five feet eleven and was a solid 195 pounds. Like most of our crew, he was a handsome dark-skinned dude. He was two years older than me. Conrad lived two buildings down from me in the Grand Towers apartment complex. He was also a black belt in karate. I knew Kim through Conrad. Kim was fine, with long legs that framed her statuesque frame at five feet nine, so when Conrad wanted to introduce me to Catherine, I said, "Hell yeah!"

Catherine was all of five feet, three inches tall, weighing a buck twenty-five. She ran track in high school and had the ass and thighs, with a slim waist to match. She was small breasted with light-brown eyes and full lips. Did I mention that she was smart? She and Kim attended public school at the Manhattan School of Science, which was the most prestigious high school in New York City. The Manhattan School of Science sent more students to Ivy League colleges than any other high school in the country.

"Catherine, this is Max," Conrad introduced us. "Max, this is Catherine."

"Hello," she offered sincerely as she held out her hand to greet me.

I quickly took her hand in mine and held it, lingering as I replied, "Hello. It is nice to meet you."

Conrad and Kim stood to the side, admiring us like they had just put together a match made in heaven.

"We thought we'd catch a movie," Kim suggested. "And then just hang out."

"Sounds like a plan to me," Catherine replied.

Catherine's voice was sweet like a song. Her affect was soft yet confident. You can tell a lot about a person by the energy, cadence, and rhythm of his or her voice. Catherine's voice revealed a temperament of innocence, full of hope, and an optimistic glass-is-half-full perspective.

I do not remember what movie we saw as the day melted into evening. Walking the streets of Brooklyn, in the theater, whenever I could, I stole glances of Catherine. I was checking her out—her hair, eyes, lips, neck, breasts, thighs, and ass. On occasion, she busted me looking, and she smiled.

All of us sat close together in the dark theater. Conrad and I bookended Catherine and Kim as they sat between us. Midway through, Catherine leaned toward me, and our arms touched for the first time.

After the movie the four of us walked the twelve blocks from downtown to the ice cream parlor on Myrtle Avenue. Myrtle Avenue was the nearest commercial stretch of blocks in our neighborhood. Whenever you had some money in your pocket, you went to Myrtle Avenue. We shopped where we lived.

Conrad and I were typical gentlemen as we paid for our dates' ice cream cones. We then walked to the basketball courts, the same courts where Adisa had come to the rescue of his older brother Saucy Sam. I sipped my chocolate milkshake through a straw and watched Catherine lick her strawberry ice cream from the cone.

The evening was quickly winding to a close when Catherine gave out a sigh of surprise.

"Paul!" she exclaimed.

A dude a few feet next to us in the ice cream parlor turned around. He was over six feet tall, had an almond-brown complexion, and was well groomed, with a basketball-player physique.

"Catherine," he returned, equally surprised.

Catherine made the first move toward him, leaving my side. The two of them hugged and kissed each other on the cheek. I turned to look at Conrad with the "What is going on?" face, and he hunched his shoulder at me as if to say, "I do not know."

Catherine grabbed the guy by the hand and walked him over to me.

"Maximus, this is Paul," she began to introduce us. "Paul, this is Maximus."

We shook hands. I shook his hand vigorously.

"Paul is one of my best friends in school," Catherine continued.

"Hi, Paul," Kim greeted him.

"We take the same AP classes," Kim stated.

"He's going to be my big brother at Harvard," Catherine announced.

I was processing all of this new information in real time as fast as I could before I had any sudden reaction that I might regret. *Paul is a guy friend of Catherine and Kim from high school, and Paul and Catherine will be attending Harvard in September*, the voice in my head said. *Got it.*

"Congratulations to you as well, Paul, for being admitted to Harvard," I offered.

"Thanks, man," he replied. Then turning his attention to Catherine, he said, "So, Cat, is this...are you..."

"Yes, Paul," Catherine replied. "Maximus and I are dating."

"Well, good for you, Cat," he replied. "Maximus, you are a lucky man. Cat has never claimed a dude, as far as I know."

Again, I was processing in my head as fast as I could. *Cat? He calls her Cat? Is that his nickname for her? I thought she did not like being called Cat?*

"Paul is exaggerating maybe a little," Catherine interrupted.

"I'll take that as a compliment," I responded.

In the obvious uncomfortable moment, we all said our respective goodbyes. Conrad walked Kim home to the Academy Gardens projects, and I walked Catherine home to Gulliver Walk. If I thought Grand Towers was a step above Academy Gardens, then Gulliver Walk was the next level above Grand Towers.

"Later, C," I said to Conrad. "Good night, Kim." I followed up with a kiss on her cheek.

Catherine and I strolled hand in hand in the shadows of the tree-lined blocks near her home.

"So *Cat*, huh?" I began.

"What?" Catherine responded, unsure of the question.

"Cat is cute," I continued. "I did not know you had a nickname."

"Yes." She blushed.

"Is that a general nickname or just Paul's nickname for you?" I said.

"Wait." She paused. "You are not jealous of Paul, are you?"

"No. I'm just—"

"Yes, you are," Catherine interrupted.

"No—"

"It is okay," she interrupted again. "I'm flattered."

"I'm not jealous unless I have something to be jealous about," I countered. "I'm genuinely curious to know if that's a general nickname or not. Like, can I refer to you as Cat?"

After some reflective silence from Catherine, she stopped walking and faced me directly.

"Cat is a general nickname, but Paul probably uses it the most. I'd rather you not call me Cat because other people call me that, and you are not just other people."

She stood on her tiptoes and kissed me. After, I grabbed her hand without a word, and we continued walking. A few yards from her apartment building's entrance, I asked, "What do you think Harvard will be like?"

"Hard," Catherine offered as matter of fact. "But I'll be ready. I was built for this."

"I have no doubt that you are."

"What about you?" she countered. "What's next for you after your last year in high school?"

"Hopefully a scholarship to play football."

"That's your plan?" she challenged. "Are you really that good?" she continued playfully.

"If numbers do not lie," I began. "I believe that I'll get some offers."

"And if not?" she asked.

"Then I guess I'll have to make it on my brains, just like you."

"I like that idea," she concluded.

As of her last comment, we were standing in front of her building. After the usual awkward silence and gestures, we came to a mutual understanding through unspoken words. We hugged lightly and quickly punctuated it with a kiss on the cheek. It was a proper first date.

That summer was a storybook coming-of-age experience for me. I worked my summer job cleaning up vacant lots for more than the minimum wage, worked out in preparation to play football, and hung out with Catherine. She did the same minus working out, though she always looked good when I saw her.

By late July, about a week before I was to return to the Ozarks for summer practice, Catherine and I agreed to continue our budding romance into the fall.

"I want you to come out for homecoming in October," I invited her.

"Is that what you really want?" she asked in disbelief.

"Yes. I'll pay your way."

"How about this?" she suggested. "We'll split the airfare fifty-fifty. You fly me out, and I'll fly myself back?"

"Deal," I happily replied.

We sealed it with our first full-tongue kiss.

Before she could actually go, we needed her parents' approval.

Like most of us, Catherine was born into a two-parent home. The length of the average union was up for debate. This modern-day phenomenon of single-parent homes had not yet been born while we were preteen children growing up. At that time, the question of how dysfunctional our homes were with both parents in them should have been a matter of concern.

Catherine's parents seemed to be a model couple—the Huxtables before the Huxtables. Her dad was the first black partner in a corporate law firm near Wall Street, and her mom was the president of a major charitable foundation. I met them two nights before I was scheduled to leave to begin my last campaign on the gridiron to earn my way to the next level. I rang the doorbell, and her father answered the door.

"Good evening, Mr. Caverton," I said as politely as I knew how without totally kowtowing.

With an infamous pregnant pause, Mr. Caverton sized me up from head to toe with eyes bulging from their sockets before he bellowed, "Well, hello there, Mr. Talisman! Your reputation precedes you."

With a wave of his hand, he welcomed me into the apartment, and as I crossed the threshold, he grabbed me by my shoulders and began to feel my arms.

"Catherine tells us you are a football player," he stated matter of factly.

Before I could answer, Mrs. Caverton appeared from the kitchen.

"Sherman," she reprimanded. "Leave the boy alone," she continued before turning her attention to me. "Do not mind him. Welcome, Maximus."

"Good evening, Mrs. Caverton," I said.

"Catherine will be out in a moment," Mrs. Caverton said in a comforting voice. "Come have a seat while we wait for her."

Damn—in hindsight, this was a classic let's-get-to-know-him-without-her-in-the-room strategy. The real motive was either to discourage a dude from courting their daughter or to scare him into marrying her—extreme behaviors either way.

"Can I offer you a beverage?" Mrs. Caverton asked me.

"How about a beer?" Mr. Caverton chimed in. "I'm having scotch, but you are too young for scotch. Boys your age drink beer."

"Water will be fine," I answered.

"Do not mind him," Mrs. Caverton suggested. "He only has one child, and it is his daughter, so…" She paused, looking directly into my eyes. "You'll understand one day."

Carefully lowering myself to sit in a single chair in the living room, I noticed that the room had to have been rarely used or used only on special occasions because the furniture did not show any worn spots that indicated regular use. In that moment it registered in my psyche that this was an important day for the Cavertons.

"So, Mr. Maximus," Mr. Caverton began as he handed me a glass of ice-cold water. "You must be training for the upcoming season."

"Yes sir, I am," I answered.

"Catherine tells me that you play running back," Mr. Caverton continued.

"That's correct," I replied.

"You don't seem that big," he countered. "You must be fast."

"I can run," I said.

"What's your forty time?"

"Four point four," I said with confidence.

"That's impressive," Mr. Caverton said flatly. I couldn't tell if he was impressed or angry because the time was impressive.

"And he's being recruited by several Ivies," Catherine interjected as she appeared from the hallway that led from her bedroom.

With that, Mr. Caverton showed the first hint of approval.

The evening went on that way for at least another hour. I felt as if I was in an interview or an interrogation. I would learn that Catherine's family were members of the local Jack and Jill club and that they vacationed to Martha's Vineyard—both reserved, at the time, for black people who could pass the brown-paper-bag test. Clearly, I could not with my coal-black skin.

Summer ended for us in early August when I had to report to football camp. Catherine and I agreed that she would visit during homecoming weekend that October. She came as planned. That Friday, she slept at my coach's house under the watchful eyes of him and his wife. I'm sure his motivation was to keep the legs of his star running back fresh for the game. Saturday came. I played well, and we won the game. I guess as a reward, the coach arranged for Catherine and me to stay in a hotel that night.

Catherine and I were two high school students experiencing the awkward dance of two inexperienced teenagers trying to have sex. Though I was not a virgin, I was far from a confident lover. My previous experiences had been just as awkward. I couldn't remember if I had ever had an orgasm. Catherine, on the other hand, was a virgin.

I remember showering first and waiting for her in bed with just my underwear on, listening to the shower run, imagining her naked under the water. Soon after, the water stopped; the shower curtain scraped back against its pole. A few minutes passed as I heard the light clinking of metal against the bathroom sink. A few more minutes, and Catherine emerged in sexy pink lingerie.

I shut off the lights in the room but left the bathroom light on and the door slightly ajar. There was just enough light for us to be able to gaze into each other's eyes but dark enough to hide our youthful insecurities about our bodies.

At the point of penetration, I remember her biting into my neck, hard enough to draw blood. We both grunted, but neither screamed out. I was in love.

The next morning, my coach picked us up and took us to IHOP for breakfast. He and his wife had ear-to-ear smiles on their faces, but they were discreet enough not to ask us anything about the night before. Afterward they drove us back to campus for the remaining hours before Catherine's flight back to New York.

The two of us walked around the football field and track before stopping at the flagpole, where we sat on the concrete edge surrounding it.

"Maximus." Catherine's voice trembled.

I was totally caught off guard because I had no idea where this sense of fear in her was coming from.

"You all right?" I asked.

"I'm okay. I had an amazing time, Maximus. The best ever."

"So did I, Catherine," I said, with relief in my voice.

"And because I feel strongly about you, I want to be honest with you." Tears slowly began to stain her face.

"What happened, Catherine?"

"A few weeks ago I went to a party on campus for Harvard's homecoming. I was having a great time, when I bumped into Paul. We hung out for a while, and then I was ready to go back to my dorm, but the girls who went with me to the party weren't ready to leave."

Catherine paused to swallow saliva stained with the salt of her tears.

"Paul offered to walk me back, and when we got to my door...we kissed."

The impact of that statement began with light-headedness followed by shortness of breath. I started seeing faint spots of light-white pollen dancing before my eyes. I was disoriented, unaware of my physical location. If I had not already been sitting down, I would have fallen down.

"Max," Catherine called. "Max," she called again. This time she gently touched my shoulder as if calling me back from somewhere else.

"I thought he was a friend," I said in a steady voice.

"He was. It...just happened."

"Noting just happens, Catherine. You made a decision."

"I know, Maximus, and I am so sorry."

"So what's up with you two?"

Again, there was a heavy pause that filled up the space in the heavy air building between us.

"We're seeing each other."

"So he's your man?"

"Not technically. I mean, obviously we haven't had sex."

True, I thought to myself. The blood on the sheets from last night coupled with the bite mark on my neck confirmed that. And with that thought came the conflicting feelings from what we shared and the breaking news that had just been revealed. I had been in love just a few hours ago.

"That's some bullshit, Catherine."

"I know, but..."

"But nothing," I rejected her claim. "It is time for you to go."

I stood up from the concrete base of the flagpole and began to walk toward the entrance of the campus, where a taxicab had just pulled up.

"Do not do this, Maximus."

"Do what? I did not do anything. You did. I'm walking you to your cab."

She picked up her bag and struggled with it as we walked separately to the cab. All I could think of was how I'd been a fool for believing that she was just friends with that dude. I did not even believe in men and women being friends without some kind of sexual tension between them. After this experience, I told myself I would stick to that belief. I was made a fool for love.

Standing beside the open taxi door, Catherine and I faced each other. I avoided eye contact until she touched my hand with hers.

"I'm sorry, Maximus. I hope you can forgive me."

I said nothing in return. She kissed me on the cheek and got in the cab. I walked away without looking back as the cab drove away.

Catherine and I did not speak for months despite her efforts to reach out to me. Thanksgiving and Christmas break came and went without any communication. Over spring break in March, I finally accepted her invitation to meet.

I went to her apartment. Her mother greeted me at the door with a long face and slumped shoulders. She hugged me, but I couldn't tell if she was genuinely sad about me and Catherine not being together or if she felt pity for me.

On the other hand, Mr. Caverton had a shit-eating grin on his face as if to say, "Thank God my daughter won't be with a black motherfucker like you. Nothing personal. It is just that in this day and age, life is still too hard for dark-skinned folk."

"Go on to the back, Maximus," Mrs. Caverton directed me.

I found my way to Catherine's bedroom, which was decorated as if her life had stopped at sixteen. It was not the room of a college freshman at Harvard.

"Maximus," Catherine greeted me with a surprisingly warm hug.

"Catherine," I returned, my pulse not a beat above normal.

"You still mad at me?" she asked.

"I wouldn't say mad," I returned. "More…indifferent."

"Wow," Catherine said in shock.

We made small talk and chitchat about the current affairs of our lives.

"So have you decided where you are going to school?" she asked.

"Yes. I'm going to accept the offer from Dartmouth."

"That's great," Catherine responded with sincerity. "We'll be archrivals."

"That seems appropriate," I answered.

"Listen, Maximus," Catherine began. "I did not invite you over to fight. I invited you because I wanted you to know that even though we're not together now, I chose you to give myself to, my virginity to, because…because I couldn't think of anyone better to introduce me as a woman to the world. At the end of the day, I need to explore the world and all it has to offer, and so do you without being committed to someone at eighteen years old."

"I hear you, Catherine. And I feel you. But at the same time, you and that dude are still hanging out."

I refused to say his name out loud, especially as I imagined them having sex and him getting the benefit of me breaking her hymen.

"I'm not with Paul anymore, Maximus," Catherine declared.

The news of their demise was music to my ears, but I stayed with the poker face.

"I'd be lying if I said I was sorry to hear that," I said.

"I know. And that's one of the qualities I like about you, Maximus."

We sat around for a while longer in silence, not knowing what to say, before I offered, "So I'm going to go."

"I know you have to go so you can get up and go train or whatever, but I'd like to play a song for you before you go."

Catherine walked to her cassette player and pushed play, and Deniece Williams's "Free" wafted through the air.

My magic potion for love
Telling him I'm sincere
And that there's nothing too good for us

But I want to be free, free, free

Let's not waste ecstasy
'Cause I'll only be here for a while

I've got to be free, free, free, oh
And I just got to be me

I must admit that I was moved in the moment to feel that Catherine loved me and just wanted to be free. But free from what, and why? Then I thought, *This is bullshit*, but I did not say it. I looked her in the eye, got up, and left. That was the last time I saw her or spoke with her until the summer break.

—

The crew and I were sitting in Emerson Park; actually, we were on the benches outside the park, near the Gulliver Avenue entrance, where we never sat on a regular basis. I think this was the first and last time we sat there. It was shortly past dusk, after playing ball, when the forty-ounce drinks and blunts began to make their way around the circle of guys.

"You know you can't guard me." Adisa directed his comment to Khahari.

"You right, but I can pull your shorts down when you are shooting," Khahari answered.

"You are crazy, Khahari," Bosida chimed in as he passed the forty-ounce of Ballantine Ale to Darwin.

Just as Adisa passed the blunt to me, the shadow of a couple holding hands and walking past us twenty yards away crossed our faces.

"Yo, Max," Adisa whispered. "Ain't that your old girl Catherine?"

I inhaled the smoke, and then I squinted as I slowly exhaled, trying to see if the woman was Catherine.

"That's her," Darwin confirmed.

No one said anything immediately after. I felt as if all eyes were on me, though I did not look around to see if that was true. I stared at the couple, saying to myself, *That is her.*

"You just gonna let her walk by like that?" Adisa challenged me.

If you have ever really taken stock in your life, there are several moments that require immediate decisive responses, and you always have a choice. The challenge is that when you are young and lacking a ton of experience, you tend to make choices that are reactive based on outside influences. As we get older, hopefully the responses become more intuitive based on experiences.

"Catherine," I called out.

The couple stopped and cautiously looked in my direction. Neither of them responded.

I began walking in their direction as I called out again, "Catherine, is that you?"

"Who's that?" she questioned.

As I approached, the light of the streetlamp illuminated our faces, allowing us to see one another.

"It is me."

"Maximus?" Catherine was clearly surprised. "Hi!"

After solely focusing on her face for the first time in months and still harboring mixed feelings of love and rejection, I turned my attention to the guy next to her. It was Paul.

There must have been something in the way that I looked at him because he immediately let go of her hand before I said a word. I leaned toward her, and she leaned in toward me. I embraced her and kissed her on the cheek. Afterward, I stood away from her at arm's length, taking her in.

"You have the nerve to bring this dude around here, Catherine," I barked at her.

She pulled away from me and closer to Paul.

I took one step toward them, and they stood still. Frozen. I wanted a physical confrontation with him. I felt that I needed it. A release. It was an adrenaline rush, knowing that endorphins would kick in once the pain began, if any. That was a lesson learned from being pushed over a banister to fall three flights or from willingly colliding your body into others at full speed over and over and over again. But I could tell that he was not up for it. And there were times, where I was from, that if it was not going to be a fair one, where both cats were willingly participating, then it was not worth it.

"Listen." I directed my attention to Paul. "Don't you ever come around this way again. Ever."

Then toward Catherine, I turned and said, "And you. You should know better."

I stood there, poised to pounce. Catherine and Paul stood paralyzed by fear.

I turned and walked away without looking back.

The feeling that bubbled within me in that instant scared and surprised me. I sensed that I could go either way—walk away or strike them both, unleashing a beating that was years in the making.

A VIOLENT RESPONSE

There were three acts of violence that imprinted their indelible footprint upon my being. Quatum was already twelve years old when I met him. Q, as he was known, lived in the middle building that made up the three towering buildings of the co-op project complex where we lived. He had been born in Barbados, and he was built as if from a black onyx rock, even as a preteen. He was everything physical that we all wanted to be, and it was all natural. Q never knew the inside of any gym or weight room. His rippling muscles came from running, jumping, and playing in the streets from sunup to sundown. Q excelled at every sport that we played as the seasons changed. In the fall we played football in the falling leaves, and in the winter we played football in the snow. In the spring we played baseball, and in summer it was basketball. Q jumped higher, ran faster, and hit harder than all of us. Like many of us, he grew up an only child to a mother who would become single. Now that I think about it, many boys in the neighborhood grew up in that type of house-hold, but most of the girls had siblings.

By his sophomore year of high school, his mother left him the first-floor apartment where they lived as she returned to Barbados to live. Having to fend for himself, Q dropped out of school. Apartment 1E became party central.

"Maximus!" Q called me one day in his deep, rumbling base of a voice in his rambunctious way. Q lifted spirits in part to mask the low space where his resided, but you wouldn't know it if you did not know Q.

"My dude," I returned.

It was Saturday morning, and I was returning from the grocery store, as my mother's custom was to send me with a list to buy food for the house. From the age of ten, I had mad chores. I did laundry, where I became intimate with ladies' intimates! I washed dishes, cooked, and shopped for groceries. On this day, Q was coming from wherever he spent his nights these days in the *Lord of the Flies* life in which he found himself.

"Come through tonight," Q said, more telling than asking. "I'm having a fete!"

"Word?" I replied as Q peeked over the top of my grocery bags.

"Word, son!" Q returned.

Q pulled a pack of chocolate chip cookies that I had bought for myself out of the grocery bag.

"There's going to be mad honeys!" he continued while opening the pack.

He shoved a cookie in his mouth and then one into mine, as my hands were full.

"I'll be there," I said, almost salivating.

I did my chores for the day and asked my ma if I could go out, to which she of course said yes because I had earned my way.

Since there were going to be girls at the fete, I put on my best pair of the three pairs of jeans that I owned and strutted across the parking lot to apartment 1E.

The thump and pace of soca music greeted me in the hall before I could ring the bell, and before I reached the door, the pungent smell of high-grade ganja seeped from under the door. As I raised my hand to knock, a guy and girl stumbled out of the apartment, and I entered before the door could close.

Teenagers were everywhere in the darkened apartment hidden from the light of day by venetian blinds and drawn curtains. Q invented day parties! The dining room table now served as a bar, with people surrounding it and serving themselves. Girls were trapped against walls, being rubbed and humped by horny pubescent boys.

I had been taught to familiarize myself with my surroundings in order to assess all possible scenarios in case I needed to use my space to my advantage, whether for pleasure or protection. I walked down the hall of the apartment, past the ajar bathroom door, where a boy and girl were kissing and feeling each other up, and past the first bedroom, where the door was fully open, and people were dancing and drinking and smoking and laughing. At the end of the hallway was the master bedroom. The door was closed, but I could hear loud voices behind it. I opened it to "Maximus!" shouted above all the noise by the host himself, Q.

"My man," he continued. "Welcome to the fete!"

"Q!" I returned. "Your party is live!"

"You ain't seen shit yet," Q announced.

Turning his attention to the girls in the room, Q introduced me. "Everyone, this is the Maximus Talisman, who is fam and who will be going to the league, so you better get to know him now. Max, this is everyone."

"Chari, be a darlin'," Q encouraged in his Bajan accent, "and go get Max a drink."

At fifteen, Chari was already developed as a woman with at least 36C breasts. She smiled at me with her light-brown eyes staring directly into mine.

"Anything for you, Max," she sang her words to me.

After she left the room, Q closed the door behind him.

"Yo," he called our attention. "Check this out."

He went into his closet with his back turned to us. After some rustling about, he slowly turned to face us to reveal a sawed-off shotgun.

While no one let out a gasp or any outward sign of surprise, there was a collective inhale that sucked the air out of the room. Either Q did not register this disturbance or, more likely, he did not give a fuck because no one, not even his mother, had really given a fuck about him.

One of the other few boys in the room asked Q to see it, and Q nonchalantly tossed the gun to him. I wanted no part of the gun, especially since I did not know if it was loaded. All I could think about was the idea of getting shot in the face and my future career ending before it started.

When the boy handed the gun back to Q, Q asked the ladies if they wanted to handle it, and all of them declined.

"You want to check it out, Max," he challenged me as he pointed the gun directly at my chest.

In the seconds that seemed liked several minutes, I grew angry by Q's challenge and not-give-a-fuck attitude for my life while at the same time I processed that to do anything except to handle the rifle could imperil my life further and my cool status in the room and indirectly in the hood. I extended my left hand to receive the offering. Q turned the rifle sideways to give it to me.

"You know it isn't loaded, right?" he asked with a sly grin.

The sawed-off shotgun was surprisingly light, as I'd expected to have to hold it with two hands. I examined it briefly before returning it to Q. The experience was so surreal that the words he spoke after to his captive audience began to fade from my ears so that I did not understand what he was saying. Simultaneously, Chari returned with a drink for me. That was my cue. I stood up and greeted her halfway across the room.

"Thank you," I began. "Is it all right if we go and dance?" I suggested.

"Of course," Chari responded with anticipation.

I led her through the dimly lit hallway back to the living room as I gulped down whatever alcohol there was in the infamous red cup to relieve the tension of the moment. Reaching the dining room, I placed the cup on the table. Feeling a bit sorry not to meet Chari's anticipation of dancing with me and whatever she thought would follow, I mouthed the words "Gotta go" to the pulsating music. I was out the front door in the next step. That was the first and last time that I would enter apartment 1E.

Over the next three to four years, I would see Q sporadically during my vacations from boarding school and college. During those years, Q had become a low-level drug dealer for the career criminals in the neighborhood. I'm talking about the ones who had been born into it versus guys like Q who had fallen into it due to being dealt a lousy hand as a kid. The career guys preyed on those less fortunate. And at the same time, the very same guys could be so benevolent to the point that they recognized that guys like me stood a chance of getting out, and they honored that idea by protecting me. That was the hood code.

The summer following my sophomore year of college, I was basically living on my own as my mother summered with her new lover on Martha's Vineyard. I had bumped into Q mostly at the park amid his comings and goings as he ran the streets. He no longer had time to play the games that most of us did as teenagers in summertime. He had adult responsibilities.

Late one night after one of my runs from 369 to the Brooklyn Heights Promenade and back, just as I got out of the shower, the intercom buzzed.

"Yes," I answered.

"Yo, MA," Q called out the initials of my first and middle name. When Q called me MA, he was in distress.

"Q. What up?" I responded.

"I'm tight on my consignment and need to pay up quick. Can you spot me some dough?" Q's voice revealed his predicament, which was high on the desperate meter.

"I don't really have cash like that, but if you need a place to lay low, you are welcome to come up," I offered.

"Nah, homie. I'mma need some loot 'cause they ain't playing."

"Why don't you stay here for a few days until you can figure it out?" I suggested.

"Thanks, Max, but these guys…" Q paused. "They'll find me wherever." His voice trailed off in resignation.

Days came and went, and no one saw or heard from Q. I bumped into G-Money three days later.

"Maximus," he began. "You heard about Q, right?"

"Nah," I said, not ready to hear the inevitable.

"They say the police found him around on Grand Avenue in the abandoned factory."

"Word," I almost whispered as my heart sank down and away from hearing the rest.

"Yeah, man," G-Money continued. "They say they found him sitting upright on the stairs with a single bullet wound to the middle of his forehead. Said he'd been there a few days. The rigor mortis had set in."

What does one say to that? I could not find any words, so I shook my head slowly and walked away.

It was not until decades later during a conversation with my mother, whose early onslaught of dementia was ravishing her short-term memory but leaving intact her long-term memory, that I was reminded of the wild wolf puppies we were, abandoned by our parents.

"One of the things I regret," she began. "Was leaving you on your own so much when you were a boy." She halted her words in reflection. Then as if gathering the courage to speak her mind, she continued, "You pretty much raised yourself."

Her thought that followed was to give herself some measure of comfort. "I did the best I could. Besides, you turned out all right."

In the moment of that conversation, I immediately flashed back to my years between ages eleven and thirteen. Not only had I been left to fend for myself as my mom had left me for days on end as she'd traveled with the boyfriend of the moment, but Q and Khahari had been in the same predicament. The three of us would run the streets until dawn as adolescents, doing nothing and having no purpose save the fact that we could. We'd often had parties at my apartment because my mother's timing was predictable, and I was able to calculate cleanup time the next day before she came home. The other boys—Bosida, Adisa, and Darwin—would hang out as long as they could before their curfew because their parents were home. For some reason, there were girls who could hang out almost to sunrise. I wondered where their parents were. We drank, did drugs, and had sex, of course unsupervised, way too early in life.

I do not remember crying for Q's death because young black boys dying was woven into the fabric of our lives. He became another casualty. The best way I knew how to honor his life was to not become a statistic.

There were three other deaths among several where I grew up that remain in the crevices of my mind. Deaths I wonder if I will ever be able to wipe out like the cobwebs they are. The first was Z-Roc.

Z-Roc was fly, all the way around. He was tall, slender, and charismatic. He was a ballplayer and a lady-killer. Some called him The Mac like in the black movies of the day. He had it made. Went off to college on a basketball scholarship until his girlfriend gave birth to their daughter. He came home and seemed to be handling his business. One day we heard that he leaped to his death from his seventeenth-floor apartment in Academy Gardens, landing on his knees, driving his lower body up and through his chest cavity.

Black Pat was knifed in a street fight gone rogue. I mean, we grew up throwing hands until cowards resorted to weapons. Lastly, there was Yellow Man Yardie, who was murdered as a result of mistaken identity. He was riding in the intended victim's BMW, which had tinted windows. The murderer was the drug dealer who Q worked for. Dude even had the nerve to attend Yardie's funeral.

Since violence knows no discrimination, I believe that I have had my share. I thank God that they did not end in my death.

—

The summer of 1974, I was twelve years old. Though my mother and father had been divorced for years, I still spent time with my dad on weekends of his convenience. He moved to Westbury, New York—Long Island to Brooklyn cats. He was a professor of music at SUNY Old Westbury.

My dad was shacking up with his latest female friend. This was before his next three wives and my four siblings, who were born by four different women. Keyanna was the name of the lady whose house he was at, and she had two sons. Zion was almost grown when I met him, and he was hardly around. He was a yellow mon as we called light-skinned brothers in the day. He was cool and comfortable in his skin and conscious of mind, being well read.

Keyanna named her youngest son Man with the idea that he would embody the characteristics of her idea of what it meant to be a man. Man was a serious cat. Even when he laughed, it was short lived. Whenever I visited my dad, Man was my running buddy.

Man was taller than me, with a wiry frame. He was not skinny. Rather he was sinewy and just as dark-chocolate black as me.

Westbury was indicative of most Long Island residential neighborhoods. The blocks were made up of houses with backyards and not a bodega or apartment building in sight. You had to literally walk blocks at times to find someone to play with.

Man knew the closest family, which was two blocks away and around three corners.

"Let's check out Kimba and his family," Man suggested. "There's so many of them that there's bound to be somebody to play with."

Kimba's house was on a hill, which was rare in this neighborhood. When we arrived, we waited at the bottom of the hill. Looking up to the house, I saw three older boys on the front porch, sitting on furniture that was typically reserved for inside a house. There were four other boys, first cousins of Kimba, who were sitting on the stoop of the porch, playing cards. Two of them may have been a year or so younger than Kimba, and the other two appeared to be slightly older. An older lady, whom I took as the mother of all the children, rocked back and forth in a rocking chair. She stared through me and said nothing.

"Kimba," one of the older boys yelled out. "Your little friend is here."

I guessed that he was speaking about Man since this was my first time here.

I heard footsteps in the house gathering speed with every step before Kimba burst through the front door and sprinted down the hill to greet us.

Kimba Leonard was slightly shorter than me, but he probably outweighed me by ten pounds with his pudgy yet burly frame. You could tell that when he got older, he'd either be obese like some of his relatives sitting on living room furniture on the porch or, with exercise and diet, he could be built like a linebacker.

Man introduced me to Kimba, and Kimba gave me a big hug that lifted me off my feet. After the two of them caught up on neighborhood gossip, the three of us stood around tossing a football back and forth between us.

Soon, some other boys from the block joined us, and we had a full tackle football game going, sans any equipment. It is interesting to feel compelled to add the disclaimer about having no equipment. It was normal for us to play tackle football without helmets, shoulder pads, nothing. Now, when you tell a person that was what you did, they look at you like you are crazy because kids do not do that anymore.

I was having a pretty good game, scoring touchdowns, intercepting passes, and making hard tackles. Kimba was on the other team, and he was playing well enough that it was obvious that he was the best player on his team. I was the best player on my team.

After one play where Kimba dove to make a tackle on me and missed, his big brother blasted him.

"Kimba," he yelled. "You gonna let him do you like that?"

Kimba looked at him, then at me. He was confused.

The next play, Kimba ran the ball, and I plowed him into the ground. He was slow to get up.

"Kimba," the same fat man yelled again. "He making you look weak! Get up."

Kimba stood and brushed the dirt off vigorously, shooting a glare my way.

"Why'd you do that?" Kimba asked me.

"Do what? Tackle you?" I answered rhetorically.

Kimba brushed by me as he returned to his huddle. For me, that meant game on.

On the next play, I intercepted a pass, and as I was about to cross the goal line for another score, Kimba charged at me to make the tackle. In less than a second—though it seemed longer than a second as everything slowed down for me—rather than easily sidestep him, I lowered my shoulder to meet his and ran him over for the score.

"Kimba," yelled another obese brother from the porch. "You can't let that happen."

Kimba looked at his older brother, then at his mother, who stopped rocking in the chair. She stood up, and as she walked to the front door of the house, she stared at Kimba, then at me. She entered the house without a word.

Kimba picked himself off the ground and stomped toward me, bumping his chest against mine.

"Hey, man," he began. "What's up with you?"

"What do you mean?" I responded, backing up from him.

"You did not have to run over me like that."

"Dude, it is football," I replied matter of factly.

"Yeah, but still," he stammered.

Then he looked toward the porch again. His oldest brother stared at him and nodded his head. I looked at Man, who stared at me with unknowing eyes.

Kimba approached me and pushed my chest with both hands, causing me to take two quick steps backward to catch my balance.

"Why'd you do that?" I demanded.

"'Cause I felt like it is why," Kimba nonchalantly answered. "Why, what you going to do about it?"

"Max," Man interrupted. "Let's go."

He put his hand on my shoulder to guide me away.

"What, you scared, punk?" Kimba challenged me.

"I don't want to fight you because you have a lot of brothers and cousins."

"We ain't gonna jump in," said one of the cousins from the porch.

I thought about it, weighing the risk-reward factors of fighting or not. I'd had plenty of fights. I'd won most but lost a lot. For me, the idea was not necessarily about winning or losing. The idea was to be physical enough to let the opponent know that win or lose, they were in a fight that they would remember enough to not want to fight me again. Ever.

"Listen, Kimba. I do not want to fight you."

"Why not? You scared? Pussy."

It always amazed me when guys called other guys *pussy*. Pussy was a beautiful place that men craved. Was it really an insult to be called one?

"I am not scared of you."

I looked at the family members on the porch. They looked at me with blank stares.

"I said we ain't gonna do nothin'," said the oldest brother.

"Kimba, I do not want to fight you."

"That's because you ain't shit."

"No, it is because no matter who wins, you are going to know that you were in a real fight. That I promise you."

With that said, I turned to walk away. Kimba rushed up behind me and kicked me in my ass.

"Then run on home, punk!"

I turned around, pushed up my sleeves, and put up my dukes. I was ready for an old-fashioned fistfight, boxing-style.

Kimba was slow and lumbering while I was quick. We sparred a bit before—*blam!*—I connected with a straight right hand after a feigned left jab,
square to the bridge of his nose, right between his eyes.

Blood immediately gushed profusely. We all were startled by the sudden-
ness and seemingly unending bloodshed. Even when his older brothers came
off the porch with towels and tissues to stop the blood, it would not stop.

"Why did you hit him like that?" questioned one of Kimba's cousins as
they now gathered around.

I looked at him as if to say, "Is that a trick question?" What came out of
my mouth was, "It is called fighting!"

Then out of nowhere, I heard, "Get that motherfucker!"

Simultaneously, four cousins attacked me. I dodged them and started
running. I made it across the street before being tripped by one of Kimba's
older brothers. I found myself sitting on the curb, knees drawn to my chest,
arms wrapped around my knees, and my head buried against my knees as
blows from feet and hands rained down upon me.

In what seemed like minutes again but was actually seconds, Man made
his way through the mob. He pulled me to my feet, and we were off and
running.

We made it to Man's home with Kimba and his cousins fast behind us,
though fading as they could not match our speed that was propelled by adrenaline and endorphins.

To this day, Man and I laugh about the great escape and how profusely
Kimba's nose bled that day. Man still sees Kimba in the neighborhood these
days, and they remain friends, the folly of our youth forgiven, though not
forgotten. I've told Man to tell Kimba hello for me, thinking perhaps it would
be good to see him again.

━━

What do you do when you have these experiences that directly tell you that the
world can be an ugly place, a place that is unfair and unforgiving? Growing
up, we learned to take everything seriously. We did not tell too many "yo

mama" jokes because it inevitably led to a fight. Because all you had was your rep, and if your rep was that you were soft, you were in for daily harassment.

You had to choose how to handle it. You and only you could make deliberate and conscientious decisions on how you would confront and address the challenges of your life.

Social scientists have called it flight-or-fight response and reflexive mechanisms. I call it survive-or-thrive responses.

So when Big Merk was pummeling Saucy Sam, Sam was in full-flight mode, though he could not escape. Conversely, Adisa was in full-fight mode when he came to his brother's defense.

Where I grew up, you either shrunk away and became hunted prey or you became the hunter. At the very least, you built up your defense and immune system to levels that protected you from being hunted, sort of the equivalent of a chameleon's camouflage. Though you may not have been the one hunting, let someone fuck with you, and he or she would see the predator in you. I chose the latter.

369 had two rivals. There was 311 Rye Place and 45 Saint John's. Those three buildings made up our playmates and housed our archenemies. We were always out to prove who was the fastest, most athletic, and the toughest. Interestingly enough, we never competed about being the smartest or doing well in school. Those among us who excelled academically usually kept it on the low, but those of us who knew the smart ones respected them anonymously. Doing well in school or having intellect was considered a gift and not something you could acquire or grow with work, time, and effort. We spent a lot of time honing the skills and crafts that we thought could be developed. My chosen craft was football. And so it was for Harrison Martin and Wilson Kart.

Harrison Martin was from 369. He lived on the third floor. Houdini, as we called him, was the prototypical opposite of me. We were the same age and about the same height and weight, but we wore it differently. He looked svelte, and I looked stocky. He was arrogant, and I was humble. Well, maybe not *humble* humble. Confident. If there ever were born rivals, Houdini and I were that.

We were rivals for years. We would race a few times each year, and the neighborhood made it an event. Sometimes he won, and other times I won. He was a better basketball player. Houdini had more finesse and panache. I was a better football player. I was tougher. And then there were the epic fights.

"Yo, Fox," Forty Gran called out to me. "What up?"

Forty Gran was one of the first cats off the block to play D1 college ball. He was a six-foot, three-inch shooting guard from Boys and Girls High School who went on to play at the University of Nevada, Las Vegas (UNLV).

Forty Gran's government name was Dyson Clay, but he never went by his government name. Every summer when he came home from Vegas with a pocketful of cash, he'd say, "If I do not have forty dollars in my hand, I ain't got a grand! Want to know what I got? Forty gran', motherfuckers!"

And when Forty Gran's money was tight, Forty Gran became known for drinking forty ounces of Olde English 800—the scourge of my community in Brooklyn. But who did not drink it at the time?

When his eligibility at UNLV ended, I was initially disheartened because surely, if anyone from Clinton Hill was going to make it to the pros, Forty Gran would!

"Yo, Forty," I called out to him one Saturday afternoon after the neighborhood summer league games came to an end due to the settling in of dusk.

"Box," he responded. "My man. What up, kid? How's ball?"

"Going into my senior year," I answered. "We're favored to take the chip, but we'll see."

"The chip would be cool," Forty responded. "But whatever happens, make sure to get yours. Recruiting season is coming."

"You just finished your last year, right?" I continued.

"Yeah, man," Forty said, his mood suddenly becoming sullen.

"What's your next move? You going to the league?"

"I have a few looks," Forty offered in a quiet voice. "Not gonna get drafted but will get some tryouts." His voice got smaller with each word.

Forty Gran never made it to the league, and he never graduated from UNLV. That was when I knew that no matter what, I would finish school, because if you did not finish school, and you did not make the league, you would probably end up fucked for life, never to escape the nightmares of the hood.

Forty Gran spent the remainder of his adult life as a transient handyman sprinkled with a few seasonal stints in jail from petty theft crimes.

On that same night that I stood talking to Forty Gran, Houdini sauntered into the park with his now signature bop in his step. It was funny how all of us could recognize one another in the dead of the night solely by the way one walked.

"What up, G?" Houdini offered.

"Houdini!" Forty Gran returned.

Then with mouth turned down and eyes starting from my toes and working their way up to meet my eyes, Houdini reluctantly muttered, "Box."

I gave him the obligatory head nod.

"Harry."

"Why you always got to call me by my government?" Houdini barked at me.

Not calling someone by his or her nickname was blasphemous in Clinton Hill.

"Because that's what your mama named you," I clapped back.

"I don't go calling you Maximus."

"That's your choice. You can call me Box or Maximus."

"I prefer Fox myself," Forty interjected.

"Well, I prefer you call me Houdini," Houdini demanded of me.

"Fox, you gonna call him Houdini or what?" Forty questioned me.

"I'll think about it."

"What you gonna do with that, Houdini?" Forty challenged.

As a few other guys in the park began to gather around, including Adisa and his brother Saucy Sam, Forty Gran approached Sam and whispered, "Yo, Box versus Houdini! Who you got?"

"I don't know," Sam began. "It is close." He paused. "I'mma give it to Box 'cause he's my next-door neighbor, and he's tough."

"True," Forty Gran added. "But Houdini is nasty."

Houdini stepped to me as I simultaneously stepped back, out of arm's reach. That was one of my standard operating procedures. Whenever presented with a potentially violent situation, I sought to stay out of arm's reach until I assessed the situation and decided on a response.

"Say my name, motherfucker," Houdini demanded of me.

"I am saying your name," I replied.

Houdini stepped toward me again, and this time I stopped in my tracks. "Harry, I'm not tryin' to..."

Before I could speak another word, his right jab caught me beneath my left eye. A welt rose immediately, and it was on. I lost the fight that day, but Houdini knew he was in a fight too. It would be our last fight because neither of us wanted to go through that pain again. I've called him Houdini ever since.

I was still in high school when I came to realize that I had to use ball, or it would use me because everyone, no matter what stage of life or career they were in, had to come to terms with the idea that eventually, the ball stops bouncing for you.

Forty Gran was living proof. He came home and became a hustler.

Why was it that in most urban neighborhoods in the United States, athletic rivalries collapsed into violent exchanges that could tragically—and with elements of the theater of the absurd—end in death?

You cannot dominate me in running or jumping or scoring touchdowns, and the girls like us equally, so...you have to beat me up?

Motivation was a motherfucker. Looking back, I realize that I really wanted to and needed to live beyond the physical and psychological boundaries of my birthplace. I decided early on that commitment, dedication, and singular focus were worth the effort to realize a dream. I had read enough biographies of successful people to know that if it worked for them, then maybe it could work for me.

One such story that resonated with me was that of Wilma Rudolph. She was an athlete, and so was I. I thought that if she could overcome polio and make it to the Olympics, all I had to do was overcome the trappings of the hood to become a professional football player.

I would run up and down the sixteen flights of stairs in 369 three times a week, and when I was not doing that, I was running the two miles round trip from my building to the promenade. My junior year of high school, I met Julia.

JULIA

Julia was a year younger than I was. I do not recall how I met her. She seemed to just appear in my life. I think I was just finishing up a workout in the backyard of 369 when I felt someone looking—not necessarily staring. I had reached my full height of five feet, ten inches by now with less than 10 percent body fat at 185 pounds. I had evolved into chiseled granite.

"Hello," she initiated the conversation.

"Hello," I returned as I took all of her in.

Julia's complexion was like rich dark chocolate. She stood at about five feet, four inches and was built on the slender side. It was her eyes that were captivating. Her spirit was on display in an unassuming way for the world to see.

"Whatcha doing?" she casually asked.

"I'm working out," I answered.

"For what?" she asked.

"I'm getting ready for the football season," I replied.

"So you are a football player," she said as she gestured with her body to expand like the Hulk as she puffed her cheeks. That made me laugh, and I decided that I liked her.

Julia worked that summer, and so did I, which was often bookended with workouts. We still managed to find time to spend together. She proved to be very understanding.

"So, Mr. Football Player," she began over the phone one day. "Can you make time for a fan?"

"Most definitely," I responded. "Let's connect tomorrow and hang out?"

"Sounds like a plan," she said. "Looking forward to it."

Maybe it was her direct manner in which she expressed herself, or maybe it was her unpretentious way. Julia did not expect anything, which meant that she could flow as the energy moved her or as she moved it. She was way beyond her years in maturity.

The next day, she was waiting for me in the lobby of 369. We embraced as if we had missed each other. To this day, I enjoy longing for someone in the sense of missing them. *Let me miss you.*

"Hey, stranger," she said with excitement. "That was a nice hug!" she continued before she kissed me on the cheek slowly, with soft lips.

"I missed you," I confessed.

We walked all over Clinton Hill and Fort Greene that day. *Where you from? What do you like to do? How do you spend your time? What do you want to be when you grow up?* Halfway through the walking tour of my neighborhood, I took Julia's hand in mine.

We ended up at the stoop that led up to the two wood-framed glass doors with lace-and-linen curtains at the entrance of the brownstone her family owned. We stood in that awkward space of "Do we hug and kiss, shake hands, wave, or what?" Simultaneously, we leaned in and kissed respectfully but with passion.

"You want to come up?" she offered.

"Yes," I replied immediately.

Julia gave me a tour of her well-appointed, decorated, and furnished home. The woodwork was exquisite and handcrafted by a real artist. I was compelled to reach out and touch it in disbelief of the craftsmanship. The use of pocket doors to make the space between the living room and the dining room fluid in terms of open or closed space was ingenious.

Now this is living, I thought to myself.

Having scanned the living room in admiration of the artwork that adorned the walls, including African masks and statues that balanced on Greco-Roman-inspired stands that stood waist high and on the oversize fireplace, I turned to find that Julia had quietly positioned herself in the middle of a tremendous couch. I imagined that one could get lost in the plush couch and its pillows or fall asleep while reading a good book by the fireplace.

"Come here," she called to me with arms held as wide as the smile on her face.

My spirit fell into hers, followed by my eyes, then my body as I floated into her embrace. Our lips met; then our mouths opened, and we kissed with eyes opened. As the kiss began to grow, our eyes fell shut. We found ourselves fully in the kiss, and time disappeared.

With the fullness of the kiss realized, we slowly pulled apart but stayed close.

"Wow, Mr. Man," Julia whispered. "That was…a kiss."

"Mmm," I sounded. "Yes, it was."

We did that off and on for at least an hour—touching each other and exploring each other's body. As I moved to caress her face yet again, the sound of keys jingling and unlocking the front door drew my attention.

"My mom," Julia mouthed.

An older, taller, and more sophisticated version of Julia glided into the living with a face that masked whatever surprise there may have been to find a strange teenage boy in her home.

"Hello, Julia," her mom's sultry voice let out in an even tone.

"Hello, Mother," Julia returned formally as she stood up from the couch to hug and kiss her mother on the cheek.

"Mother," Julia began the introductions. "This is Maximus, and Maximus, this is Mother."

I stood to greet her and extended my hand to shake hers.

"I prefer Mrs. Robinson to Mother, especially when being greeted by anyone other than my daughter," she offered with a wry smile as she extended her hand to meet mine.

"Good evening, Mrs. Robinson," I offered in return.

"And who are you, Maximus?" Mrs. Robinson asked.

"Maximus is the football player I was telling you about," Julia interjected. "Remember, I told you I met him while he's around until he returns to boarding school in August?"

"So you attend a fancy boarding school, do you?" Mrs. Robinson responded.

"I wouldn't call it *fancy*," I answered. "But it is a boarding school."

Mrs. Robinson pivoted toward the kitchen, which was in the rear of the brownstone.

"Well, I'm going to make dinner, and you are welcome to stay," she offered. "I'd love to hear how a handsome black boy such as yourself ended up at boarding school, in…" She paused in thought. "Minnesota?"

"Missouri, Mother," Julia corrected her mother.

"Thank you for the invite, Mrs. Robinson," I began, "but on such short notice I can't stay. I still have some training to do."

"Well, your loss, but do come again," she answered.

Julia walked me to the door and reached for my hand out of eyesight of her mother.

"You told your mom about me?" I asked.

"Of course," Julia answered matter of factly. "My mom is my best friend. We talk about everything. Who do you talk to about everything?"

I was not ready for that question. After hesitating and truly considering the question, I responded, "No one. At least there's no one person that I talk to about everything."

As she opened the front door to escort me to the first step that led down several steps to the street, Julia turned to hold my face in her hands and said, "Well, I hope you find a confidant with whom you can share all of your secrets." With that, she planted a deep wet kiss on my lips and in my mouth.

"Good night, Mr. Maximus."

I jogged home that evening, replaying the day spent with Julia. Several blocks into the run, I stopped at a traffic light, waiting for the light to turn green, and I smiled a wide grin that would make a stranger ponder the source of my joy.

After reaching home, I headed straight for the shower, where I thought more about Julia and even started planning for the next experience with her. I turned the shower off and toweled off the dripping water before tying the towel around my waist and walking directly across the hall to my bedroom, where the first thing I did was pick up my notebook where I kept track of my workouts.

"Legwork on stairs 3x, abs, stretch, back," read in part for the next day's workout, and then reality smacked me in the face. I could not hang out with

Julia anymore. It was not a choice. It was not a decision. It was a visceral reaction. There was no way that I was going to be as good as I wanted to be for that upcoming football season *and* be able to spend time with Julia.

The next time I saw Julia was where I had met her—behind 369, along the walkway that parted the grassy areas. I finished my last sprints. With hands clasped on top of my head, I walked slowly toward her as I caught my breath.

"Hey, you," I breathed.

"Not bad there," she answered. "A little slow on the last one, but I'll let you slide."

I smiled a weak smile, and Julia noticed.

"Cat's got your tongue?" she offered.

"Nah, just tired," I said but my body language revealed more.

"That may be," she began, "but I'm sensing a different vibe. What's up?"

Julia had been straight with me the entire two weeks we had hung out—exactly six times we were together. I owed her the respect of being straight with her. It was the most difficult conversation I'd had to have up to that point in my life.

"Julia…" I paused in careful consideration of the words I would choose to express my sentiment. "I can't see you anymore."

"You are joking, right?" was Julia's immediate response. When I did not answer right away, she shifted her weight to her right foot and stood a little taller as she straightened her back.

"I'm not joking, Julia. I dig you beyond measure, but I can't rock with you and work and get ready to play ball."

"So you are dumping me so you can work out to play football?" Julia questioned.

"I'm not dumping you. I just need a pause."

"Really, Maximus? You need a pause?" Suddenly, Julia started laughing out loud. "You are really serious about this?" she continued.

"I am, Julia, and it is the hardest decision I've had to make because I dig you like that."

"Well, apparently not," Julia retorted.

The silence between us for a moment was deafening before Julia broke it.

"Max, I can't even be mad at you. I understand what playing football means to you. I'm just sad that there isn't room for me."

Looking into her eyes, I could find no words. Julia reached to embrace me, and I held her tight. My head buried into her neck, and I inhaled the scent of her hair and perfume. Deeply.

"I'm sorry, Julia."

She kissed my cheek and walked away. I watched, thinking she would turn around. She did not. It was the last time I saw or spoke with Julia. But I remember her.

—

I do not apologize for my life. Some have called me *beautiful* and *kind* and *generous*; others have called me *monster* and *mean* and *selfish*. I have been—and still remain—all of those, I am sure. Through it all, I have made maximum effort to be more *beautiful* than *monster*. Of late, I am at peace with being a beautiful monster. In doing so, I would advocate that those who needed my beautiful self in their lives received that from me. And to those who received the monster, your life called for a monster as a springboard to your beautiful self. Maybe you should thank me.

What do you do when people have done their best with what they have, and it falls way short? Forgive?

So when I do not speak at times, it is because I have learned to be silent because friends have died due to misspoken words. And when I lie, it is sometimes because it is difficult for me to trust, and sometimes I do not want to deal with the consequences of truth. I have known people to trust and tell the truth only to have it used against them. And that has resulted in death at times. No one should have to experience death so young.

—

I ended up attending Dartmouth the fall after that fateful encounter with Catherine and Paul. I was the starting tailback on the freshman football team.

Though the Ivy League did not award athletic scholarships, it did recruit athletes and find ways to make attendance affordable.

Allow me a disclaimer on the whole Ivy League thing. Proper etiquette among Ivy graduates is to never say outright that you attended an Ivy League institution. I only mention it to say that I appreciate a rigorous learning environment and that I understand that in part, it had nothing to do with my wit, grit, and determination. It was not only due to my aspiration but also to fortune and grace and sacrifices of loved ones. Simply stated, get the best education you can, and use it to make a contribution to the well-being of humanity. That being said, imagine a Brooklyn cat like me in the Ivies! My whole freshman year, I was on my Jack-Nicholson-as-the-Joker vibe like, "Wait till they get a load of me!"

My Dartmouth experience was apparently unique among African American students. In some of my conversations with black students post-graduation, many said they had hated their own Dartmouth experiences. Some said they had endured the constant barrage of racist micro-aggressions and slights on their intelligence as a badge of courage upon completing the four-year torture chamber. When I told some of them that I enjoyed the challenges of my experience, they said it was because I was a football player, and therefore, I had access to the entire Dartmouth experience as lived by non-African American students. While that may have been true, I was not without the perils and pitfalls that came with every journey. Perseverance through adversity is where men are made.

On the idea of meritocracy—until it is an inconvenient truth.

Hanover, New Hampshire, was a magical place shielded in the Granite Mountains of the state from the outside world. As you approached the college along Interstate 91, the steeple of the library rose above the evergreens as the only hint of a bustling small college town.

Athletes who played fall sports showed up for summer training about two to three weeks before classes started, when the majority of students returned to school. For me and at least one hundred other football players and countless other athletes in dozens of sports, this meant that we were on campus in early August. For me it meant sweating my balls off trying to elude heatstroke and dehydration in eighty-plus-degree heat that felt like one hundred under the helmet and pads.

As we were dressing for the first practice, Petey Corrigan from Tyler, Texas, swaggered into the locker room with the intent of making an entrance.

"What's up, fellas?" he exclaimed. "Who's ready to give up their spot to me?"

Petey was five feet, nine inches tall and all of 165 pounds. The room fell silent at his unprovoked announcement. Petey played running back, which was the same position I played as well as at least ten other athletes in the room. While what he said caught the attention of the entire team, the running backs, including me, took exception to the proclamation.

"What?" Petey asked rhetorically. "Y'all do know that I will be starting soon because I was an all-state and all-American tailback."

A collective sigh was let out in the locker room, followed by pockets of laughter.

"What's so funny?" Petey demanded to know.

The freshman quarterback who had been the number one recruit that year casually walked by Petey on his way to practice and nonchalantly obliged Petey with a response.

"Dude, we're all all-state and all-Americans. Why do you think we're here?"

With that, he tossed a towel over Petey's head, and everyone laughed. Though Petey would play sparingly his freshman year, and despite his flashy speed and moves, his slight build was not made to withstand the violent collisions that every football player had to endure on a constant basis. On the other hand, I thrived on the gridiron my first year.

I split time in the starting rotation with Bidzill Adahy. Biz, as we called him, was from the Abenaki tribe from Massachusetts, and his name meant "he who was strong and lived in the woods." Biz was a half inch taller than me, and though we weighed about the same, his body mass was distributed heavily in favor of his legs—his thighs and calves were massive, whereas his chest looked as if he never lifted weights. Biz was fast but not as fast as me. He was not quick, but I was. He was tough but not as tough as me.

Toughness is underrated, and most people do not have a clue as to the origins of toughness. I was tougher than Biz because my life had been tougher, therefore raising my threshold of pain physically, mentally, and spiritually, for better or for worse. Nonetheless, I earned Rookie of the Year honors because the numbers did not lie. I had a monster season.

Going into our sophomore year, I was projected to be the number one tailback. But in football, as in many performance-based workplaces, you are only as good as your last performance. I ended up getting nicked on my right hip with a hip pointer. If you have ever had a hip pointer, you may consider wishing it on your worst enemy depending on how sadistic you can be. My sophomore season ended before it began.

Biz stepped in, and the team did not skip a beat. He went on to have a historic season for a sophomore in recent memory, and though I was healthy going into my junior year, the coaching staff handed Biz the keys to the kingdom. This was where it got interesting.

Typically, in the code of sports, players who were ranked first in the depth chart did not lose their position to injury. Even if the backup performed well, when the starter was healthy enough to compete, he or she would have an opportunity to challenge the backup to regain their place in the rotation. That did not happen for me. In the summer between my junior and senior season, I would learn why the protocol of allowing the starter to earn his position back after injury was not afforded to me.

Spring semester of my junior year, I failed a comparative psychology class that focused on comparing various schools of thought on the mind—from Freud to Piaget, B. F. Skinner, and Carl Jung. Suffice to say, I was not cut out to major in psychology. I changed my major to organizational sociology, which was simply the study of human social interaction within social structures. The bigger challenge was that I had to attend summer school in order to be eligible to play football in the fall.

While I did not have to take a psych class that summer, I did have to take a humanities course. With the summer class offerings reduced to a bare minimum, my options were severely reduced.

Conrad Coatright was a defensive back on the football team. At six feet three and 215 pounds, he fit the bill of what you would want in a safety. Conrad was from Milford, Connecticut, which was the wealthiest city in the state. Suffice to say, he did not encounter someone like me on a daily basis. You could say we were polar opposites. He was a Republican, and rumor had it that he wrote for *The Dartmouth Review*, which was the most vilified college newspaper on campus. At the time when most of us were engaged in sit-ins in the administration office to divest investments from apartheid South Africa at the time, *The Dartmouth Review* was recommending investing more money.

Nonetheless, there was something about sports that brought people together. Perhaps it was the idea of sharing a common cause. Sports may have arguably been one of the closest endeavors to meritocracy we had. Conrad and I recognized and respected each other's talent and acknowledged that we needed each other to be successful.

"Max," Conrad called out to me from across the campus square while jogging up to me. "I hear you need a course this summer to stay eligible for ball?"

"True," I responded.

"A bunch of us are in the same boat," he said matter of factly.

The casualness in which he said it caught me off guard. I had been embarrassed that I had to go to summer school in order to remain eligible to play football because I had failed a class. Conrad said it as if it was something that happened all the time.

"We're taking Professor Morehead's summer lit course on the American classics. We'll spend the summer reading shit like *The Great Gatsby*, *For Whom The Bell Tolls*, and other cool shit."

Professor Morehead, I said in my head.

I wanted to say, "You mean the same Professor Morehead whom every black student avoids because he is the faculty advisor for *The Dartmouth Review*?" I guess Conrad could tell what was going on in my head by my facial expression, which read, "You are joking, right?"

"Max, don't worry about it," Conrad interjected before I could answer. "We've already spoken to Morehead about you taking his class. He likes you."

"Really?" I exclaimed.

"Yes, really," a voice with an Austrian accent startled me from behind me.

I quickly turned to see Professor Morehead slowly approaching from a few feet away. He was in his late forties to early fifties. It was hard to tell because he smoked and drank whiskey practically every night as he regaled students around the fireplace in his campus apartment. Professor Morehead was a stocky five feet ten with the gait of a retired and injured rugby player.

"Hello, Professor," I greeted him.

"I'm guessing you are having trepidations about joining my class this summer—and for obvious reasons," Professor Morehead stated.

"I'm considering it," I responded.

"Well, let me assuage your fear," he returned. "Despite what you may think of me based on rumors and innuendo, I believe in a fair fight and equal opportunity, and you, my dear young man, have not been given one. And though your American football is not nearly as challenging as its predecessor, my dear rugby, I enjoy watching the game and how you, in particular, play it. Unbeknownst to you, you have not been given a fair chance since you were injured because your fellow competitor has a personal relationship with the coach."

He paused, smiling, evidently amused by the confusion showing on my face as I processed what he was saying.

"Plainly said," he continued, "Mr. Adahy, while in high school, babysat Coach Yardley's children as he, Mr. Adahy, was being recruited by said coach while he, said coach, was at Brown University before finally ending up here and thus bringing Mr. Adahy along with him."

I stared at Professor Morehead as my mind said to me, *So I lost my starting position because Biz babysat Coach Yardley's kids?* I turned to Conrad, who had a look of sympathy on his face while nodding affirmatively as if he heard my thoughts.

And that was how I learned that sports as a metaphor for meritocracy was selective and opportunistic at best.

I decided to take the class, which ended up being a great idea. I read several American/Western European classic novels such as Dosteovsky's *Crime and Punishment* and Hemingway's *The Sun Also Rises*. I also learned how to write. Despite what I'd heard about Professor Morehead, which had been supported in part by the fact that he was the faculty advisor for that hideous rag of a paper, he turned out to be more than fair.

The end of summer term was upon us, and the last class had just ended. As we were exiting the lecture hall, Professor Morehead called to me.

"Maximus Talisman," he announced.

I made my way toward him through the throng of students casually leaving the room.

"Yes, Professor?"

"Max, my dear man, you have done well for yourself in my class."

"Thank you, sir," I answered.

"Do not thank me. Thank yourself for completing the work. I want you to remember that you are more than a football player. You have a brilliant mind."

I stared at him, not knowing what to say because he had just told me not to thank him.

"You can thank me now," he stated nonchalantly.

I smiled. "Thank you, sir."

"Good luck this season."

With that said, he turned on his heel and exited through a different door than the students.

Outside, Conrad was waiting for me.

"Congratulations!" he exclaimed.

"For what?" I returned.

"You got an A."

"How do you know?"

"He told us. He likes you."

I nodded in silence and smiled, thinking how interesting the world was.

I can unequivocally announce that football saved my life simply because it sanctioned the rage and violence that percolated inside of me. I'd had many fights between adolescence and college. Thank God for football.

—

In October 1982, Dartmouth traveled to Boston to play Harvard. I had two touchdowns and rushed for 150 yards, and we won the game.

A few days before the game, I'd received a letter from Catherine. She was aware of the game and invited me to visit her afterward. As the team was boarding the bus back to Hanover, New Hampshire, I was the last to saunter out of the locker room because I was not returning to campus with the team.

Catherine was alone, waiting for me to appear. As I did, she rushed to hug me.

"Maximus," she called my name while burying her face in my chest.

Before I could react or decide to return the embrace, Catherine removed herself from me, her face aglow.

"You played well, Maximus," she offered praise.

"Thank you," I answered.

"Looks like your game not only travels, but it transfers from high school to college."

"So you are a scout now," I said sarcastically.

"A thank-you would be nice," she responded.

"You are right. Thank you for the compliment."

We took a cab back to her off-campus apartment. It was a well-appointed studio in the Back Bay section of Boston, across the river from Cambridge, with a water view back toward the pillared buildings of MIT.

"Are you hungry?" she asked.

"Famished!"

Catherine set it out that night, as we would say. She cooked some salmon with asparagus and rice pilaf, complimented with a pinot noir.

After dinner, we sat together on her couch, working on our second bottle of wine, overlooking the river. She laid her head on my shoulder, and in complete silence we listened to Sade's "The Moon and the Sky" from her *Soldier of Love* album.

It had been almost a year to the day that Catherine had given me her virginity. As she moved with love in her heart this second time, I moved with no more than lust. We sat there experiencing the shared space and energy. The balance in the vibe between was in harmony. It was the timing. We were two people whose time had expired.

Over the next few years, during the days of my youthful indiscretions in college, indifference became my default feeling—if that is even a feeling. The highs and lows of romance would never catch me in its jowls again.

Football became the Novocain to my emotional pain. Besides, it was legalized violence.

THE AWAKENING

Robert Frost wrote the following in his poem "The Road Not Taken":

> *Two roads diverged in a yellow wood,*
> *And sorry I could not travel both*
> *And be one traveler, long I stood*
> *And looked down one as far as I could*
> *To where it bent in the undergrowth;*
> *I took the one less traveled by,*
> *And that has made all the difference.*

Though the poem is more about choice than circumstance, there are still elements of making choices within one's circumstance hidden in the verse.

Growing up, we learned about motivation. There were times that we manufactured anything good to escape the bad and trauma committed against us as children who were not socially and emotionally developed or equipped to manage the abuse. Permanent scars are sustained for a lifetime—if not throughout generations—and are monumentally difficult to overcome. Sad to say, many of our wounds are self-inflicted from the era of slavery. One could make a case that the trauma is in our DNA. It is good to know that via evolution, DNA strands can also evolve, which is why it is paramount that we continue to do the best we can with what we have and where we are because with visions beyond our lifetime, our children can live beyond the trauma.

When you are growing up, and all sorts of fucked-up shit happens to you, and there's no real rhyme or reason for it or justification, that's when you become bitter and you say, "Fuck it, it happened to me, and so I'll make it happen to others."

If you are fortunate enough to evolve through the bitterness, you'll come to learn that your experiences do not give you the right to inflict harm on others. Easier said than done. Rather, the idea becomes, how would you have liked to have been treated? Act upon that idea.

I was reckless in my college days and shortly thereafter.

From the span of my freshman year at Dartmouth to two years thereafter, I personally knew and hung out with four young men who died of AIDS. Once, I hung out in a cocaine bar and even smoked crack—once.

—

"Max," Wanky called me one evening while I was home for spring break my sophomore year in college. "Let's go hang out with Banks and his boy. I heard they got that new high."

"Word," I responded. "Let's get it."

Crack was just on the scene. I had tried marijuana and cocaine at that point. I did not take to cocaine because all it did was keep me awake when I wanted to go to sleep. Marijuana allowed me to be creative and to escape the trappings of the matrix, but it made me sleepy when I wanted to stay awake.

I picked up Wanky, and we drove to Banks's house. His parents had left him the three-story brownstone in Bed-Stuy when they had retired and moved to Virginia Beach, Virginia. Though I knew Banks from elementary school, Wanky knew him most recently because Wanky's nephew went to the private school where Banks taught English.

Banks stood at six feet, two inches but seemed shorter and rounder because he tipped the scale at three hundred pounds. His complexion was butterscotch, and he was always sharply dressed and well-manicured. From fifth grade on, all of us had known that he was different. That he did not fancy women. We did not have a name for his difference, but we accepted it because inherently, we all knew that all of us were different in some way, and we all needed and expected to be accepted in our differences.

Wanky and I pulled up on Halsey Street and found a parking spot directly in front of the house.

"We're in our flow," I announced to Wanky.

"What?" he asked incredulously.

"When things happen easily in your life without effort, like us being able to just pull up and find a parking spot without having to look for one," I explained, "you are in your flow."

"Okay," he answered skeptically. "Whatever you say."

Wanky was laughing as he exited the car.

We ascended the nine steps to the parlor level of 227 Halsey Street, where Banks was already waiting for us. The door was open, and Banks greeted us with open arms.

"Maximus," he exclaimed in his dramatic fashion as he hugged me and air-kissed me on both sides of my cheeks.

Banks did the same to Wanky, ignoring Wanky's feigned protest.

"Boy, stop," Banks demanded. "Welcome to my palace," Banks continued as he led us from room to room and down a narrow spiraling stairwell with wrought iron railing to a cave-like den.

"This is where the magic happens and dreams come true—where you can be anything you want," Banks announced before plopping into the wraparound couch.

He fell into his friend, whom Wanky and I had yet to meet.

"Maximus and Wanky," Banks began. "This is the interior decorator extraordinaire Derrick. Derrick, this is my elementary school classmate, alpha male number one, Maximus—and his first cousin and wonderful uncle to my best student, Tyrus. This is Wanky."

Derrick stood up to greet us with two glasses of Veuve Clicquot. The four of us clinked glasses and toasted the evening.

After some surface conversation that included topics such as the differences between public and private school education, Banks interrupted with a call of "Time for some party favors!"

I had never seen a crack pipe before. Crack pipes were prettier than weed pipes or bongs. I guess that was the allure. The all-glass encasement with curvatures attracted the eye. Derrick was the first to light up. As he inhaled slowly and steadily, the white smoke made its way slowly through the sleek lines of the pipe, capturing my eyes with every turn of the pipe. I was caught in the trance of chasing the white dragon.

Banks was after Derrick, followed by Wanky. By the time my turn came, I had seen enough of how to do it that I taught myself. The three of them were totally high as I began to inhale. I had never seen a drug force its will upon men so strong and so quickly. For me, one inhale was all it took, and I was instantly high. No wait time. However, the thing about crack was that it lasted as long as it took to get you high, and that was why its slaves craved it and were willing to do anything they needed to do in order to get it.

The high was so impactful that I was glad it did not last. Yet I was still high when I saw what followed. Banks leaned over and kissed Derrick full on the mouth with lips open.

I turned to look at Wanky just as he did the same to me. Our eyes met and messaged the same thing to each other.

"Did you see what I just saw?" our eyes spoke simultaneously.

In sync, we both stood up.

"It is late, and I still have to drop Wanky home," I announced.

"Already?" Banks replied.

"Yeah, man," I continued. "Thanks for having us over."

I was moving with deliberation, which did not allow for the same pleasantries as when we had arrived. When we got in the car, Wanky exploded.

"Yo, what the fuck!"

"I know," I replied. "I thought it was the high until I looked at you, and your face confirmed that you had seen what I saw."

"That shit freaked me out," Wanky said. "Not that I have anything against gay people. It's just that I had never seen them kiss up close and personal."

"Exactly," I contemplated.

It was close to three in the morning when I reached home and began calling up every woman I knew for a booty call. Most did not answer, and those who did said no. The next morning, I called them all to apologize. I never smoked crack again.

—

Even before some of these devastating events began to occur in my life, I distinctly remember being acutely aware of the injustices in the world.

"Ma," I said to her one day. "Why is it that people who love God seem to suffer so much, and people who do not even pray seem to be having a good life?"

I went to Sunday school every Sunday. Lloyd Jackson and I would get up on our own at ten years old, get on the number fifty-two city bus, and ride the fifteen blocks to Greene Avenue to attend Jeremiah Baptist Church. No one else in our households attended church.

Lloyd and I were the same age and about the same height, but he was skinny and lanky with two buckteeth on a face that had sunken cheeks accented by a huge Afro.

His aunt Geraldine was the Sunday school teacher, and she was redbone fine. Overall she was slim, but her smile and how she treated us made her the most attractive woman we knew at that time.

Her "Good morning, Maximus" was enough to make my day.

I wanted to be a good Bible student for her. And before we left church, her kiss on the cheek and her "Tell your mom hello" to Lloyd warmed my soul until the following Sunday.

The whole church-religion idea was an odyssey most of my life. Soon after divorcing my mom, my father converted to Sufism, which was defined as Islamic mysticism. I must have been on the cusp of thirteen when my dad approached me about it.

"Son, I want you to convert to Islam," he declared.

My immediate thought came out of my mouth.

"Would I have to change my name?" I asked.

"Yes."

Again, first thought, first words.

"I do not think I want to do that."

This particular exchange between us was unlike most others, in that it felt more like a demand from him than a negotiation or request even.

One particular request has stayed with me all the days of my life.

Up until my junior year in high school, I had not been exposed to any illegal drugs. That year, my mom was snooping through my room as she was prone to do, when she found some weed.

"What is this?" Her voice was shrill as she held up a dime bag of cannabis.

Speechless, I stood silent.

The next day, my father was at our apartment, though he had abandoned it years ago.

"So your mom tells me that she found some ganja in your room," he began.

I nodded.

"Well, you know I smoke, right?" he continued.

I thought it was a rhetorical question since surely he had to remember taking me on his weed-buying runs in his baby-blue 1972 Volkswagen from the time that I was maybe eight years old.

I did not answer him but returned a blank stare as if to say, "Yeah, dude, I know you smoke. Do you know that I know you smoke?"

"I smoke to support my creative mind space when I'm composing music, and I only smoke in my home."

He paused, waiting for a response, I supposed. I was thinking that he was sharing his rules for acceptable weed-smoking conditions.

He continued, "I thought you were an athlete?"

"I am," I barked back.

"Well, you can't smoke ganja and be the best football player that you can be, can you?"

"Probably not," I reluctantly answered.

"If that's the case, then you have to make a choice," he said. "Either you are going to smoke ganja and jeopardize your athletic career, or you'll stop. Your choice."

I quit that night.

In hindsight, that was one of the best Jedi mind tricks my father ever played on me, and it is one that I use often. He used his influential power to guide me to discover my own answer, or at least it felt that way.

The conversation about converting to Sufism was not the same as the conversation we had about smoking weed.

A SON DID RISE

Despites the wretchedness of my youth, I also choose to remember the good experiences throughout my journey.

To this day, there are certain times of the year when I am called to the road or plane or whatever mode of transportation is required to travel. My mom programmed me this way because we would travel whenever she had a break from teaching. This particular break was spring recess or, as we called it, Easter break.

After my ma divorced my dad, my ma would carry on the noble pursuit of travel, and she acted upon her new lease in life by dating a few good men. She did not date them all at once, but rather she was a serial monogamist. One such man was Roy Jackson.

Roy was a high yellow man from Greensboro, North Carolina. He was the obvious product of a mixed relationship from the days of white masters raping black women. His hair was wavy, and he sported a thick mustache that embodied the style of the seventies. Standing at six feet, three inches tall and with a muscular build, he resembled an aging athlete, though he had never played organized sports in his life. Spending most of his youth outdoors playing or working the land that his family rented from the white overseers had molded his body.

Nonetheless, Roy was mindful of the privileges his light skin brought him, understanding the fence he straddled between black and white. He strode with a humble confidence that made him kind toward those who were kind to him. He was charmingly disarming.

My mom met him at one of my aunt Beulah's Friday-night card parties. In between hands of poker, Roy noticed my mom casually hanging around the game, a part of the scene but not in it. He approached her as she leaned against the wall, a cold beer in her hand.

"So are you going to stand there all night, or are you going to join the game at some point?" Roy asked.

"Well," my ma began. "I do not know where you come from, but where I'm from, we say hello or good evening when we begin a conversation." Her laughter punctuated her sentence.

"Forgive me," he responded. "My name is Roy Jackson." He extended his hand to hers.

"And I am Ava," my mom announced. "And no, I do not play poker, and I do not cook, either, before you ask," she proclaimed with a cackling laugh. "I mean, I can cook, but not that good and not that often."

Apparently Roy took to my mother's sass because he took her to lunch the next day. Roy took an interest in me as well, often including me on weekend getaways. About a year into dating my mother, he decided to take my mom and me to meet his folks in North Carolina. It would turn out to be one of my most memorable road trips.

In the tradition of black people traveling around the country, we left hours before sunrise in order to get halfway by around noon so that when we stopped, it was daylight. We'd have lunch out of the way somewhere near a gas station. As always, my mom had made some fried chicken and mac and cheese wrapped in tinfoil. I was not yet a teenager, and this was the early seventies. We could not count on finding a friendly place along the road that would be willing to serve us.

As we continued our journey, I fell asleep stretched out on the back seat of the '69 white Cadillac with the white interior.

"Wake up, my prince," my mom gently called to me. We had arrived in Greensboro.

I slowly pulled myself up from my prone position to sit upright, knocking balled-up tinfoil and ginger ale cans to the floor of the Cadillac. I was still groggy from sleep, so I thought I was dreaming based on what I saw.

The gray deadwood shack of the slave days struck me first. There were two or three people sitting on the porch in rocking chairs. The narrow doorway was screened in with a creaking screen door with holes in its netting and had one window on each side. My eyes tracked down the two creaky wooden steps that led down to the dirt path that led to the dirt road. I looked left and right to see that the house rested on cinder blocks that raised it off the ground. A mangy dog rested in the cool shade under the shack. I continued to pan left and right, and I could see houses several feet apart that looked just like the Jackson's.

My mom and Roy were out of the car now, and Roy led the way up the two steps to greet his people. My mom followed behind before stopping half-way up the dirt path to turn back to me and motion me forward with a wave of her hand as she mouthed, "Come on!"

Reluctantly, I slowly pushed the car door open and walked up the dirt path to where my mother was, all the while looking around in disbelief.

This is straight out of slavery days, I thought. *People still live like this?*

Roy had hugged all three people on the porch by the time my mom and I climbed the two steep steps that required deep knee bends for a twelve-year-old to climb.

"Ava, this my mom," Roy introduced his mom to my mom. "Ava, this is my mama, Marlene Jackson."

Ms. Marlene Jackson was a solid woman. Came from good stock was what they'd call it. She stood around five feet six, but she looked taller due to her girth. She had a big bosom and wide hips from the DNA embedded in her since some of us had been used as breeders. What was most striking was the contrast between her cotton-white hair and her cast-iron skin. Unless you understood the secrets of the South, it would have been hard to believe that Ms. Marlene had given birth to Roy.

"Good afternoon, Ms. Jackson," my mother offered.

"Call me Ms. Marlene," Roy's mother answered.

"Then hello, Ms. Marlene," my mother returned.

"Mom, this is Ava's son, Maximus," Roy continued.

"Hello, ma'am," I replied.

"Well, ain't that special?" Ms. Marlene stated. "Mr. Maximus here is so polite," Roy's mom exclaimed while at the same time hugging me to her ample bosom. Then she held me at arm's length.

"And handsome too," she continued. "Y'all get your belongings and come on in the house and get settled. Supper 'bout ready too."

I looked at my mother as if to say, "This is where we're staying?"

"Roy, you and Ava get the boy's things too. Maximus, dear, come on inside with me, and I'll show you around, and you can help me in my garden to gather what we need to make the living juice."

Ms. Marlene swung the screen door open, and I hurried in behind her so as to not get slapped with the whiplash of the spring-hinged door. There was no second door or real door, though I took notice of the hinges where one would go. Ms. Marlene noticed that I noticed too.

"Do not mind that, ya hear?" she said, laughing. "Down here in the summer ain't no need for a door due to the heat. We puts it in after the fall."

Within just a few short steps, we were already standing in the living room, where three other adults sat on a couch just big enough for the three of them, and another adult lay in a single bed in the corner of the room as all four watched a thirty-two-inch black-and-white television.

"Come on through." Ms. Marlene guided me. Down a narrow hallway, we passed a kitchen on the left, then a bedroom on the right and one last one on the left. We walked all the way to another screen door in the back of the house that led to the backyard. The tour did not last five minutes.

As we pushed open the screen door, I smelled the vastness of Ms. Marlene's yard and garden. It was a delicate mix of cow or horse manure and flowers and fruits and vegetables.

"Help me down," she asked of me.

I held her hand as we gently made our way down two wooden steps that were identical to the ones in front of the house. Once we reached the ground, I attempted to let go, but Ms. Marlene squeezed my hand just enough to keep it in her palm.

"Walk me to the garden, and help me look after some things," she directed.

The garden was well guarded with wired fencing all around it. If any animal got in, I was sure they'd have a hard time getting out, if they did at all.

"I have all of God's nature right here to make the juice of life," Ms. Marlene said proudly. "Look here," she continued. "I got my kale right here—cucumbers and beets over there. Some ginger, garlic, and, most importantly, the turmeric. Then I got me lemon and apple trees back yonder. All of that with some apple cider vinegar juiced down makes what they call the elixir of life."

Ms. Marlene shut the latch of the chicken-wire fence that guarded the garden.

"What's that?" I asked, pointing to a black pot that lay bare in the open grass in the corner of the garden.

"That, my dear Maximus, is the family vat that has been passed down since we got here from Africa. It is a deep fryer."

Ms. Marlene headed in the direction of the vat, and I was drawn along as if by a magnet.

"This was modern stuff back in the early days. Easy as pie. All you had to do was make a fire under it, get you some oil or lard, and you could deep-fry everything. That's what's gonna cook our fish tonight, hon."

On the way back to the house, Ms. Marlene quickly pointed to her left, and if I hadn't been swift, I would have missed it.

"And that over there is the shower and outhouse."

I stopped in my tracks as Ms. Marlene carried on. I stared at the wooden box, then looked back at her for explanation. There would be none. She made her way up the stairs; then the screen door clanged behind her. I found myself in the backyard alone as dusk began its descent upon the earth. It was just a few moments before I realized that I was alone, outside in the country, and I hustled into the house.

When I caught up with Ms. Ms. Marlene inside, everyone was gone except for Roy and my ma, from what I could tell. My ma ended up in the kitchen, talking with Ms. Marlene as she prepared dinner. I joined Roy on the porch as dusk fell upon the dirt. Just then, a candy-apple-red sedan pulled up in front of the house. With a honk of the horn and a wave of a woman's hand to Roy, who waved back, the car pulled off in a cloud of smoke. When the dust settled, there stood the most beautiful girl I had seen in the whole world during my entire twelve years on earth.

Antoinette was a southern girl if ever there was one. Like me, she was also twelve, but she seemed different. Her caramel skin was flawless from the day she was born. Her natural hair fell in careless curls around her shoulders. She was lean like a boy from playing outside all day, but she was definitely a girl.

Carrying a cardboard suitcase, she effortlessly sauntered up the porch, almost taking the stairs in one bounding leap.

"Evening, Uncle Roy!" Antoinette exclaimed, dropping the suitcase and almost knocking her uncle down with a hearty embrace.

Roy was able to hold her weight for a few seconds before guiding her back to the porch landing.

"Hello to you, my beautiful and smart niece," Roy announced.

I stood, patiently waiting to be introduced, which did not take long.

"Antoinette, meet Maximus," Roy introduced us. "Maximus, this is my favorite niece in the world, Antoinette."

I extended my hand to meet hers as she seemingly extended hers with the same eagerness that I had.

"Hello," I stammered. Up close, she was even more beautiful.

"Hello, Maximus," Antoinette offered. Then she whispered, "I'm his favorite niece because I am his only niece."

"And even if I had another one," Roy interjected, "you'd still be my favorite because you are the first."

We all chuckled before Roy headed inside the house, leaving Antoinette and me to fend for ourselves.

Antoinette carried most of the conversation. At twelve, I had not spent a lot of time engaging girls in conversation. If we weren't playing RCK (that's Run, Catch, and Kiss to the layman), I really did not know what to say to them.

Talking with Antoinette was like talking to an adult, only she was a girl.

"Where you from?"

"How old are you?"

"What grade are you in school?"

"Do you play sports?"

On and on, Antoinette drove the conversation. Every question she asked me and that I answered, she answered equally.

She went on to show me around the yard, almost the same tour as Ms. Marlene's but from a kid's view. Antoinette's lens was different than her grandmother's. Both were beautiful, but hers was just different and better. Just like watching a good movie the second time. You tend to see more. This time when we went to the garden, Antoinette directed our efforts to actually picking some fruits and vegetables.

"For breakfast," Antoinette determined.

Dinner that night was memorable because it was so simple. So southern. No matter how modest the home was, the company, the food, the drink, and the conversation engrossed you until time stood still, and the world fell away. In all my travels around the world, my mantra was born that night in Greensboro, North Carolina—good food, good drink, good company, good conversation—in that order.

Having lost track of time with the excitement that came from meeting new people along life's journey, bedtime arrived. Apparently, judging by the way people began to move knowingly as I remained seated, the sleeping arrangements for the night had been set. My ma and Roy went to one bedroom, and Ms. Marlene, Antoinette, and I headed for the other. With showers taken and teeth brushed, Ms. Marlene made us kneel and say the nightly prayer: "Now I lay me down to sleep…"

After, Ms. Marlene landed in the middle of the queen-size bed that squeezed into a room built for a full size at best, and Antoinette and I ended up on either side of her.

Close enough, I thought.

Easter Sunday could not come soon enough! I awoke to the smell of jasmines, peaches, and fried pork.

After we ate, the house was quiet as everyone seemed to be excited about the prospect of going to church. Roy and I got ready on the back porch so the women would have the comfort of the house.

"Let's go," Roy announced as he and I walked around the side of the house to the front. I sauntered past the only window to the bedroom where Antoinette and I had slept with her grandma as the ultimate chaperone. I caught a glimpse of Antoinette as she adjusted her slip while admiring herself in the full-length mirror that hung on the back of the bedroom door. The angle of the mirror was such that Antoinette could see me eyeing her through the window. Our eyes met in the reflection. I was startled and prepared to run, but Antoinette's eyes remained calm and inviting. After complimenting smiles toward each other, I continued to the front of the house.

Though I was a fan of church because of my infatuation with my Sunday school teacher around that time, church down South was nothing like church up North. Or should I say, church up North was nothing compared to down-South church.

Everything was longer. The choir sung longer. I remember them singing.

> *I'm a soldier*
> *In the army of the Lord*
> *I'm a s-o-l-o-l-dier*
> *In the ar-r-my*

Then the pastor preached for almost an hour and a half, or at least long enough for me to lose track of time in delirium. It must have been 110 degrees inside the packed one-room church. Sweat was pouring from brand-new shirts, skirts, and blouses. People were oblivious, caught up in rapture. I was lost in it all as the choir chimed in during the climax of the preacher's sermon with the following:

> *I do not know what you came to do*
> *But I came to praise the Lord*
> *Well, I do not know what you came to do*
> *But I came to praise the Lord...*

Antoinette was caught up as expected. This was home for her. Watching her across Ms. Marlene's swaying belly that again had made its way between us, I admired the rhythm of collective souls caught up in praising their God. I had to admit that I found myself caught up in the euphoria of celebrating God. Again, time became what it was—a manufactured tool to measure experience. I was free of it in this moment, carried away by the sheer experience of church.

"It is now the hour," the preacher began, "where we welcome our guests to this house of worship. So if this is your first time here, I'm going to ask you to stand. Say your name and where you're from."

The piano player tickled the ivories a little softer as the preacher spoke, and the drummer drummed lightly. My mind told me that the preacher was speaking to me, but I did not see anyone else stand, so I remained seated. Sitting on one side of me, my mom stood proudly.

"I'm Ms. Talisman, and I'm here today with my son from Brooklyn, and we are glad to be in the house of the Lord one more time. Praise the Lord."

The congregation responded with, "Praise the Lord."

"Go on." Antoinette prodded me with a nod of her head.

I rose slowly with reluctance.

"My name is Maximus Talisman, and I'm from Brooklyn," I stated simply and matter of factly.

"Come on down here, son," the preacher called to me. "I feel a special message in my heart for you today."

My heart sank a bit because now I was called to be on full display, which was not what I'd signed up for. I brushed past Antoinette, Roy, and a couple of other folks before making my way up the aisle to the preacher.

"Saints, I need y'all to gather 'round this young man, fo' I hear the Lord saying to lay hand and pray for him."

The elders in the church approached me from their various stations in the church. Swarmed by the ushers, with the women dressed in white and the men in black suits, and the deacons and deaconesses coming in their robes from the choir section, in minutes I was at the epicenter of a prayer vigil. There were so many gathered around me that after so many had lain hands on me in prayer, the others laid their hands on their peers, as that was the nearest they could get to me.

"Dear God," the preacher started praying. "I hear you saying that this boy is one of your special ones."

"Yes, Lord!" was spontaneously shouted out throughout the sanctuary.

"I hear you saying that we need to build a hedge 'round him to protect him from those who would do him harm as to prevent him from fulfilling his purpose on earth."

"Hear our prayer, Lord," came a voice from the pews.

"We stand in the gap today, Lord," the preacher continued, "to say we will not allow that. Satan, get thee behind thee, and leave this child alone!"

"Hallelujah!" came shouts throughout the sanctuary.

"We proclaim these words in Jesus's name. Let the church say amen," the preacher ended.

But the laying of hands and the people shouting and dancing continued for three more minutes. I had to admit that I felt a higher vibration of my life energy, and the energy among the people was vibrating at a higher frequency. My spirit was moved by the connection to the spirits of the people in the room. I knew that there was something in the universe that was bigger than me. I would come to know grace and mercy because of this.

Down South, church had another element that was hands down better than up North. After church in Greensboro, people hung around for hours sharing a meal and catching up with people they hadn't spoken to since last Sunday. With it being Easter Sunday and all, there was also the Easter egg hunt with a silver dollar going to the child who found the golden egg!

Back then, the church mothers used real hard-boiled eggs that they had painted an assortment of colors except for the one egg they had colored gold.

"Let's search together," Antoinette suggested, to which I immediately nodded. "I know all of the mothers' best hiding spots," she confessed.

Antoinette and I found early success as we found a half dozen eggs, none of which were the golden egg. As everyone ran around frantically in failed attempts to find the golden egg, Antoinette stood still, listening. To what, I did not know, but I did know she was searching without moving.

"Come on," she directed.

I followed her as she was led against the flow of children who assumed they'd already finished searching in the direction we were headed. Around back of the church, Antoinette took her time walking and searching. The yard of the church was fenced in with a white picket fence that was about chest high for us. In the corner farthest away from the church itself was a section of fence that had been torn through and had yet to be mended. It was just big enough for a ten-year-old child to squeeze through.

I was drawn to that space just as Antoinette was, and we approached together. While the grass inside the fence had been mowed with diligence, the blades beyond the fence had not been touched in what looked like many seasons, if not years. The grass stood knee high in spots.

The broken fence hole was not big enough for Antoinette or me to squeeze through, though we tried. Kneeling at the broken entrance, Antoinette and I looked at each other with pessimism. In that instant, Antoinette's face began to literally glow with an idea.

She reached her arm shoulder deep through the hole in the fence and began to pat through the tall grass just beyond the fence. On the fifth gentle pat, her searching palm came to halt. Antoinette turned to me and smiled with hope. Slowly she pulled her arm and closed hand back to our side of the fence. Releasing her fingers one by one, she revealed...the golden egg!

When we were presented with the silver dollar, the church mother held it in front of both of us. Antoinette turned to me; at the same time I turned to her. I gestured with a nod for her to take it.

That evening, the elders let us walk home together. Alone. No chaperone. We walked toward the sun setting at the end of the road. We talked about the events of the day and how amazing it had been. Halfway to Ms. Marlene's house, Antoinette slipped her hand in mind, and we walked the rest of the way in silence.

I will forever remember Antoinette and my time in Greensboro, North Carolina, because it was pure and innocent.

RECKONING

The time when one is called to account for one's actions.

"Max," Khahari began. "Remember when we used to ring your doorbell so you could come out and play?"

We saluted one another with a clink of glasses filled with Ketel One Vodka on the rocks with lemon twists, raised to celebrate life. We were forty years old now, sitting on the veranda at Marine Park Golf Course after a round of golf.

"Yeah, man," I reminisced.

At least three times a week, my ma had given me piano lessons because she had taught piano lessons in school. So of course her son had had to take lessons.

"We'd ring the bell," Khahari continued. "And you mom would answer. 'Come in,' she would say. 'Have a seat. Maximus is almost done with his lesson.' We were too afraid to say no."

"I know," I chimed in. "I felt bad for y'all but glad for me because it made my practice time shorter."

"Well," Khahari interrupted. "If felt like forever to us."

"That was obvious," I interjected. "Because y'all stopped coming by!"

We laughed out loud.

"Yeah, man," Khahari admitted. "After a while, we just said we'd catch you outside instead of being held hostage."

"That's some funny shit," I concluded.

Each of us took a sip of our drink, silent in reflection.

"You know we grew up in some dysfunctional shit," Khahari said.

"That's probably an understatement," I returned. "And the real madness is that we thought it was normal."

"Exactly," he said. "The deep shit is that we do not talk about real-life issues as men because no one taught us. So we'd all be experiencing shit that we thought was unique to us alone, and we thought it was up to us to handle shit, when all along most us were facing the same shit."

"Imagine life had we just spoken to one another or had an adult to talk to," I pined. "Do not get me wrong; I think the adults in our lives did the best they could with what they knew."

"We gotta do better, bro," Khahari chimed.

I thought about our people.

None of us had had any real successful romantic relationships growing up.

We hadn't been able to protect our mothers, resulting in extreme ideas of mother-son relationships. We had either been overprotective, doting and childlike à la Peter Pan, or distant and adversarial.

BOSIDA

After dropping Khahari off at 369, I bumped into Adisa on his way to visit his mom.

"Have you been to see Bosi?" Adisa asked me.

"Nah, not yet," I responded. "You?"

"Nah," he answered.

"It is time to go," I decided.

After attending a Catholic high school in Brooklyn, Bosida had attended Morgan State in Baltimore, Maryland. He had not graduated because his newfound freedom in college had been too much to bear as he futilely chased women. Bosida had always worked at jobs but had never had a career. In his midforties he had become a stalwart at our neighborhood church. Joining the church had been the thing to do for many black men who had been beaten down by the pursuit of the ever-elusive American dream.

Bosida had volunteered in the church's real estate ministry, traveling extensively throughout South Africa. Unknown to him for some time, the travel had led to a buildup of blood clots that had led to an aneurysm that would leave him incapacitated for eight years.

Adisa and I arrived at Brooklyn Hospital on Dekalb Avenue. My gait immediately became noticeably slower. Word on the street was that he and Lola had recently reconciled after nearly twenty years of not speaking.

That happened a lot in the hood. Teenage sweethearts went their separate ways after turbulent breakups only to find comfort in one another after finding that their untreated dysfunctions of their youth kept them from loving and being loved by anyone other than one who had lived through the same.

Bosida and Lola had gone to hear some live jazz in Fort Greene on an October evening—Indian summer, we called it. On the walk home afterward,

Bosida had collapsed and lost consciousness. They said he went four minutes without oxygen. It was enough for him never to wake again.

The night before I went to visit Bosida in the hospital, I'd had this dream. Bosida, Adisa, and I had been walking down a street, probably in Brooklyn, when I'd realized that Bosida was walking around and talking as if nothing had happened. I'd cried with delight and told him that I loved him, and he told me back. He'd complained that his leg hurt. We'd walked a little farther. I could not recall our conversation or if we had even had a conversation. I did know that we had enjoyed being together. After a while, I had hailed us a cab so Bosida wouldn't have to walk anymore. In the dream, I had believed he would be healed.

Nothing could have prepared me for what I saw when we entered room 703. Bosida was being fed oxygen through a foggy tube, and brown sludge was being poured into him for food from another tube.

I did not last six minutes before the stale hospital air coupled with the sight of my best friend on earth lying in an invalid state overwhelmed me. I cried like a baby. Tears poured out, streams running down my face to the floor. I gasped for air in between sobs, grasping for breaths before convulsing shots of spasms threw my head back and forth.

Adisa was his usual stoic self. He had perfected the silent scream within to mask the pain.

That January, cats from the hood rolled twenty deep to host a Super Bowl party in Bosida's hospital room. Soon, monthly visits deteriorated to once every six months. The pain of seeing him in that state of being was too much for our psyche to bear, in part because if it could happen to him, it could happen to us. It was not until years later that I realized that to visit Bosida was for him and not for us, and therefore the sacrifice was worth it.

But after years of hoping and praying for even the smallest of change and seeing none, good intentions could go to hell.

Secretly, we discussed putting a pillow over his head—he was breathing on his own now and had only a feeding tube. Starving him to death did not seem like an option.

Adisa and I vowed to assist the other in death should we meet Bosida's fate.

KHAHARI

Khahari attended the University of Miami on a baseball scholarship. Like Bosida, he dropped out after his sophomore year. Unlike Bosida, Khahari had great success hunting women on campus.

Again, without the full complement of a college degree, Khahari was employable but not career minded.

New York became overwhelming, and so like many African Americans whose families had fled North and had since fallen on hard economic times—participating in the great reverse migrations—Khahari moved to Darlington, South Carolina, the home of his second wife's grandmother. As Jay-Z is attributed to having said, "Wherever you go, there you are." Khahari could not escape his penchant for women and liquor nor the dark cloud of being a hard-to-employ man in part due to his blackness.

Khahari and his second wife, Belinda, were a good match on paper. They were both of dark-chocolate complexion with traditional features of southern blacks from the days of our ancestors. Belinda was built strong from the ground up, with tight features that you could tell would get overbearing and loose with age. Turned out the make-or-break feature between them was the fifteen-year age difference. As the younger partner, Belinda could not relate to some of the topics of conversation that Khahari enjoyed engaging in. Conversations between them became increasingly rare, save for the everyday mundane small talk that most couples partake in out of obligation to get through the day.

Life between them became challenging because she did not get his jokes, and he did not understand her generation's variation of the English language. A slowdown in sex resulted.

I recall Khahari telling me how the conversation went down.

"Darling," Khahari introduced the conversation, "how come we ain't fuckin' like we used to?"

Belinda snapped back, "Probably 'cause when I have to get up and go to work at the diner, yo ass be laying up in the bed."

Not long after that, Khahari waited for Belinda to find REM sleep before he crept beside her.

"Darling," he whispered in her ear. "Belinda," he softly called after she did not respond.

This time she stirred and turned to find a 45-caliber pistol pressed to her temple.

"You my wife," Khahari commanded. "And my wife is going to fuck me when I want, whether I work or not."

Belinda went to work the next day and never returned. They say she moved in with a coworker who was a lesbian. Earlier in their relationship, Khahari and Belinda had tried unsuccessfully to coax the woman into a ménage à trois.

Finances were always a challenge. When a woman worked, and a man did not, it was often insurmountable.

I used to tell Khahari, "My dude, all she wants to see is that you are making an effort to find work, especially since she has to work."

"But I'm disabled and can't work. Besides, my disability check will stop."

"Then get something off the books; even if you pumped gas, she'd respect the effort. At the very least, go out in the morning when she leaves, and look like you are looking for work."

We laughed, followed by contemplative silence. It was years later—after Khahari found himself alone, having moved deeper South to Alabama because that was where his disability check got the most traction—that he finally found work in a meatpacking factory.

Like Bosida, Khahari found religion and joined the local church, where he sang in the choir.

DARWIN

D-Knowledge ended up marrying his second girlfriend in his life and having four children—three boys and a girl. They moved into his wife's childhood home that had been willed to her upon her parents' deaths. Darwin represented the best among us, though he had the same proclivities as his father.

"Yo, Max," Darwin introduced the conversation six months after his wife gave birth to their last child. "When is it okay to tell your wife who gave you three boys and a girl that it is time to lose weight? 'Cause I'm not feeling it, bruh."

"That's a tough one, bro," I answered. "There probably is no good time."

"Exactly," Darwin responded. "That's the problem because I feel like I can't express myself."

"If you and Erica are the friends that I think you are, you should be able to say what you feel. It just depends on how you say it. But wait at least a year from the last baby."

"It has been more than a year already."

"I know." I laughed. "I'm the godfather."

In August of 2001, Darwin and his wife hosted one of their now infamous Brooklyn backyard barbecues, where food and drinks were overflowing. Smoked ribs, grilled salmon, jerk and curry chicken, mac and cheese, fish, chicken, and steak kebabs. Whatever you drank was in stock at their bar. Old-school Caribbean music permeated the background but did not overwhelm conversations. People came from out of town for a Darwin barbecue. The energy in the space was positive. The whole crew was there: Adisa, Khahari, Bosida, a few others, and me.

"Yo, D," Adisa called to Darwin. "What your Knicks gonna do this year?"

"I do not know, bruh," Darwin returned. "But I do know that one-hundred-million-dollar contract they signed Allan Houston to is gonna come back to bite them in the ass!"

"Man, the Knicks ain't gonna be shit," exclaimed Khahari.

We laughed with roars, tossing back Heinekens. Later on, Darwin caught my eye as I was talking with his dad.

"Maximus," Darwin called to me.

I turned my head away from my conversation, toward his voice. He was making his way past a few guests as I noticed a woman trailing him. Soon enough, the two of them were upon me, face to face without anyone in between.

"Max, I want you to meet someone." The way Darwin turned to present this woman signaled a level of importance he assigned to her.

"Nola, this is Maximus. Max, this is Nola."

I reached to shake her hand as she reached to embrace me. Her embrace won the day.

"So glad to meet you," she offered. "Darwin has spoken of you so much that I feel as if I know you."

Nola was five feet seven, about 145 pounds with ample breasts, curvy hips, and a muscular ass. She wore her hair natural, as did most women in our circle. She wore a colorful blue-and-orange African-print head wrap that allowed her hair to peek out between the folds in the wrap to show its brilliance.

Nola, Nola, Nola, I repeated in my head, attempting to recall any mention of her in conversations with Darwin. *Nola. Yes!* It came to me.

Darwin had dated her while he had been at Morehouse, and she had been at Spelman. They had stayed in touch after graduating but had never managed to be in a monogamous relationship, though they were always open to being in each other's lives.

"Nola," I said happily. "Darwin has mentioned you as well."

Over Nola's shoulder, I could see Erica shooting laser beams with her eyes into the back of Nola's head. Then she stared down Darwin and to me with the look of "Max, how could you?" and "I bet you knew all along!"

I knew that Darwin and Nola had dated in college and had been in touch over the years—as recently as the last few months. I did not know that he would invite her to his annual barbecue in his own backyard.

Later that night after everyone departed, Darwin and I remained alone in the backyard.

"My dude," I began. "What are you thinking?"

"Max..." Darwin paused. "I do not know. All I know is that I'm not happy."

"Well, you are gonna have to figure this shit out real quick 'cause I know Erica is not having it."

"I know bro." Darwin was resigned. "Erica and I already had that convo."

"What did she say?" I asked.

—

"Listen Darwin," Erica had started. "I know things ain't been right between us lately."

"What you talking about, Erica?" Darwin had defended himself.

"Stop, Darwin," Erica had interrupted. "Let's not pretend anymore. I know you've been in touch with your ex, Nola..."

"How you know that?" Darwin had returned.

"Does it matter?" Erica had answered. "All I know is that me and the kids are here for you, and we're going to be here. You have to decide if you want to be here. But one thing we ain't gonna do is have you steppin' out with your side chick. You gonna have to make a decision."

Darwin had stared in disbelief as Erica had kissed him on the forehead and had gone up the stairs to the parlor floor of their family brownstone.

—

"Damn, B!" I offered, in disbelief myself. "That's cold blooded and loving at the same time."

"Tell me about it," Darwin responded.

"So why bring ole girl to the crib tonight?"

Darwin stared at me before speaking. "Because I think I'm going to make that move. The only thing holding me back is the kids. I don't know if I can handle not seeing them every day."

"Okay," I began. "Let's play out the scenario. Where you goin' if you leave?"

"Back home, I guess," Darwin surmised.

"So you're going to go back home and sleep in your old single bed in the room you grew up in?"

Darwin nodded as he likely pictured the scenario.

"Why not move in with Nola?"

"'Cause I do not really have shit to contribute like that."

"And you won't because Erica is going to make you pay child support, and who knows when you'll see your kids."

"True," Darwin said matter of factly.

"Let me ask you a question. When you married Erica, if someone would've told you that for thirty years of marriage, you may have five years of hell or more, would you still do it? Knowing that twenty to twenty-five years would be great, but you'd have to get through the five to ten years of shit, would you still have married her?"

Darwin was deep in thought as if he was rewinding his life to his wedding day and then, just as quick, fast-forwarding through a thirty-year marriage.

"Yeah," he concluded. We sat in silence for a minute. "Thanks, bro. I receive that."

Out of all of us, Darwin and his wife were the only ones to remain married.

ADISA

Adisa was the first among us who attended an HBCU (historically black colleges and universities) to not only graduate but to graduate on time in four years. His dogged determination served him well. Adisa was as steady an adult as he was a child. He had a plan, and he worked through adversity.

Adisa took a job working for the city's youth-development department. He directed a yearlong after-school program in Bed-Stuy, Brooklyn, at a local elementary school. Over the twenty-some-odd years that he worked there, his space of work became a neighborhood safe haven, and for that, upstanding citizens and criminals alike respected Adisa.

His first wife, Norma, cheated on him and left him for some guy she ended up leaving as well.

His second live-in "wifey" was the baby mama of one of the cats who ran in our general clan, so it really was a bro-code violation to be with her. But Adisa thought he had done it the honorable way.

"Yo, Raheem," he had begun. "I know that you and Karima aren't together anymore."

"True," Raheem had acknowledged.

"I'm here to ask you," Adisa had continued, "if it's cool if I see Karima."

Raheem had looked Adisa in the eyes calmly and had coldly said, "Yeah, man. If she's with it, why not?"

Karima had ended up moving in with Adisa, bringing her and Raheem's daughter to Adisa's house in Long Island. She had even moved the dog in. Less than eight months into the relationship, Karima and her daughter moved out and left the dog. It was not until another three months later that Adisa found out that Raheem and Karima were still fucking.

Who was wrong, and who were we supposed to feel sorry for? No one spoke about it—as if it never happened. There were always these one-thousand-pound gorillas in our rooms that everyone pretended not to see.

After a while, Adisa and Raheem were cool enough to hang out with each other in a peripheral sort of way. Karima seemed to disappear into the background fabric of the neighborhood. She slowly faded from the scenes of the block parties and house parties.

TIME WAITS...

Time is the only commodity that we can never get back. It does not replenish itself. As such, it can have a way of crushing the life out of some of us.

My cousin Roxanne had a baby boy at seventeen. I never saw her after that. She moved around often from apartment to apartment, borough to borough, and even state to state, most times in and out of shelters. I heard she named her son after me. I never met him.

Roxanne died of AIDS shortly before her son's fifth birthday. Her brother Tuma, raised the boy. Maximus, her son, grew up, and at twenty-six years old, he embraced his feminine side and publicly declared his transsexual identity and began dressing as a woman.

Tuma moved to Buffalo, New York, to live with his other sister, whom he and Roxanne had been separated from by the foster care system when he was two years old. Now in their midthirties, they still found themselves entangled by the same system. Tuma helped raise her two adopted children. At fifty-eight years of age, he was unemployed, with very little prospects except for his monthly disability check of $1,200.

Wanky and Tank chose to be homeless. Both had children, and both were estranged from them. Wanky's daughter was born mentally disabled due to drug use by him and the baby's mother during the mother's pregnancy. The Agency of Child Services took the baby away and institutionalized the girl as a preteen. Officials had determined that the girl suffered enough her whole life with her parents. Her parents' initial response was feeling relief from the burden of being two parents who could not care for her. In the long run, it drove Wanky mad. He did not actually know he had been driven mad. What madman admitted to madness? His life reflected that of a madman. Thus, in madness, he embraced his ability to live as a homeless man.

Tank fathered several babies by several women. He never stayed long enough to get to know any of his children. Missed birthdays and holidays turned into years. Rumor had it that Tank was so far removed from his children that he could walk right past them on the street and not even recognize them.

MAXIMUS

Despite the obvious strains in my relationship with my father, including wanting to kick his ass for hitting my mom, he and I had a relationship of mutual respect for the most part and with all experiences considered. There were good times and bad.

Life's beat-downs were mitigated by a talent that I pursued through hard work, travel, education, and God's extra grace and mercy reserved for fools and babies.

My worldview was shaped by education and travel—experiences evidenced the fact that our humanity trumps all ethnic divisions, which are social constructs to legitimize greed and oppression.

I, too, bounced around from job to job, with two years signaling my time to move on between each. I did not become career minded until I understood and embraced the idea that one's career or lifework is that which gives him or her a sense of purpose toward advancing the well-being of humanity.

From a macro-view, I choose to believe that life's been good, all things considered. The single most influential factor in my life's progression is arguably the few "rabbis" I've had along the way. A good mentor is worth his or her weight in gold. The angels sent me along my life's path since birth, just as the midwife who birthed me had alluded to, and guided me through the gauntlet that is life. As a result I have been afforded experiences such as attending boarding school as well as one of the finest colleges in America, if not the world, and living abroad.

—

Around my twenty-seventh birthday, I found myself adrift, moving around a lot until I landed a roommate—an old college friend. That spring, three of my fraternity brothers from college decided to join me on a vaca to Trinidad for Carnival. Though our housing situations were tenuous at best, collectively, we had enough money to rent a four-bedroom villa on the side of a mountain with sea views from all of the bedrooms along with an infinity swimming pool. Even twenty years after the experience, I remember it well. I kept the bedroom sliding doors open at night, the white linen curtains billowing in the trade winds; I awoke one morning to stand on the balcony to greet the day. I looked far out to sea and saw a dark sheet of cloud that was clearly delineated from the rest of the sky. It was fascinating to see a clear blue sky and sunshine in one part of the sky buffeted against a dark-gray line of sky. As it moved across the horizon, I could see that the dark sheet was actually a rain line followed by sheets of rain over the ocean. It was too far out to sea to rain upon me. That night, the four of us went out on the town. That was when I met Toni.

Toni had been born on Tobago and had flown home from New York to enjoy Carnival as she had done every year since she had become an adult who worked and could afford to pay her own way home. Toni was as dark as me and almost as tall. Her teeth were whiter and straighter than mine, and her strut was bolder than mine.

In the midst of an outdoor party in the street somewhere in Port of Spain, Trinidad, our eyes met across the street before I turned away. The next thing I knew, she was standing next to me, tapping me on my shoulder.

"Excuse me," she began. "Were you just staring at me from across the street?" She mouthed the words, but I could not hear her over the loud music.

"What?" I shouted.

This time she moved in close enough to where our bodies touched as she repeated her question with her mouth close to my ear.

"I wouldn't call it *staring*," I returned in her ear.

We went back and forth this way, learning each other's names and finding out that we both lived in New York City. We partied a few nights in Trinidad before committing to see each other back in New York.

Toni and I dated long enough to spend time at family gatherings and to become an exclusive couple. After a year, with our mutual friends starting to get married, Toni asked me when I was going to marry her.

When? I thought to myself. A bit presumptuous, I believed, but at least she had been consistent in who she was from the day I'd met her.

My overall impression of Toni was that she was an outstanding party partner. On many a Friday night, we would polish off a fifth of Absolut Vodka before eleven o'clock at night. I was not sure that made for a life partner.

"Let's do this," I suggested in May of that year. "Let's move in together, and at the end of the year or by next May, we can decide to get married or move in a different direction."

"Deal," she responded and shook my hand firmly like a man to seal the agreement.

At the time, I was running my own fundraising-consulting firm and worked out of town as an on-sight resident consultant to a client in Providence, Rhode Island. In my years of bouncing around from job to job, I had spent a couple of years working for the United Negro College Fund. Initially, I had been so enamored with the organization and the work they did on behalf of historically black colleges and universities. However, the seemingly patriarchal hierarchy that prioritized longevity over objective measurable talent quickly disillusioned me. At the same time, I thank the UNCF for being my springboard to entrepreneurship.

I would typically drive from Brooklyn early enough on a Monday morning to get to the office by eight o'clock and come home Friday nights by seven o'clock at the latest. I had some spiritual moments along those drives.

Three o'clock on a Monday-morning drive back to Providence. On a December day, the snow came down heavily enough to impact visibility on the road and enough to stick to the ground, making driving conditions slick. It was still closer to night than day, with no sight of dawn on the horizon. It was also a time when many trucks were on the road.

My senses seemed dulled by fatigue, and I relaxed my focus on driving during a mile stretch of straight road. In a split second as my eyelids grew heavy with sleep, the SUV swayed ever so gently just a nudge to the right side of the lane. It was just enough for me to slightly lose control of the car on the icy road.

The car swerved left and right and began to skid. Instinctively, I did what I had been taught in driver's education—steer into the skid. No longer skidding, I glided down the center lane of the three-lane highway. The car was perpendicular to the lanes instead of parallel as usual. That meant the front windshield was facing the side of the road. I had to turn my head to my left to see down the roadway. But when I turned my head to look out of the passenger-side window to see what was behind me, I saw an eighteen-wheeler bearing down on me.

As my car came to a slow halt, all of the traffic behind me did the same. The truck came within half a car's length of hitting me. It close enough that I could only see the grill of the truck.

Realizing that I was safe, I steered the car in the right direction and returned to the drive. Less than a quarter of a mile into the journey, I felt a voice say, "Hey, man, I'm here."

With full and undivided attention, I calmly turned my head to the passenger seat. The essence of my father was present. I was being comforted by the spirit of my father, who had passed eight years prior from a heart attack. I smiled and was made still in the peace of the moment. I have always felt the comfort of the Talisman ancestors.

—

Less than two months into our agreement, Toni was pressing.

"So what are we going to do?" she demanded.

"What are you talking about?" I returned.

"About getting married," Toni answered.

"You cannot be serious right now. We haven't lived together for two months yet. We agreed on a year."

"Well, I can't wait that long," she concluded.

In hindsight, that should have been a trigger signal that this relationship was headed to an end.

"I'm prepared to stick to our agreement. What do you want to do?" I asked.

"I'm not waiting around a year for you to say you aren't going to marry me."

"Who said I wouldn't marry you at the end of a year? And why did you agree to move into my space with that understanding?"

Crickets were what I got in return. Not a word came from her—just a blank stare.

Being the gentleman that I imagined myself to be, I agreed to let her stay in my duplex pad until the end of August because that was the time she said she needed to get her money together to move out. We also agreed that we would see other people. Again, hindsight being what it is, of course she was already seeing someone, unbeknownst to me. The caveat was that she would not bring anyone to my pad.

—

When you are in flow with the universe, instinctual signs appear. It was a Wednesday, mid-afternoon in July, when God signaled to me that it was time to go home. I drove the damn near four hours back to New York that evening. It was after ten o'clock at night when I arrived at my duplex pad; all of the lights were on, which was unusual for that time of night on a weeknight.

I did not think anything of it at the time, and thus I was not sneaking into my own crib. I unlocked the front door as usual and casually stepped up the three stairs that led to the living room. Every light on the first floor was lit, but no one was there. As I headed up the stairs to the second floor, I called out, "Hello?"

There was no response, though I did hear rustling as if someone was scurrying about. I reached the second-floor landing, where the bathroom faced the staircase. There were two bedrooms. The master bedroom was to the immediate left, and the smaller bedroom was to the right of the first bedroom.

Both bedroom doors were closed, with the door to the master bedroom ajar enough that a knock would push it open. I knocked.

"Hey," I offered to a disheveled Toni, who was sitting on the edge of the unmade king-size bed. When I say *disheveled*, I mean looking as if she was done with her workday and ready to go to bed: scarf on her head, no makeup, contacts out, and glasses on.

"Hey," Toni replied. "I did not expect you home in the middle of the week."

"It was a spur-of-the-moment thing," I answered. "Everything okay?"

"There's someone behind the door," Toni confessed out of nowhere.

Standing at the threshold of the door and with her admission, I pressed on the door slightly with the intent on opening it as far as it would go. After opening a few more inches, it stopped as it met resistance.

"Hello," came the voice of man I'd never heard before and whose head popped out from behind the door. I scanned down from his head to see a bare chest. I could go no farther.

In a purely visceral reaction, I let out a cackle of a laugh followed by "Aw, hell no" as I turned to enter the second bedroom to take off my shit.

"I know you do not have another motherfucker in my crib!" I announced.

Dude was like, "I did not know she had a man living here."

"How could you not know with all of these trophies and plaques and shit up in here?" I demanded to know.

"I did not know," he replied sheepishly.

"Here's what I know," I began. "By the time I finish taking off my shit, you better be gone."

There were no words exchanged for the minutes that it took me to change into some sweats and a T-shirt. During those few minutes, I was able to calm down to a rational level, down from the potential insanity of the moment. During that time, the internal conversation in my head went like this: *It is not like she's your woman. Yeah, but still she violated your space. Exactly! That's why I need to wail on the motherfucker. Nah, yo. It is never the dude's fault. Always the chick's fault because she let him do what a man does. True. But still, if he's still here, I gotta rock his motherfuckin' bell!"*

I opened the door to the second bedroom, ready to put in work. The door to the master bedroom was wide open. Dude was nowhere in sight, and Toni remained in the same position as when I had first seen her that night.

"He's gone" was all she said.

Damn, I thought. He hadn't made a sound. He was out like a ghost—quick, fast, in a hurry. *Good*, I thought, because at the end of the day, a confrontation with unknown results had been avoided.

As I focused on Toni sitting on my king-size bed, all I could think was, *Fuck, I can't fuck, let alone sleep, on my king-size bed again.*

"I thought we agreed not to bring people into our space?" I began rhetorically.

"We did, but I did not know you were coming home," Toni responded.

"What the fuck does that have to do with anything?" I shouted.

"I mean, if you did not come home, you wouldn't have known that he was here. I thought you only came home on weekends."

Wow, I thought. *Now I know why I didn't want to marry this crazy bitch.* I stared at her in disbelief.

"Come here," she suggested, extending a welcoming hand to me.

I approached and stopped shy of touching distance.

"Do you want to fuck me?" she asked in her most seductive voice.

Wild eyed was how I would describe my look at her. She must have noticed because she scooted herself back onto the bed a few feet, not knowing my response. My thinking was, *I know she did not just offer to fuck me! Maybe I should and just choke the shit out of her.*

I did not say a word. I called her cousin, who was a good friend of mine.

"Hello," Edolphus answered. Edolphus was an accountant who did my taxes.

"It is Maximus," I began. "I came home tonight and found your cousin in my crib with another dude."

"No, man. Do not say that." He let out a pained sigh.

"Real shit. I need you to come and get her before I do something crazy."

"Say no more. I'm on my way."

With that, I hung up the phone and turned my attention to Toni.

"Pack a bag. Your cousin is on his way to get you before I kill you."

Toni moved to touch my arm. I snatched it away before the touch.

"You have until August fifteenth to be out. I won't come home until then, but when I do, you better not be here."

I stayed at the duplex until Edolphus arrived. Toni was ready when he rang the bell. He and I shook hands.

"Sorry about this, bro," he offered.

"Not your fault," I responded.

Toni brushed by me without a goodbye. I had not been expecting one.

A SAFE SPACE
TO LICK WOUNDS

I returned to Providence bent on putting this experience behind me. As such, I spent many a lunchtime at the Lion's Den, the local strip club. As a frequent customer, I became known by name, and I knew many strippers by their stripper names.

Ironically, my sole client at that time was the Roman Catholic Diocese of Providence. Day and night, I was meeting with priests and parishioners, advising them on why and how to raise money to support Catholic endeavors. In between those times, I lived at the Lion's Den.

As a younger man, I had not been one to frequent strip clubs, merely for the fact that I did not understand the logic of spending hundreds of dollars just to get a hard-on and maybe to have an orgasm in one's pants from dry humping. It made more sense to go to a whorehouse or hire a professional to receive real sex. Nonetheless, strip clubs were safe because of their non-penetration policy.

I would usually sit at the bar, have an actual lunch and a drink, watch sports on one of the two televisions that hung from the ceiling, and wait for bored strippers to sit with me and engage in conversation as they waited for the next customer or their regulars. Oftentimes I would give them a modest tip for their time because everyone needed to make a living in America. That was how I met Francesca.

Francesca was a second-generation Italian. Her hair was jet black and naturally curly from her ancestors probably mixing with the Moors who had come across the Eurafrican Mediterranean Sea to Sicily, where Francesca's great-grandparents had been born. Francesca's skin was olive in complexion, which told the story of black people and European people loving one another. She stood at five feet, eight inches, with long legs and heavy breasts.

"So good afternoon sir," Francesca introduced herself.

"Good afternoon, lady," I returned.

"No need to be so polite. We are in a strip club." Francesca looked around the club. "I'm Aurora." She extended her hand.

I reached for it, held it firm but gently in mine, looked her in her green eyes, and replied, "Austin."

"So, Austin, what brings you in here like…every day?"

I chuckled in reply between swallowing some *penne alla vodka* and a swallow of sauvignon Blanc.

"Lunch."

"That's it?" Francesca replied incredulously. "Out of all of the places you could go for lunch, you choose a strip club on a regular basis?" She gave me the side-eye and tilted her head. "I'm not buying it," she concluded.

"It seems fitting based on where I am in my life at this time," I replied.

She seemed to feel my vibe and did not probe further. I signaled that I had finished my meal by tossing the cloth napkin onto the plate.

"Where you from?" she asked.

"Brooklyn."

"New York, huh?" Her voice rose at the end. "What brings you to Providence?"

"Work."

"What kind of work?"

"I'm a fundraising consultant for the diocese of Providence."

"No shit," she said in disbelief.

"Why do you say it like that?" I asked.

"Only because everyone down here knows that the Catholic priests are the biggest perverts in America."

"Allegedly," I retorted.

Again, I got the side-eye.

There was no denying the allegation. At the time, the diocese of Providence, Rhode Island, was under scrutiny as having the most lawsuits filed against them in America for child molestation. My job was to help priests raise money for diocesan-wide projects, which entailed some nights alone with priests in the rectories.

Rectories were posh pads that priests got to live in for free. It was a nice gig if you could get it. I'd had conflicting experiences with Catholic priests.

I remembered meeting the bishop of the diocese. It had been at church service, and during communion he had shaken my hand. It had been electrifying. I recalled thinking that he was truly a man of God—one who lived their convictions and did not cause harm to others. He was one who served wholly. On the other hand, there was Father Gerald.

Father Gerald—or Father Jerry, as he liked to be called—was a dead ringer for Uncle Fester from *The Addams Family*. He was disarmingly charming and humble, with self-effacing humor. One night after a fundraising executive committee meeting, Father Jerry had invited me to the rectory, which was adjacent to the main chapel hall. You did not even have to go outside to get there.

It had been winter, with snow on the ground, just after the Super Bowl. Basketball season had been starting to warm up.

"Maximus," he had begun. "Why don't you come by the rectory and join me for the game tonight? Washington is playing the Knicks."

His voice had been so inviting on a winter night in a place where I had not known many people, and my hotel room had been a drag. Besides, I had wanted to test the theory of perverted priests for myself. I'd figured I could take the fat fuck if the situation got out of hand.

The rectory was modestly furnished. What stood out was the detailed woodwork that looked rich, as if the craftsmen had taken their painstaking time to perfect it.

"Have a seat," Father Jerry had gestured to me with a sweep of his hand, directing me to a grain-leather single-seat lounge chair. He had disappeared into the nearby kitchen, emerging shortly after with a tray of snacks, two rocks glasses—one filled with ice, the other without—and an unopened bottle of Macallan 12. He had set the tray on a serving tray next to the hard wooden chair with a seat cushion, where he would sit.

"Do you prefer your scotch neat or on the rocks?" he had asked.

Caught off guard due to the notion that men of God were not supposed to drink, I had been slow in my response.

"Neat," I had responded.

"Neat it is," he had returned as he opened the bottle and made a meticulous pour for each of us.

Talk between us had been limited to during commercials, as both of us had been into the game. He had done most of the talking, asking the general questions about one's life: Where are you from? Where did you go to school? Small talk. After the Knicks won the game, and as he returned to the kitchen to clean up the food and drink, I had stood to put on my coat.

"Leaving so soon?" Father Jerry had questioned.

"Yes. I have a long day tomorrow that starts early."

"Well, as you can see, the rectory is full of rooms, so feel free to stay," he had suggested.

It had never crossed my mind to stay, but I was curious as to why he would even ask.

"No, thank you, Father," I had stated. "Thank you for the drink."

"And thank you for the company."

On my drive home I had thought that he—like many priests, I imagined—was a lonely man, and that the priesthood had made him so. No wonder some priests fucked little boys. I had cringed at the thought. They were only allowed to be alone with the altar boys. *Who decided that?* I had wondered. *We covet that which we see the most. Priests should be allowed to marry women.*

—

"So do you have any juicy priest stories?" Francesca asked over the booming strip-club music.

I thought about telling her the Father Gerald story but decided not to because it was against my code to make fun of another's misery.

"Nah. So far all the priests I've encountered have been respectful."

Francesca burst out with laughter that turned heads in the club.

"Whatever you say, Brooklyn," she said with the accent of Brooklyn. Francesca grabbed my hand and said, "Come get this lap dance."

I got up from the barstool and allowed her to lead me to the VIP section. The bouncer at the entrance stared me down as Francesca led me through.

"What's up, Big Reg?" she said to him as she patted him on his ass.

"Let's go over here," she continued, directing me to a corner couch in the proverbial dark booth in the back.

I sat down and spread my legs to get comfortable as Francesca went to work. We talked as much as we bumped and grinded.

"So what's your real name?" I asked.

"I told you," she replied. "What's yours?"

"Austin."

Francesca stopped gyrating on me. "For real?"

"If Aurora is your real name, then Austin is mine."

Francesca's laugh was infectious.

"Okay, that's fair," she continued. "My Catholic name is Francesca. So what's yours?"

"I'm not Catholic, but my government name is Maximus."

"Stop playing," Francesca demanded.

"I'm serious!"

"That's fucked up because Maximus is worse than Austin," she concluded as she went back to gyrating. She hugged me around my neck and pressed her bare breasts against my chest.

Not that I needed any more incentive to go to the Lion's Den for lunch, but now there was a sense of purpose as Toni began to fade from view.

Francesca and I began seeing each other outside of the club.

"You should come by my house for dinner," she offered one day in the middle of a particularly sexy lap dance. How could I say no?

"That sounds like a plan." I accepted the invitation.

On the drive to her place two days later, I attempted to talk myself out of it, but usually when I gave my word on something like this, I tended to keep it.

As I pulled up to the house, I was immediately impressed. It was on one of those blocks you would see on television with the white picket fence, where people would leave their doors unlocked.

As no cars were parked on the street, I pulled into the driveway and parked behind at least three other cars that I could see. I entered the side pathway of small gray slates of granite embedded in the grass that led to the front door.

Ding-dong! Ding-dong! went the chiming doorbell.

It took a moment for someone to answer the door, and since I had never rung the bell on a house so big, I struggled with how long to wait before ringing it again. Just as I was about to push the button a second time, the door opened.

"Hello?" came the ascending voice that came with a question, from the mouth of an older man whom I assumed was Francesca's father. He was short, around five feet, six inches, and stocky with a muscular frame, wearing a crisp, fresh-out-of-the-box wife-beater.

"Can I help you?" he asked, looking me up and down.

"Good evening," I began. "I'm here to see Francesca."

The man, who indeed was her father, examined me from head to toe before directing me around to the back of the house.

"She's 'round back." He motioned to me with a nod of his head to his right.

I retraced my steps and made a right near the parked cars in the driveway, squeezing my way past. I shortened my gait to accommodate the downhill slope.

Ain't this some shit, I thought to myself. *Dude is sending me to the back of the house. This is bullshit.*

Reaching the plateau that matched the depth of the house and turning right to walk under the extension of the upper floors of the house, I looked to my left to see a wide and long backyard—a well-manicured lawn extending to an amazing view of the Narragansett Bay. I turned to knock on the door of what turned out to be an entirely separate apartment from the main house.

"Hey, you," Francesca greeted me with a kiss on the cheek.

"Hey." I returned the kiss and added an embrace before handing her a bottle of pinot grigio.

"Thank you. Come in, and welcome to my space. It is not much, but it's mine." Francesca opened her home to me.

Two steps into the doorway, I was in the living room, which was separated from a den area by the couch. Past the living room were two steps that led up to the bedroom on the right and the kitchen and bathroom on the left. Both could be seen through window cutouts in the wood-paneled walls. Though her apartment was small, it was truly quaint and spacious enough for one person. Besides, the backyard and view of the bay were worth it.

"This is really a cool pad you have," I commented. "And your backyard and view are beautiful."

"Yeah, I love it here," she replied.

"So I met your dad."

Francesca laughed out loud.

"What's so funny?" I said with a smile.

"Nothing. He's a piece of work. I'm sure he looked you over."

"How did you know?"

"Don't worry; he looks everyone over. Come open the wine while I finish cooking."

Francesca prepared a traditional Italian meal that first night. Tomato-and-mozzarella appetizer with decorative basil leaves. Penne pasta in a pesto sauce followed by chicken parmesan and a mixed salad with oil and vinegar. Lastly she served tiramisu for dessert. We finished the bottle of wine I had brought, and she opened another bottle as we moved outside to sit in wicker rocking chairs under the overhang of the main house. We talked about everyday mundane topics, getting to know one another until the moon rose on the cloudless night. We returned inside, and I dried dishes that she washed. Later, I sat in the living room while she excused herself to the bathroom. She soon returned in modest but sexy loungewear, not quite lingerie. She straddled me just as she had in the Lion's Den, but with the energy of just a girl at home.

Stripper sex was amazing!

Francesca and I hung out for the duration of my contract in Rhode Island. As great as the sex was, some of my most memorable moments were outside of the bedroom, such as when we went to The Capital Grille in downtown Providence. Our last week together was spent with me reading to her in the bathtub every day after her shift at the Lion's Den. I read *The Bridges of Madison County* to her. Much like the end of a good book, our time during my retreat in Rhode Island was over.

HURT PEOPLE...

Like many of life's experiences, the best of times are too often born out of the worst of times. One of the most life-altering moments as an adult came through heartbreak. First was a lover's heartbreak, and then came my own.

Reina was a Peruvian queen. She was born in the beach town of Máncora, which was just over the border from Ecuador. While her parents and siblings had managed to migrate to Brooklyn, Reina still had extended family living in Peru.

I met Reina while trading stocks in the city. She was a desk clerk who processed trading orders. All five feet nothing of her—at maybe a buck twenty—commanded respect. She was curvy in the sexy Latina-woman way. Her jet-black straight hair framed her face just right so that you could not help but focus on her eyes. Yet you were drawn to her lips, especially when she spoke—as if you were reading her lips. I was drawn to her without hesitation.

"Good morning," I would greet her every morning.

"Good morning, Maximus," she would reply out of professional courtesy.

I would attempt to engage her in conversation, which she obliged me as a matter of being colleagues.

"So what do you do when you're not working?" I finally asked.

"I spend time with my family," Reina stated.

"Hanging out with family is important," I returned as I continued that train of thought before she interrupted me.

"Listen," she began to lay down the law. "If you are trying to ask me out or are planning to ask me out, do not—because *A*, I do not date people at work, and *B*, I am in a relationship."

"How's that working out for you?" I asked.

Reina craned her head sideways and looked up at me, paused in thought. Staring.

"You know," she began seriously, "I haven't thought about that. That's clever, Mr. Talisman. Let's see: my family is stressing me right now, and I'm the oldest child, so...and as far as my man, it is not much of a relationship."

"So what are you going to do about it?" I replied.

"It is not that easy," Reina rebutted.

"Maybe it is," I returned. "You just haven't figured out how."

It was late in the workday, and everyone was heading home. As I exited the office doors onto the street just a little later, I saw Reina standing still as if waiting for someone.

"You want a ride home?" I offered.

Reina looked me up and down as if able to read my motive behind the offer.

"You don't even know where I live."

"I do not. But I live in Brooklyn, and you live in Brooklyn, so it can't be too far."

"How do you know I live in Brooklyn?" she demanded to know.

"Anyone from Brooklyn knows a Brooklyn girl. Bushwick, right?"

Reina stepped back, and with a gasp of air she let out, "Oh my God! How did you know that? That's incredible."

"'Cause I know Brooklyn. Come on." I guided her toward my car, which was parked around the corner.

We went through the usual twenty questions that men and women ask each other in the early stages of courting. What was different this time was that I genuinely wanted to know, more so than other times, and I felt that she wanted to know me.

She directed me to a residential street in the Bushwick section of Brooklyn.

"Pull over here," she directed me past a few trees on the now noticeable tree-lined street illuminated by streetlamps in the city night.

"So this is where you live?" I asked.

"No. My sister lives here." Reina cocked her head to the side so the bang on her forehead wouldn't cover her eyes. "I do not know you, so I'm not going to let you know where I live just yet. I texted my sister and let her know exactly who I was with just in case." Then she smiled. "Besides, my block is super ghetto. I do not think you're ready to see it."

"I've been on a few blocks in my day," I stated with confidence.

"We'll see, Mr. Talisman." Reina bent over and quickly pecked me on the cheek with soft lips. "Good night," she sang.

A week later we went on our first date. It was a movie at a theater in Queens because we did not want anyone to know we were dating. Working together made it awkward to be seen in public before we determined where the relationship was headed. Soon after, she invited me to her sister's house for drinks and to meet her sister and her sister's husband.

After pausing to catch my breath at the top of the stairs of the four-story walk-up, I slowly approached the first apartment door of the two doors on the floor and knocked. I heard bare feet approach the door, striding hard and deliberately. Reina snatched open the unlocked door quickly.

"Hola," she sung. "*Ven.*" She gestured with the wave of her arm for me to enter the apartment.

As I crossed the threshold, I presented Reina with a bottle of an Argentinian Malbec.

"So this is what it looks like inside the house that turned out not to be where you actually live when I dropped you off the first night," I noted to Reina after she opened the door to let me in, followed by a kiss on the cheek.

"You are so observant, Mr. Talisman," Reina responded with satire dripping from her tongue.

Though it was her sister's apartment, it could have easily been hers because Reina did as much cooking that night as her sister did. The family still followed decades-old traditional male and female roles, where the women were in the kitchen, and the men were gathered in the living room around the television, drinking beer. I felt right at home.

Reina's sister, Sacha, was two years younger and five inches taller than her big sister, Reina. They were as close as sisters could be. You could tell Reina was older by the deference Sacha gave her big sister. Reina had informed me that her sister was a school psychologist who worked with immigrant children as they became acclimated to being in New York City public schools. When Reina introduced me to Sacha, Sacha gave me a big embrace.

"Welcome to my home," she exclaimed. "Reina has told me so much about you."

"Thank you for having me over," I responded.

"Marcelo." Sacha turned her head in the direction of the living room to call for her husband.

"*Qué?*" Sacha's husband yelled back from the living room.

"Por favor, Marcelo, come and meet Reina's friend."

I could hear Marcelo marching toward the foyer to greet me. We were about the same height, but he was fifteen pounds heavier than me and looked as if he had a perpetual five-o'clock shadow to go with scruffy hair that looked as if it hadn't been combed in days. He did not seem to mind.

"Welcome to my house," he bellowed to me before reaching me. He extended his hand to greet me. We shook, followed by a bear hug.

"*Bienvenido a mi casa,*" he shouted as he ushered me into the kitchen. "You want a beer?" he asked me while shoving a Modelo into my hand. "Come." He guided me into the living room while I was still saying thank you.

I looked back at Reina as if to say, "Help!" She just waved me away.

One of Marcelo's friends was sitting in a folding chair, watching soccer. It was World Cup time, and Peru had made it to the first round.

Marcelo's friend could have been his twin brother in terms of unkempt appearances. He interrupted his yelling at the television for a few seconds to acknowledge my presence with a head nod and quick "Hola."

Marcelo's friend was his colleague from work. Both of them worked at a local bread factory that was under the Williamsburg Bridge in Brooklyn. It was one of the last remaining old-school factories in an area where abandoned factories were being turned into loft apartments.

"Please," Marcelo invited me. "Sit down and relax. We have lots of beer!" he exclaimed while raising his bottle to clink with mine in celebration.

I took a seat on the couch, which almost sank to the floor. As I took a swallow of the ice-cold beer, I was thinking that it was going to be difficult to get up.

Marcelo and his friend started speaking fluent Spanish, which was too fast for my broken Spanish ears to hear or for my mind to comprehend. I watched their mouths and facial expressions to decipher what they could have possibly been speaking about. After a few minutes I gave up. My head was hurting.

As soon as I turned my attention to watch the soccer match on the television, Marcelo and his friend became aware that I was left out of the conversation.

"*Lo siento*," Marcelo offered. "How you say in English…I'm sorry."

"*No hay problema*," I replied. "*Yo entiendo Espanol un poco pero non mucho.*"

Marcelo and his friend laughed at my attempt to speak Spanish, but they showed admiration for the attempt by saluting me with their beer bottles raised high.

Marcelo drew close to me but stopped just before the proximity that would have compelled me to back up to maintain my personal space, and he whispered in a hushed voice, "We were speaking of our *amantes*. You know, girlfriends. My friend was saying, about two days ago we were at the hotel with our *amantes*! *Mucho caliente!*"

Marcelo made a clapping sound with one hand as he whipped his hand so fast that you could hear the sound between his fingers as they clapped against each other.

I did not know if this was a trap of some kind. I mean, I didn't know these guys at all, and they were sharing some pretty intimate details of their lives with me, a complete stranger. Perhaps they were attempting to bond with me on a male hormonal level. I stared, nodded my head, and smiled at the entertainment provided. But I did not say a word.

Astonishing, I thought to myself. Even if I'd had an amante, which I did not at the time, I wouldn't have told these guys.

"Maximus," Reina called to me just in time. "*Por favor*, come—we're about to eat."

"Marcelo," Sacha yelled from the kitchen. "*Ven a comer!*"

When dinner was served, I learned that traditional South American families stood on ceremony and took it seriously. As an invited guest in the household for the first time and as a potential long-term suitor, I was served the national dish of *pique a lo macho*, which consisted of bite-size chunks of beef, sausage, onions, spicy peppers, boiled eggs, and fries.

Later that night, Reina allowed me to drive her home.

"Thank you for spending time with my family and crazy brother-in-law," Reina said apologetically.

"Thank you for inviting me. I had a good time. Your brother-in-law is cool," I offered.

Reina leaned over to kiss me good night, and I turned my head to face her so that our lips would meet. She paused, inches from my face. Our eyes locked on one another before she moved in with passion. The kiss was full, deep, and electric as lips parted and tongues entwined. Just as suddenly as it began, it ended.

"Good night," Reina chimed as she opened the car door to leave.

"Good night," I replied and watched her until she disappeared into her apartment building.

As I drove off, I surveyed the block. Reina had been right. The block was hot. In the hood, you could tell the weather by how many people were outside. On this evening, more than half the households were outside sitting on the stoops, leaning on cars, shooting dice in the street, or slap boxing. Younger children were playing in the water from the fire hydrant, jumping rope, and playing skelly or hopscotch. To the untrained eye, there was nothing nefarious about the neighborhood being out en masse. A closer look from someone who knew what to look for revealed drug sales going on near the corners of the block and people sitting in cars, drinking and smoking ganja. That was where criminal plans were often born.

The courtship of Reina was old school, with a lot of family interaction. It was mutual in the sense that I met her family, and she met mine, and everyone loved each other.

Lovemaking was exceptional. Being called *papi* at the moment of climax by an authentic Latina woman was memorable!

Reina and I spent most of our leisure time together, and after six months of dating, I was moved to make a bigger commitment.

"So what do you think about us moving in?" I asked one evening after work at her place as she changed out of her work clothes and into loungewear.

"Huh?" she coughed out.

"You didn't hear me?" I responded.

"I think I heard you, but I'm not sure. Did you say we should move in together?"

"I did."

"You think we're ready for that?" she questioned.

In my mind her hesitation and questions meant no.

"I don't think I'm ready, Papi. I've just gotten out of a marriage about a year and a half ago to my high school sweetheart. He put me through hell. The dirty motherfucker gave me crabs one time, and I ended up picking them off of him. So I'm not ready yet."

"I receive that," I replied. I was shaken for a minute, but I understood and was in agreement that now would not be a good time to move in together.

I was at a place in my life that I was beginning to discern the signs that revealed the potential journey of a relationship. This instinct coupled with learned behaviors from previous relationships, romantic and nonromantic, triggered an emotional pullback for me. We were clearly not in the same space, which begged the questions of when and how we would get there. So until such time, I decided we should enjoy this time of a mutual journey that the universe had conspired to on our behalf for reasons still unknown.

Never had I been one for hanging out late at night, clubbing. Reina loved to party. She would go out till almost dawn on a regular basis. Most of the time was spent on the dance floor for hours. Strictly Latin music—merengue, salsa, bachata. I hung as long as I could until the core essence of who I was asserted itself to say that this was not how I wanted to spend my time. But it was how Reina wanted to spend her time.

We still spent plenty of good quality time together because her party time was my sleep time, for the most part. Again the signs appeared. Diverging interests led to space for new interests. Besides, the notion of Reina out dancing with guys in the sexual gyrations of the music did not sit well with me.

A year and a half into the relationship, our families remained close, and Reina and I were as close as we could be without living with each other or being married—both of which I wanted. The desire for marriage was brought about by the idea that if we married, we would live together. See how that began to work? The universe had already sent me the signs that revealed the limitations of the relationship, which should have helped me decide to either live within the boundaries of the relationship or get out of the relationship. However, I wanted to move the boundaries in order to fit my perspective of what the relationship should be. Reina had already told me she did not want to live together, and the fact that she had recently left a tumultuous marriage most likely meant that marriage was not on her mind. We were playing a masquerade in the relationship, only we did not know it at the time—at least not on a conscious level. That space between the conscious and the subconscious remained a mystery where it was hard to tell what was real from what I told myself to believe. We were biding our time until the situation changed— when we could take steps toward a deeper, more permanent commitment—or until the universe arranged the goodbye that neither one of us was prepared to make. All the signs led to a deeper commitment.

That summer we took a trip to her country because she wanted me to meet her family. We planned to stay several weeks so she could show me the beauty of South America.

We began our trip with a stop in Quito, Ecuador, where Reina had an aunt and uncle she wanted to visit. We visited one of the local tourist vendors on the earth's equator where they demonstrated the earth's gravitational pull. One of the most popular demonstrations was how water drained at the equator. Directly at the centerline of the equator, the water drained straight down.

"That is why we do not have hurricanes or twisters," the native woman explained in broken English. "But we do have volcanoes."

She went on to demonstrate that south of the equator, the water drained in a clockwise rotation, and north of the equator, water drained counterclockwise.

Reina and I traveled north to the province of Esmeraldas before heading south toward the Galápagos Islands and then finally to Lima, the capital city of Peru.

"I want you to see your people in my country and why I can see you," she exclaimed.

Seventy percent of Afro-Ecuadorians lived in Esmeraldas. It was amazing to be around people who looked like me but spoke another language. They seemed to be equally fascinated by meeting me!

—

Most associate the Galápagos Islands with Darwin's theory of natural selection, almost to make it at least a cliché, but it lives up to its intriguing and fantastic reputation. Finally, we set upon Peruvian soil.

We flew from the Galápagos to Lima. Reina decided that we had spent enough time on the road, so she had her *tio* meet us at the capital airport to drive us directly to her family village of San Lorenzo, a small fishing village along the beachside of the country.

Over the course of a three-hour drive, Reina and Tio Mafi spoke in Spanish as I surveyed the landscape. There was no way that I was going to sleep because the terrain was rugged. The roads were not secured with guardrails, and there were times where we found ourselves riding along a cliff's edge. As I peered out and looked down the side of mountains, imagining our ten-year-old van careening down the slope, my heart became faint, my stomach woozy, and my testicles tingly. As time passed, the landscape meandered from city to mountain to farms and finally to the shore of the sea.

"Look, Papi," Reina directed. "That's San Lorenzo." She pointed out of the front passenger seat window. "This where my parents were born, first met, and were married."

I inhaled the ocean air deeply and then held my breath. In the silence of the moment, I could hear my heart beat, and I felt its rhythm. The view from the elevated roadside that wound its way down to sea level was reverent.

Entering the town of less than one thousand inhabitants was like entering a deserted place. It was close to dinnertime, and everyone in the town was either at home preparing or eating dinner, or they were at a neighbor's or relative's house doing the same. Most often, the neighbor was a relative.

As we pulled up to Tio Mafi's house, where we would sleep in separate rooms because we were not married, at least fifty people—men, women, and children—were waiting for our arrival. The half of the invited villagers who stood outside the wood-and-mud house with cutouts for windows but absent actual glass were mostly children. The other half—adults, elderly, and a couple of babies—were inside the house. The heat from the stove was stifling. There was not an air conditioner in sight. One chicken strutted throughout the house, with children chasing it at times while the adults ignored it. Gave new meaning to "playing with your food."

Relatives mobbed Reina as soon as she got out of the car.

"Tia Reina, Tia Reina," the children screamed her name while pulling at her blouse and jeans.

At her height, she was lost among the wave of children.

Reina called them by name and seemed to chat with several of them, taking seconds to say something specific.

"Look at you," she'd say to one. "Your braces are finally off. Your teeth look beautiful."

All of her comments were affirmations that anyone could embrace, yet each child embraced the comments uniquely.

I followed Reina, and in her wake I, too, was welcomed with open arms and the curiosity that accompanied first-time experiences. In this case, I was the first black man ever seen by the locals who had never left the village.

I made it into the house, where Tio Mafi had already delivered our luggage to our rooms. Reina patiently introduced me individually to every adult in the house. I must have said "*un placer*" thirty times.

Darkness erased day, and candles were strategically lit through the house to provide accent lighting in most of the rooms. Only the kitchen had an overhead light. The other rooms were lit with candles.

On my way to my room—which was Tio Mafi's daughter's room, converted into a guest room for me, which meant that his daughter would be sleeping in his room with him and his wife—I saw several women in the kitchen, working almost assembly-style. Two women were plucking a chicken, two were washing a chicken, and one was seasoning a chicken while two chickens were in the oven. Two other women were preparing other provisions such as yucca. I lay on the bed in my room, staring at the ceiling as the sound of voices speaking Spanish lulled me to sleep.

———

Morning came early in the village, where chickens, cows, and a sundry of other animals roamed free. The trumpet of the roosters that walked freely throughout Tio Mafi's home woke me at dawn. Everyone else seemed not to notice as I silently roamed the hallway to the kitchen for some water and finally walked out to stand on the porch. Cows and chickens roamed the dirt streets as the tiny town slowly stirred to wake.

Reina joined me on the porch, and we watched as the townspeople lived their day. Local shops opened, men herded cows, and barefoot children chased chickens into coops.

"Come inside for breakfast in a few," Reina whispered close to my ear, her breath caressing my cheek. "We have a busy day."

I didn't know if it was the smell of the cooking food or the daily habit that honed one's internal clock, though I suspected both, but everyone in the house seemed to simultaneously appear from all corners of the house to get their portions of breakfast. The same ladies who had cooked dinner were dishing out food buffet-style. Adults and children got their plates and found space throughout the house because there was not enough room at the kitchen table. I was invited to sit at the table for six.

We spent the rest of the day out of the house, walking about the town. The first destination was to the cemetery to offer respect to Reina's ancestors. After, the men and women split. The men seemed to huddle around me and thereby herded me away from Reina. Every step added distance between us. I peered over and around the sea of men and women who stood between Reina and me until she and I made eye contact.

"You'll be fine," Reina mouthed. "See you later," she yelled before being tugged by the laughing ladies surrounding her.

Our men's journey ended at the lone soccer field and stadium in the town. It was the typical home field model where the home side was twice as long and high as the visitors' side. I was to learn that most towns in every South

American country had a soccer field. The stadium in San Lorenzo was built to seat at least five times the population of the town. My interpretation of Tio Mafi's Spanish mixed with broken English was that the dream of "build it, and they will come" did not become manifest. Instead, local children gathered to play sandlot soccer, and old men played league soccer on Friday nights.

Climbing the stadium stairs to the top, I turned around to see the beach and ocean over the visitors' side of the stadium. Tio Mafi and a few of the other men—there were about twelve of us in all—simultaneously pulled brown paper bags filled with homemade liquor from their jacket pockets.

The conversation in my head went, *Have you ever tasted grain alcohol? You might as well be drinking straight rubbing alcohol. Gasoline is what they should call it. I have heard of people going blind drinking that shit.*

"*Toma una copa,*" Tio Mafi offered.

One of the other men passed around small clear-plastic cups.

I received the pint bottle in a bag and poured some in my cup as three bags passed in a clockwise rotation.

Oh, shit, was what I said in my head as I coughed enough for the men to laugh. I was buzzed almost immediately. After three sips, I was done. The day was still young, and I had to pace myself to get through without passing out.

From the stadium, we walked behind and between houses and down dirt roads until we turned right onto the main street, which was paved. On the same side of the street about two short blocks away, we entered an open-air pool hall. The front doors and roof were retractable—not mechanically but manually. The women were already there.

"Hey, Papi," Reina greeted me with a kiss on my cheek and a strong embrace.

"Hey, you," I returned. "I missed you."

"Aw, Maximus, I missed you too," Reina answered.

We played pool and drank cases of beer for hours, closing down with the owner. Dinnertime meant the town officially closed for the night. The second night of our five-night stay was reserved for family business and for paying homage to home.

The light of the full-moon night shone through windowless panes in the walls. Accompanied by modest lamplight and lots of candles, Reina sat in the middle of the lone couch in the house, sandwiched between Tio Mafi and his wife. She began with them.

"I bring greetings from our family in New York," Reina began in Spanish. "My mother and father give special greetings for hosting us and welcoming Maximus."

She gestured toward me. I was posted in the back in the corner, taking in the scene—lost in the experience. I nodded in acknowledgement and tipped my Huari beer bottle toward Reina.

"For Tio Mafi." Reina turned to her uncle and handed him a shirt.

This went on for hours as Reina handed out gifts to her family members. Mostly she gave them clothing, from socks to underwear to combs, brushes, and toiletries. She provided some essentials for which they were grateful. I marveled at the sincere thanks the family showed Reina and the joy she radiated from being able to provide for so many in her family.

In the wee hours of the night, when most had gone to bed, Reina sat with the elders in the family. She represented her parents in their absence.

The discussion turned to who would be next in the family to be sponsored by Reina's family to immigrate to New York. For two generations, Reina's family had selected families and a few children to come to New York for a better life. When a family was selected, the father would come over and work until he could afford to bring his wife and children. Sometimes the wife would come and work as well, and the child or children would stay in Peru with relatives. When a child was being sent, it was usually a teenager who would stay with an established family before going on to college, which was the expectation. I admired the fortitude, courage, and patience that accompanied a vision beyond one's lifetime. The collective consciousness of a people gave rise to hope and change. My sleep that night was deep in a newfound peace in knowing that ideas such as perseverance, sacrifice, and hope were real.

On the three-hour ride back to the airport in Lima, I thought about San Lorenzo. I thought about drinking white lightning and praying to God not to die. And then I thought about the children and how happy they were with the simplicities of life. Everyone in San Lorenzo seemed at peace. Compared to the havoc and chaos of most of our in-the-matrix lives, the simple life had value to which all of us could aspire. Out of all of the places I have traveled, San Lorenzo will always remain a vision of peace and joy.

I returned to New York more in love with Reina than before we had left. At least I thought it was love. I immersed myself in Reina's life, family, and culture. For Reina, it was life as usual because she lived the way she had always lived before me.

She was kind to my family as well, and we spent time with my people, so it was hard not to feel a sense of equity that way. Nonetheless, Reina was not in the space that I was. I'm talking about the settle-down, see-you-every-day space. She was in the space of "I'll see you on weekends and not necessarily every weekend and maybe once during the week." It was uncomfortable for me because that meant I had to find ways to spend my time. Knowing myself, it was better to avoid temptation than to resist it because I was not so good at resisting.

I did not resist well, especially knowing that Reina was out dancing on the regular. That meant that in the name of cultural dance, her body was pressed against another man's body, moving in synchronized sexual ways. Those ways reminded me of back-in-the-day basement house parties with the black light. As such, my default position, the place where confusion and hurt led to instinctual responses, came forth to provide comfort. I reconnected with an ex-lover.

—

Paula and I met during freshman year in college. She was tall, slender, graceful, and funny. Born in Granada, she came from a prominent family of doctors and lawyers for many generations. She was from the type of family that vacationed on Martha's Vineyard. I was not born into that ilk, though I was certain that I was qualified to be a part of it if I chose.

Paula could not give me the time of day in college. Not because she did not want to but because she could not. She needed to date an upperclassman whose family came from a similar socioeconomic background. The dude she dated despised me because he knew Paula wanted to be with me because she was drawn to me with all of her body, mind, and, most importantly, spirit. We all knew it, and there was nothing he could do about it. Whenever we were together in a social setting, I would flirt with Paula openly in front of him because both of us knew he could do nothing about it because at the end of the day, I would fuck him up. I knew that she chose him because his background lent itself to a more stable future whereas I was wild, free and unpredictable, but I was young and hurt.

Years after we graduated, Paula and I saw each other from across the room at a political fundraiser. The candidate had just begun his twenty-minute speech when we made eye contact. We squirmed and winked and smiled the entire time until we could rush across the room to say hello.

"Hello, Black Boy," she began.

"Black Gurl," I returned. We shared a long embrace.

It was as if time returned to those longed-for days of college. Time is funny like that, isn't it? Only now, we could act upon years of repressed desire and lust.

This was years before I met Reina. Paula and I had an affair spanning at least a decade with years off in between. As of the start of my relationship with Reina, I had not seen Paula for years. She was back now.

While Reina was out at the dance hall, Paula was in my bed. Then Reina came to my place late one night after dancing and drinking. She rang the bell incessantly until she suddenly stopped.

"Is everything all right?" The apprehension in Paula's voice was distinguished.

"Yeah, everything is cool," I replied, calm on the outside, nerves combusting on the inside.

"I do not want to cause any trouble," Paula finished.

I turned to her in bed as she lay in my arms, naked. Eye to eye, I said, "You are not."

I was sharing a flophouse with another down-on-his-luck cat. We had separate bedrooms and shared a bathroom.

Like most nights, when my neighbor was not home, I did not lock my room door. The bedroom door was a quarter of the way open before I realized it was moving. That was how slow it was moving. For the remaining three quarters of it opening, I was too paralyzed to act. Though I could not see her yet, I knew that Reina was opening the door. Reina must have entered the building when another transient tenant had opened the door.

In this moment, everything moved in slow motion. The door opened in slow motion. Reina's fingers wrapping around the door, pushing it open, were in slow motion. I pushed Paula to the edge of the bed, where she voluntarily slid off to hide—in slow motion.

Paula disappeared before Reina saw her face, but Reina knew I was not in bed alone.

"I tried to call you," Reina almost just mouthed the words. Her voice was faint. "When you did not answer, I thought something was wrong. I just came by to see if you were all right."

"I'm okay," I answered sheepishly.

There was silence as Reina stared at me in disbelief.

"Hi," Reina spoke in Paula's general direction. "I'm Reina."

Paula sat up enough from the floor to show her head at eye level to the mattress.

"Hi," she returned, embarrassed.

"Did he tell you he has a girlfriend?" Reina asked.

"Yes," Paula said.

Reina began to cry. "I'm so sorry. I shouldn't have come."

With that, she left the room in a quick gait. The front door of the brownstone building slammed shut before I could move. Paula stared at me. I glanced at her before I instinctively grabbed the T-shirt and slacks lying on the floor. I managed to slip on some sneakers as I raced to catch Reina.

By the time I made it down the stairs to the sidewalk outside, Reina was at the corner, where her sister was waiting in her red Camry.

"Reina," I called out.

She stopped near the car but did not turn around. I ran to reach her, and when I was within steps of touching her, Reina whirled around.

"Why, Maximus?" she wailed at me through a hail of tears.

"I'm sorry, Reina."

"But why, Maximus?" Reina continued.

"There is no *why* to explain it away, Reina."

"I know that," she responded. "But at least tell me something," she begged me. "I need to know something, Maximus."

I looked to the ground, searching for answers. I slowly picked my head up to see Sacha sitting in the driver's seat of the car with the engine running. Her face seemed to say, "Yeah, why, Maximus? And do not look to me for answers. I want to know why as well."

"You want to know why?" I began reluctantly. "When I first met you, I wanted to be with you in a serious way. I asked if we could live together. You said no. You weren't ready. And then with all of your partying and dancing until sunrise sometimes—dancing with other men how you dance. I did not think we were ever going to be as serious as I wanted."

"Why didn't you say anything?" Reina pleaded with me through tearstained eyes.

"What was I going to say? Hey, Reina, please stop going dancing, and definitely stop grinding up on guys? Hey, let's move in together?" I asked rhetorically. "I already asked you that, and you said no. You were in a space where your life was not flowing with mine. Not enough for next-level shit. I didn't want you to change because I asked you to. I took whatever part of you that you gave me, and this"—I gestured with the sweep of my arm back to my apartment—"is me filling a void."

"Well, I hope it was worth it," Reina offered as she walked to the passenger side of the car and got in.

Sacha rolled down her window as it started to rain. Her eyes were sad and red.

"Damn, Maximus. I thought you were the one." Sacha sounded disappointed before driving off.

You know when you were young, and right before your mom or dad was about to whup your ass, and they said, "This is going to hurt me more than it hurts you"? I did not know if that was true in this experience. In fact, I would bet that it was not. Yet I felt it to be of a similar feeling. My heart ached for the pain I had caused Reina and for the irreparable damage it had inflicted on our relationship.

Paula was gone when I got back to my room. I flopped in bed and smelled our sex-making, pondering upon the risk-reward value of the experience. I would never encounter her again. The conversation in my head went like this: *Here I am doing the same that Toni did to me, and maybe she did it for the same reasons I did. Two sides of the same coin? Timing can be a bitch.*

WALKABOUT

After my journey with Reina ended, the rare confluence of the gravity of a series of love experiences—coupled with the hunger for emotional reflection and the resources, time, and money—led to my walkabout.

In Australian Aboriginal culture, a walkabout is a rite of passage for males to undergo a journey where they live in the wilderness for as long as six months to make the spiritual and traditional transition into manhood. I did not have six months to take my walkabout, but I knew it was my time for one.

It was early August when I set out for the Florida Keys. It took all of a night's sleep to plan my destination and the stops along the route. I chose the Keys because I was drawn to the allure of Hemingway spending a lot of time there, drinking and eating and writing and writing more. The bohemian culture appealed to me as the perfect place to write.

Since I planned to spend about fifteen days roundtrip, I decided to stay at Hawks Cay in Duck Key, midway to Key West. Online, it seemed secluded enough yet modern enough to accommodate the recluse in me at this time of my life and my desire to indulge in amenities such as private poolside cabanas with butler service.

I decided to write a blog. I called it *Life at the Precipice*. Its inauguration entry was written on day one of the walkabout.

Saw the sun rise in view of the full moon yesterday morning as I crossed the Verrazano Bridge, were my first words. *Silence as the wind swirled through, in and out of the car, was welcomed. Before I left, my mom asked was I going toward something or leaving something behind? I responded, both.*

When I called Khahari, who was living in Virginia at the time and who was one of my planned stops, the question he asked was the most asked by all who dared to ask.

"You are going to the Florida Keys alone?"

"Yes."

Day 5

It is 4:00 a.m. I'm awake and after a shower, shave, and packing, it is moving day. I'm on my way to Fayetteville, North Carolina, to see my friend David who transplanted there about five years ago with his family. We're scheduled to watch his son, Monk, compete in a junior county championship in golf—what else? His tee time is 8:30—I have a three-hour window to get there. Being on the road is exhilarating. It is a blessing and a privilege to see another dawn because it is the sun's rising that brings hope and anticipation of the possibilities for the day. A song from my CD player brought tears to my eyes. Something by Sting when he was with The Police. And I reflect—I'm on this journey, not necessarily to run from or to anything but rather to take inventory on my stock as a human being. Why now? I need a clean break from work in order to sustain the level of excellence that is beginning to permeate the culture. We received an A on our school report card! Yes! Secondly, my father died when he was forty-eight or forty-nine—I do not remember now. How sad. And as I approach forty-six, I am determined to outlive him— but even if I do, black men make it to what—sixty-nine? Do we make it to seventy? I'm getting my plan together to live at least until one hundred—but a good one hundred! Lastly, I've hurt a lot of people—some really special people, and I do not want to do that anymore. Part of that is letting go of my hurts. I'm talking about avoidable pain—and not necessarily the hurt that comes

*from everyday living. I know that I have hurt some of you read-
ing this blog, and I ask for forgiveness—God knows. It was one
hundred degrees today in North Carolina! Wow! I looked in the
mirror and said to myself that I can't get any blacker—beautiful baby! Played a round of golf with David—I know I was not
supposed to play, but...I won and played better than I had in the
last four outings.*

*It is now 7:59 p.m., and I'm in a Wendy's parking lot in
Laurinburg, North Carolina, waiting for my aunt LouAnn to
get home from church revival. By the time I reached my forties,
Aunt LouAnn had remarried and moved back to her hometown
in North Carolina since all her kids were either grown or dead
by then. Driving down the country roads—some of them are
actually dirt roads—reminded me that my family migrated to
New York, which undoubtedly was too cruel for many of them. I
imagine that deep down we're just country folk. It is a different
world down here. I can't understand some of the people when
they speak, and it is not just the accent. It is like some of them
are using different words—like a different vocabulary. And the
insects are three times as big as in Brooklyn. Insects on steroids
down here! I'm here for one night, and then comes the long haul
of the trip—from Laurinburg to Delray Beach, Florida. Let's
call it ten hours over Wednesday night to Thursday morning.
Peace.*

I did not know it at the time, but that would be the last time I saw Aunt
LouAnn before she passed. I would grow to miss watching basketball with
her. Both of us were Knick fans. Even when I was not near her, I would call,
and we'd end up talking about trades and coaching. That was what we did the
last time I saw her. Sat on the couch and watched basketball.

Day 11

Say it with me: P-A-R-I-D-I-S-E. Duck Key epitomizes tran-
quility. Blue skies with clouds breezing by, sheltered beneath
white cabanas—people lounging poolside with wait service as
Bob Marley languishes in the background, "Emancipate your
mind from mental slavery!" Welcome to my world! Okay, it
could be a little quieter—there are a lot of children here, but
there is an adult side of the resort. Today was a wonderful blend
of responsibilities—I paid some bills combined with carefree, lib-
erated living. And the day is not done. Gonna take a nap, shower
up, and have dinner out on the resort. If you haven't experienced
it, I encourage you to date yourself, if only a few days a year. I
think the result will be a you who makes a paradigm shift to live
differently or a reenergized you to continue living as you are with
your best self. One noticing—why am I a noticeable minor rep-
resentation of people of color among a sea of Caucasians—there
is a Latino family here, and I did see one other person of color,
but you get me—while the service staff is predominantly people
of color. We are evolving as human beings, but there is a ton to
be done—I remain curious and vigilant. Peace.

—

Day 14

On my way back—I made it to Petersburg, Virginia, in the
morning. Played golf with Khahari, and during the round, I
realized that I want to stay on vacation. I do not want to go to
work, and I do not want to play competitive golf. As a result, I
got my butt whupped. Which came first, the whupping or these
feelings? The feelings came during the round while I was playing
well. So that was an indication that the feelings were authentic.

I do not miss playing golf. I like the relaxed, reflective artist in me. How can I remain centered amid the firestorm of New York City and my work? Help! Damn! The closer I get to New York, the more I feel/anticipate the pace and stress—though I do look forward to reconnecting with all of you, but in a different capacity. So please allow me to reintroduce myself!

—

Day 18—"Journeys Begin and End at Once"

Brooklyn, baby! Approximately three thousand miles and eleven cities in seven states over eighteen days—driving. I'm home, and it is weird and familiar at once. Driving across the Verrazano Bridge and onto the BQE was strange, as if I was on autopilot. Was I driving, or was the car driving me to my apartment and then to work? I finally found a name for my car, and it is... Scarlet. Do not tell me you do not have a name for your car? Something does occur between man and machine after such an intimate time together. I was actually in the New York City area late Saturday night, driving through the remnants of Hurricane Bill. Sheets of water poured down, and yet I remained centered, knowing that all is as it is meant to be—nonchalant yet engaged. I haven't written since Friday, so in the meantime, I visited my brother on Saturday. Tonka is my youngest brother. There are four of us, and I am the oldest. We all have the same father and different mothers, so you can imagine the challenges of staying in touch. It has been fourteen years since I spoke with him or saw him. I am grateful to our sister, Sasha, for making it happen. She and I have brunch or dinner on a monthly basis—that's the premise, at least. She has been the linchpin, and I am thankful for her. Now all we have to do is contact Marcus, and we can begin to complete the circle. Driving to Tonka's in Maryland, I saw our dad smiling in heaven. Bro, you have every right to have been angry. At the same time I hope that you can see that I did what I thought was right in the moment. At the end of the day, we can agree to disagree, but our love must transcend.

Strange how golf is. Remember I said that I did not feel like playing competitive golf? Sunday, I played in a tournament, shot an eighty-three, and won a trophy! The reason(s)? I did not expect to win. I told myself that I should approach the game like a child plays any game—with enthusiasm and fun. Lastly, I constantly reminded myself that the only shot that matters is this shot.

Today, I went to work with great energy and focus. I now anticipate a great year ahead, while at the same time I feel ready to receive what it may bring. This evening, I was telling a friend that while I feel emotionally detached from so much, I feel thoroughly connected in a spiritual way. It should not be taken as a lack of caring but rather as an act of faith. I know that the Bible supports this somewhere like in Ecclesiastes or something.

After work, I went to my spot, Night of the Cookers, to have dinner alone. I opened my laptop and continued to draft a writing regarding my first year as a principal while eating salmon penne.

Things I learned or remembered or both along my walkabout:

- *It is important to take care of yourself on a daily basis, even if it is just twenty minutes a day.*
- *Symbolic gestures can be very important.*
- *Surrender can be a sign of power—especially to God.*
- *Life is constantly unfolding—do not be ashamed of the wrinkles.*
- *Fear is an abomination of love.*
- *Freedom cannot exist with fear.*
- *I am one cool dude!*
- *I am an artist!*

- *Journeys can be physical, mental, or spiritual—separate yet at the same time synergistically together.*
- *Once in tune with your God flow, you see the magic in everyday living—you can see the benchmarks clearer, and you become spontaneous in action.*
- *There's a very thin line between being selfish and selfless.*
- *Positive energy is invaluable.*
- *The universe really does conspire on behalf of our well-being.*

I begin where I left off in my life's journey—with a different energy and perspective, constantly growing and evolving. Thank you all for your patience and indulgence. Life is good!

While in the Keys, I bought an authentic puka-shell necklace from an old lady sitting on the side of the road, teaching a girl who looked like her granddaughter the time-honored tradition. I screwed the ends of the necklace that fit almost like a choker around my neck immediately upon purchase. To this day, it reminds me simply to be true to my journey. I have never taken it off.

I encourage men and women to sojourn on at least one walkabout in their lives. The most fortunate of us get to experience several walkabouts in life, whether for a few days or months or years.

A few days in Brooklyn, back from my walkabout, I found myself in Reina's neighborhood. There were times while we had been together that I had used her mailing address. I had to go to the local post office to pick up a package. Surprisingly, the wait in the post office for the package was super short. I left the post office with a bounce in my step because I knew that day, when phenomenal events were occurring such as virtually no wait at the post office, was a magical day. I looked both ways before crossing the street and unlocked my car door remotely to time it so that I could just open the door and glide in. I turned the ignition to start the car, and then I looked up at the car parked in front of me. As I backed up slightly, I was able to read the license plate. UR4GVN.

I will forever know Reina's passionate embrace.

THAT THING MARRIAGE

You would think that someone like me, based on my experiences, would not get married. My experiences led me to become relatively selfish. When one's life has been based on survival of the fittest, one can easily grow that way. It was not until after my second marriage ended that I sought the wisdom I could have used while in the struggle. That wisdom came by way of my uncle Bottom Gut. His real name was Jerome but everyone called him Bottom Gut because he said that every decision he made came from the bottom of his gut and it never steered him wrong.

"What's the secret?" I asked him as a twice-divorced thirty-something.

"You mean to staying married?" he'd read my mind. Then answering my question before I fully asked, he continued. "That's easy—three things you gotta remember. One, if you are in it for a lifetime, you have to be prepared for some bumps in the road that take a while to smooth out. For example, if you were thinking that you are going to be married for forty years, and someone told you that of those forty years, five years would be shit, would you stay for thirty-five good years? That's one application of the idea of 'for better or for worse.' Number two, this too shall pass. Sleeping with someone else cannot be the deal breaker. Monogamy is not a natural behavior for man. It is a learned behavior. Three, whatever shit you think that you take from her, she probably takes twice as much from you. So before you start to mention some crap, sleep on it for three nights, and if you wake up on the fourth day and are still pissed about it, then it may be worth a conversation. All you youngins want the thirty-year anniversary but do not want the years of hell to get there. It doesn't work like that."

My aunt Myrna, my father's baby sister, who was married to Uncle Bottom Gut, when asked the same question, simply said, "When you can't love 'em like a husband anymore, love 'em like a brother until you can again."

It was not until I was in my forties and had read Don Miguel Ruiz's *The Mastery of Love* that I even began to understand real love. For me, it is not in a relationship where I do not feel free.

I came to understand that the traditional, conventional form of a monogamous marriage is not meant for me, at least not in this lifetime. I had been spending invaluable time and effort trying to fit into a confining definition of romantic love. I found myself lying to people and mostly to myself. I betrayed my life experiences and natural instincts because to do otherwise would not allow me to fit into the norms of our society.

As I continue to evolve and to be honest with myself and, in turn, with others, I am becoming free. Are you free?

This is not to say that it is all about having multiple sex partners. Though, I do not believe that it is natural to have one partner for all of your life. It is to say that over the course of a lifetime, it is reasonable to love more than one person and to have several relationships with the opposite sex that do not include sexual intercourse.

I remember when my second wife found out I was not honest with her about my fidelity to her. *Cheating* is a silly word that is disrespectful to the process of the human experience of finding love.

Nina was straight from Uptown Harlem, almost to the Cloisters, which sat at the edge of water that separated Manhattan from the Bronx. It might as well have been the Dominican Republic itself. I met her at a client presentation when I ran my own philanthropy consultant firm named The Alexander Group. Nina was the program director for Girls Who Work, a nonprofit organization that trained teenage girls from her neighborhood to find their voice and purpose in the world and align it to a career.

Nina was built like a brick house, as we called a woman built like her. At five feet seven and a muscular 145 pounds, she evidenced the African essence in her hips and thighs. Her breasts stood up naturally, and I loved to watch them sway without a bra. Nina was super intelligent and no nonsense about her work. She had an edge to her that made it difficult to approach her, at least in the traditional prey vs. predator way. You had to come correct, as some would say.

"Good afternoon, Mr. Talisman," Nina greeted me on my first visit to the organization's office in Washington Heights overlooking the George Washington Bridge.

"I am Nina Mendez," she introduced herself with a firm handshake. "I am the program director here at Girls for Work."

"Nice to meet you," I replied.

"We're excited to hear your presentation today and about the possibilities of partnering with you to grow our mission."

"The feelings are mutual," I returned.

Nina led me into the boardroom that was outlined on one side by floor-to-ceiling glass windows that framed the Hudson River and the New Jersey Riverside hills on the other side of the bridge. The other three walls were decorated with the faces of black and brown girls representing the South American and Caribbean countries where they came from.

I gave my presentation on the idea of philanthropy. It was not the typical pitch about philanthropy, which was the notion of fundraising. Rather, I talked about the original idea of the word.

"The idea of philanthropy," I began, "speaks to the love of humanity. In that love, we engage in endeavors that support and promote the well-being of all people. Our endeavors come in many forms and can be understood in the simple phrase that many of our mothers said to us when we were growing up. 'Whatever you decide to do with your life, be the best at it. Even if it is a street sweeper, be the best street sweeper you can be.' That street sweeper is the sanitation worker of today, who, I may add, earns a good salary with benefits and great vacation time. The sanitation worker who understands his contribution to humanity through the work understands that he or she helps to maintain the health of a community. There have been periods in history where people have been wiped out due to plagues that came from a lack of sanitation. The sanitation worker isn't just picking up garbage. They are a part of the process of saving lives. Similar to the work all of you are doing here at Girls Who Work. I see it as more than finding jobs and careers for your clients. Employment should be a by-product of finding one's purpose to contribute to the well-being of humanity in general and the community specifically. My work, should you decide to partner with me, is to create a plan to help them find their voice. My essential question in all of this is, what will be your verse in the poem of life?"

As I ended, I looked around the room and could see all eyes riveted by my words. My eyes landed last on Nina, and it was as if she saw inside of me.

"Impressive, Mr. Talisman," Nina offered as she led me out of the conference room. "Do you really believe everything that you said in there?"

"Absolutely. Otherwise I wouldn't say it. Do you believe it?"

I was startled by her skepticism and found it refreshing at the same time. I would come to know why Nina was that way and how it came about.

"I do, but I know the world doesn't believe it," Nina replied. "Because if they did, we wouldn't need organizations like Girls Who Work to help girls of color find their purpose through careers."

"True," I countered. "But we're going to shift your model to helping them find their purpose for being in the sense of contributing a verse philanthropically. When we do that, finding a career is the easy part."

"I'm going to hold you to that, Mr. Talisman," Nina demanded. "I have another meeting to attend, so Marta will walk you out the rest of the way."

Again, Nina extended her hand for a firm handshake. This time there was extended eye contact.

Marta was Nina's secretary.

"This way, Mr. Talisman," she greeted me with a smile.

At the elevator, I asked Marta, "So what's the deal with Ms. Mendez?"

"What do you mean?" Marta asked.

The elevator doors opened to an empty compartment, and I entered.

"Is she in a relationship?"

Marta laughed and said, "Yes, she has a boyfriend," as the elevator doors closed.

I did get the contract and worked closely with Nina for six months. In December the organization held its annual holiday party on the Friday before it closed until after the New Year. Nina was center stage, holding court with her wit, and everyone laughed and drank and ate from trays passed around by waiters. I stood at the periphery of the action, close to the bar.

"Bartender," I called. "Ketel One on the rocks in a rocks glass with a lime, please."

"Right away, sir," came her quick reply.

I watched her pour, and after she presented the drink to me, I noted to her, "Generous pour. Thank you."

"You are welcome," she responded.

I left a twenty-dollar bill on the bar, then turned to walk toward the sliding glass doors that led to a heated balcony area overlooking the Hudson River.

"Thank you," the bartender called out to me, holding the twenty-dollar bill above her head.

I stood close to the powerful heater spewing warm air in contrast to the chilly winter air. It was cold but bearable with temperatures hovering around forty degrees. It was a snapshot moment to take in. Another year was ending, and another one was on the horizon. What did it hold for me? I pondered.

"There is the mystery man," came Nina's voice, so close that it startled me.

I was caught mid-swallow.

"Do not choke on my behalf," Nina joked.

"Not at all," I returned.

"You are not a closet introvert, are you?" Nina asked sarcastically.

"Why do you say that?" I chuckled.

"Well, let me see. The party is clearly over there." She pointed toward the people dancing on the makeshift dance floor. "And not only are you as far away as you physically can be from over there, but you are literally outside in December."

"Your perception is impeccable. I'm not a crowd person per se. I prefer one-on-one conversations, though I can be good in crowds or in front of people."

"Clearly," Nina interrupted.

"Thank you," I replied. "I was just taking time to take in the scene and started to think about what next year looks like."

"So what do you see?" Nina pushed my thinking.

"It is not clear yet," I announced. "But it doesn't need to be right now. I trust the universe to unfold itself to me as I am prepared to receive it."

Nina eyed me incredulously. "What?" She laughed.

"I've learned that the universe always conspires on our behalf. It is up to us to decipher the messages along the way. I confess that I haven't always been good at it, but I'm getting better, and I'm better than most."

"Really?" Nina laughed.

"Yes," I replied—in absolute belief to Nina's disbelief.

Seeing my conviction, Nina ceased laughing and began to seriously ponder the possibilities.

After the holiday party, I did not see nor hear from Nina for over a year. We did not exchange numbers that night because she did not offer, and I did not ask because I assumed she was still in her relationship.

—

Due to my success with Girls Who Work and a few other nonprofit organizations, I landed a six-figure deal with a trust-fund foundation to promote my idea of the philanthropic mind-set.

I received an email inviting me to a meeting to present to the board of trustees.

"Dear Mr. Talisman," it read. "As your reputation precedes you based on the work you have accomplished over the years with reputable organization such as Girls Who Work, the Board of Trustees at The Trust Family Foundation invites you to present your services for consideration of partnering on our next project."

I was excited and intimidated at once by the prospect that those who had resources to support the actuality of theory were considering my work. I prepared feverously.

I arrived half an hour early at the foundation's offices in the Dumbo section of Brooklyn.

"Good morning, Mr. Talisman," the executive secretary greeted me with a British accent, revealing her Bajan roots. "Please follow me."

I followed the tall slender caramel-complexion model type to the wood-and-marble-decorated executive suite, where the board of trustees would be meeting.

At exactly 10:45 a.m., the sixteen board members began to file in, one after the other.

I had to admit that the diversity of the board was encouraging and representative of New York City power brokers from all five boroughs. Men and women were almost equally represented, with one or two more women. The human spectrum was also well represented with black, brown, and white people present. The age range of the members was wide, from about thirty to sixty-five. The attire of all was strictly business, as the presentation was likely going to influence how they would invest some of their philanthropic dollars over the next ten years. I was in my signature navy-blue Armani suit with a matching navy-blue suede boots with zippers on both sides and a white button-down linen shirt with cuff links and no tie. The sun-bleached puka-shell necklace was on full display.

Fifteen board members had entered when the next-to-last person appeared across the threshold. It was Nina Mendez.

My eyes locked on her in surprise as she gave a quick glance and smile, unnoticeable to anyone else in the room. The board members took their seats around the oval-shaped mahogany table. I stood at the exact opposite end from Nina. We were at the farthest ends of the table. The chairwoman of the board was an older black woman with a lioness's mane of white-silver hair. She sat midway on the side of the table that faced the door, with her back to the windows.

"Welcome, Mr. Talisman," the chairwoman welcomed me. "The foundation board members have read your seminal work on the idea of philanthropy, so much so that we wanted to hear from you on ideas that may influence our work around this country, supporting organizations whose missions are social justice and equity."

"Thank you, Madame Chairwoman," I began my address. "What is a philanthropic mind-set, and why should you want to develop one? The idea of a philanthropic mind-set was born out of wonderings about the state of humanity and a curiosity as to our purpose for being. I am not so mad as to suggest that I know our sense of purpose. I will submit that deep at our core instinctual levels, we all crave to know, sense, or understand our purpose for being. It is arguable that we also have a sense of that purpose. We either fear its power for us and/or it has been beaten out of most of us in one way or another. So what is a philanthropic mind-set? Let's first establish a working definition of *mind-set*. Mind-set is, very simply, the state of your mind at any given moment or the general state of one's mind. For example, if you want to lose weight, most people think about a plan or strategy to lose weight, and they set goals. But why is it that some people succeed, and some do not? I say it is the mind-set. The individual who truly wants to lose weight, wants to keep it off, understands that a lifestyle change must occur. The core idea is that the mind-set must understand the fundamental purpose of losing weight. That purpose must be able to sustain the action needed to keep the weight off. Hence, a lifestyle change. Your mind-set is the activation center that determines success or failure. Discipline is the main ingredient to developing a productive mind-set. It is the willingness and ability to activate and sustain purposeful action toward maintaining a philanthropic mind-set. Let us define *discipline* as having the self-control to do what you have to do to achieve a desired result, even when you do not feel like doing it. You say you want to learn to cook, and you sign up for the course that will take several months to complete and requires attendance a few Saturdays a month. The third Saturday, it is cold and rainy, and you 'tied one on' last night. You decide to skip class. An exercise in the lack of discipline as defined herein. These are some of the character-development skills we must attain to live the life we want. The guy standing next to you in the cooking class may just want it more than you do. Maybe he's just more disciplined. Creating and developing a philanthropic mind-set requires discipline. Philanthropy is defined as engaging in endeavors to advance the well-being of humanity or the human race. The premise is that there is one race of people, and that is the human race. Our current definition of *race* is a social construct designed to divide and conquer the people."

I canvased the room and saw all eyes focused on me. My eyes landed on Nina last, and there I stayed, silenced for what seemed like eternity. Nina gave a subtle nudge of her head as if to say, "Continue."

"So my proposal to you is this. Allow me to facilitate a series of workshops for all of the CEOs of the nonprofit organizations that you fund, in order to develop their sense of a philanthropic mind-set."

There seemed to be a reflective pause before the chairwoman began to clap, followed by similar applause from all.

"Thank you for the thought-provoking presentation, Mr. Talisman," the chairwoman offered. "The board will convene privately, and then we'll have a brief Q and A followed by a decision whether to proceed to the next stage, which is the details of a contracted partnership and all that would entail."

She ended with the directive, "We'll take a fifteen-minute recess before we reconvene. Mr. Talisman, please give us half an hour before the Q and A."

Several members shook my hand on the way out of the conference room. Nina was last, and as she approached me, she gently grabbed my elbow and led me to the elevator.

"Hey, stranger," she whispered.

"Hello, Nina," I returned. "I'm surprised to see you here."

"Is that a bad thing?" she questioned.

"Not at all. It is a beautiful thing, I suppose. Just surprising. What happened at Girls Who Work?"

"Success happened," Nina said matter of factly. "The Trust Family Foundation became our biggest donor and liked our work and the work I did with Girls Who Work—so much that they made me an offer I couldn't refuse."

"And what was that?" I asked curiously.

The elevator doors opened, and Nina gave me a nudge inside as she stayed in the hallway.

"The chance to change the mind-set of decision makers across the country."

As the elevator doors closed, she enticed me with, "See you in thirty!"

I ended up across the street at the Blue Ribbon Brasserie with its white tablecloth service and expansive wooden bar with gold railing.

"Grey Goose martini, dirty. Three olives," I requested.

"Right away, sir," the bartender responded.

It was shortly after midday, and though the bar was not completely empty, there was enough room at the bar so that the stools on either side of me were empty.

The bartender poured a perfect martini, and I drank it perfectly. I took my time with each measured swallow, placing the glass to rest on the bar between each sip. All the while I contemplated the idea of securing the contract and all that it would mean and the meaning of reconnecting with Nina in a most serendipitous way. The vibration of my phone interrupted my contemplation.

"They're ready for you, Mr. Talisman," the executive assistant's voice cooed across the telephone line.

I secured the contract that entailed five years of facilitating quarterly meetings with CEOs and executive directors of nonprofit organizations from around the country that were funded by the Trust Family Foundation.

A week later, Nina and I met for a celebratory dinner at The River Café, which sat on the river's edge on the Brooklyn side of the East River, overlooking downtown Manhattan.

"I guess congratulations all around are in order," I said as I raised the crystal flute of champagne to clink with Nina's glass.

"I agree," she returned. "You have secured the most lucrative contract in your young upstart consulting firm."

"And you," I interrupted, "have embarked on your journey to change the world."

"I think we're both committed to doing that," Nina chimed.

Our waiter brought the appetizers. I had the pear salad with roasted Anjou pears and toasted pumpkin seeds. Nina enjoyed the handmade ricotta gnocchi. For the main course, Nina ravished the Colorado rack of lamb with arugula pesto while I chowed down on the Mediterranean Sea Bass fillet. It was a meal for kings and queens.

"So, Ms. Mendez," I began. "Is your boyfriend still around?"

"What are you talking about?" She seemed startled in her response.

"Well, last I inquired, you were in a relationship."

"And to whom did you inquire?"

"The secretary at Girls Who Work."

Nina delicately put her fork to rest on the edge of the china plate.

"You mean to tell me that you asked about my relationship status over two years ago?"

"I do not recall it being quite two years, but yeah, I asked about your status early on."

"Early on," Nina laughed. "I can't believe you."

Her face became flush.

"You okay?" I asked.

"Yes. Why do you ask?"

"Because your face became very…" I hesitated. "Flush."

"I'm good," she chuckled. "Why didn't you say anything?"

"What was there to say? You were in a relationship, and I did not have any reason to think you would be out of it, and we were working together, so I fell back."

"Why are you asking me now? We still work together."

"Technically, yes," I answered. "But not directly, as in we won't be in the same office every day. In fact, I probably won't see you that often. And it has been one to two years since I last inquired, and things change in that time. So are you going to answer the question?"

Nina let out a hearty laugh that turned some heads in curiosity. She immediately noticed the attention she had attracted and lowered her energy to bring calm. She inhaled deeply and swallowed some champagne before clearing her throat.

"I am not currently in a relationship," she announced. "And you?" she asked before drinking more champagne.

"I am not in a relationship."

With that, we were off into the courting game. We talked about everything we needed to know to ascertain the direction of our budding relationship. We talked about our families. Nina was the oldest of seven siblings. We shared our family histories and how our families came to New York City. We discussed various topics such as sports and politics.

We were so engrossed in the conversation that we did not notice that we were the sole remaining dining party. The wait staff graciously gave us the space to be.

When we walked outside of the restaurant, our cars were waiting for us as the valet stood shivering in the cool night air, standing close to a portable heater.

"Thank you." I tipped him for both cars.

"You are welcome, sir," he replied.

I walked Nina to her car door that was already open. The first embrace was always key for me because it was filled with anxiety and anticipation. We flowed into each other's arms and stayed for a moment.

When we unclenched, we stood close, eyes locked.

"Let's do this again," Nina offered.

"It would be my pleasure," I returned.

And so began the season of Nina and Maximus. We were inseparable for almost six months. We did everything together, including attending my college reunion and traveling to amateur golf tournaments up and down the East Coast.

In month seven of our courtship, I proposed marriage to her, and she said yes! We had a destination wedding to Turks and Caicos, renting a home with five bedrooms and an in-ground swimming pool.

We moved into a two-bedroom brick home with a decked-out backyard in Garden City, Long Island. Our home became the center of life for our families, as we often hosted parties and family holiday dinners. We spent plenty of evenings in front of the wood-burning fireplace, drinking red wine and making love on the shaggy carpet. Life was good—until it was not.

Four major events happened within three years of our wedding day. The first, Nina gained thirty pounds within our first year of being married. It was not so much the fact that she gained weight. It was the circumstances under which she gained weight. Mind you, I never stopped making love to her because of it.

When I first met her, she was in the gym three times a week. Our first date was a spinning class. We hired a personal trainer four months before our wedding. I thought working out was a lifestyle. It turned out to be a passing fancy.

The second event surrounded the idea of the micro-aggressions that I experienced as a black man almost on a daily basis. When I say a daily basis, I am not exaggerating, and it was not always from a racist perspective of white people perpetrating the aggressions. There were times when it came from black women and Caribbean people who saw a difference because I was born in Brooklyn.

The racist interactions were the most painful, and I thought Nina would be a comfort and at least a sounding board. There were too many times when we went to dinner only to find ourselves to be the only minority couple—and a mixed minority couple at that.

"Good evening," the hostess would always greet us kindly. "Do you have reservations?"

"Yes," Nina would often respond. "Talisman is the last name."

We had adopted the habit of Nina responding because for some reason, people seemed to respond easier to her as opposed to responding to me. There seemed to be a slight tell of struggle to wrap their minds around the energy that came from my black body.

"Right this way, Miss," the hostess would direct us.

Hello! I would scream in my head. *I'm right here as well!*

Many times we would have to specify seating before we arrived, especially when we were familiar with the layout of the restaurant. If we did not, we found ourselves in the time-out area near the kitchen or the bathroom, having bypassed several empty tables.

"Excuse me," I would stop the hostess just before she arrived at the designated table. "Is it possible for us to sit here?" I would point to a more desirable table.

"Yes," came the hesitant response, which was more the norm than not.

There was the occasional "I'm sorry; those tables are reserved."

"Hello," the waiter would introduce himself or herself. "I will be your waiter for the evening."

"Good evening," we would return in our most pleasant voices as the waiter poured our water.

Then the waiter was gone just long enough for me to wonder what was taking so long.

"Are you ready to order?" he or she would ask ever so gently so that I could not tell if it was sincere or dripping with sarcasm.

Having grown used to it taking so long on many occasions, I got into the habit of ordering everything at once.

As you can imagine, it took an extraordinary time for food to be served. This was relative to other couples being served before us who arrived at the restaurant after us. These couples were white.

"Dinner was wonderful, babe," Nina would begin in the car ride home.

"The food was delicious, but the experience was bullshit," I would return.

"What do you mean?" she would ask.

"Really?" I replied with disbelief. "The blatant disrespect in service because we're black."

"I do not think it was that, hon," Nina offered.

"If not, then what was it?"

"Maybe they were busy."

This became a pattern between us, and I grew tired of explaining my worldview. I began giving Nina the side-eye to ask how she could not see what I saw.

The third blow to our marriage came at my birthday party that Nina threw for me in our home on September 27, 2014. As usual, ever since we moved to Long Island, we hosted events that represented not only our diversity but our commitment to diversity, though our neighborhood did not represent the same.

I recall the first Saturday after we moved out there. I went to retrieve the weekend edition of the *New York Times* from the lawn where the newspaper boy had flung it. I was in my robe and slippers, probably stumbling from a night's drinking. It was not until I had already picked up the paper and was rising from my stooped position before turning to head into the house that I saw them, and they saw me. Three families—husbands and wives with two to four children each, all Orthodox Jews—were walking in the street on their way to synagogue. I later learned that Saturday was their Sabbath and that they did not use electricity or, apparently, gas since they were walking and not driving.

"Where have I decided to live?" I would ask myself regularly.

Nina was a creative hostess. She was organized and precise, with no detail going unnoticed. I had played golf on my birthday the following Saturday at the annual tournament I hosted for sixteen of my golfing buddies. When we returned to the house after the round, several guests were already present, along with several people I did not know. Since moving into the neighborhood, Nina had come to make friends with many neighbors, all of whom were…drumroll, please…white.

As night wore on, and everyone was seemingly having a grand time as food and drink flowed, I happened to bump into two guys standing in the hallway near the kitchen, which passed to the backyard. Antonio, Nina's brother-in-law, was chatting with a friend of his who had tagged along to the party with him.

Antonio was Greek and proud of it. He was squat at five feet seven and 190 pounds. He worked for the transit department in the railroad division, fixing the tracks. He was in the ironworkers union, and he spent most of his days underground.

"Maximus," Antonio exclaimed. "Dude, your parties are epic!"

"Thank you," I returned. "Glad you're enjoying yourself."

"Your wife is the best. You are so lucky!"

"Yes, she is," I answered.

"Pardon my manners," Antonio continued. "Let me introduce you." He moved aside to present his friend. "Maximus, this is Dan. Dan, Maximus."

Dan and I shook hands firmly.

"Dan and I work together," Antonio announced.

The small talk continued to shrink until there was nothing left to say to fill the space of silence. It was a month removed from the Michael Brown execution in Ferguson, Missouri, and I was curious to get the perspective of white men who were in my house.

"So what do you think of the Michael Brown killing?" I flat out asked.

"Was that the one where the cop shot the guy in the street, and they did not come get his body for hours?" Antonio asked.

"Yes," I answered.

Dan stood with his eyes diverted to the floor. Antonio took a deep breath and looked at the ceiling. I stared at Antonio.

"He should have listened to the police officer," Antonio said flatly and matter of factly.

"That doesn't justify the cop shooting an unarmed man," I countered.

"I heard that he struggled with the officer and that the officer feared for his life," Antonio responded.

"What did the officer stop him for in the first place?" I asked, knowing the answer.

"I honestly do not know," said Antonio.

"For walking in the street," I answered my question.

We went back and forth for a few minutes more before I realized that we were not going to agree. The tone of the conversation was cordial enough, but still Antonio's disposition turned my stomach because we were in my house, and he did not have the sense of etiquette to dodge the question as politely as possible, or he just did not give a fuck. Perhaps I should not have asked the question.

Nonetheless, I bid good night, walked upstairs, and went to bed as the party was winding down.

Nina roused me from a drunken state about a half hour later.

"Babe, you okay?" she rubbed my back gently.

"Yes."

"What happened? Why did you come upstairs?"

"I thought it best before I cursed out some of your guests."

"Oh. Okay. Do you feel like coming downstairs to say goodbye to the last guests leaving?"

"No. I do not think that's a good idea. Just tell them I don't feel well. Too much to drink. Whatever."

I was not a "whatever" person, but once I had gotten there, usually I had reached the point of no return.

Finally, the most significant blow to the marriage was the controversy around whether to have a baby.

Just before deciding to date exclusively, I had asked Nina, "So how do you feel about babies?"

"I do not need to have a baby. I'm the oldest of seven siblings, and I've raised them like a mother, so I'm good," she had ended with a laugh.

"That's cool because I'm not looking to have children."

A year into the marriage she said, "I want to have a baby."

"What am I supposed to do with that?" I asked.

"What do you mean?" she returned.

"I mean, I understand that you apparently changed your mind, but I haven't changed mine."

"So I guess the fact is that I love you enough not to have a baby, but you don't love me enough to have a baby," Nina declared.

"That's not fair," I replied.

I would remain committed to Nina, but it would come with many nuances.

My work with the Trust Family Foundation had come to an end almost a year before Nina and I were married. I decided to work with community-based organizations that were more local and grassroots in the neighborhoods of Brooklyn that were closer to where I grew up. Basically, I bypassed the money for the work. I would supplement my income as a consultant with a few high-paying clients, but my passion was the underdog who could never afford my expertise. It was through my work with the Brownsville Recreation Center, known as the BRC, that I met Wanda.

Wanda was a single mom who desperately sought a male role model for her son since his dad had abdicated his responsibilities. Though she had been in Brooklyn since she was twelve years old, she was straight off the boat from Trench Town, Jamaica. Wanda was sassy, salty, and prideful, even if it meant acting against her own best interest at times. But she was willing to learn and grow under the right conditions.

I had been noticing her off and on for about a year. Whenever I went to the BRC, typically once a week, I would see her picking up her son or dropping him off. I never spoke to her, and she never seemed to even glance my way, but I always saw her dancer's booty and thighs. I once remarked to the program director of the BRC, "Who is that?" as Wanda walked her nine-year-old son out of the BRC one evening.

"Mm-hmm, Mr. Talisman," the program director responded. "I've seen you checking her out."

"A man can window-shop, can't he?" I answered.

"Who am I to judge?" she returned. "That's Ms. Bryceson. Her son is in the science-and-technology program here at the BRC."

I stood admiring her walk away from afar.

It would be months before there was any further mention or contact with Wanda.

In fact, it was February of the following year before I would see Wanda again. It was just after the most recent nor'easter dumped more than a foot of snow on New York. I was on my way to the local cleaners, and I saw her at the bus stop.

"Hey, you," I called.

She hesitated until she recognized me through my car window. "Hey, sir," she responded respectfully.

"You need a ride?" I offered.

"Sure. I'm actually headed to meet a friend. We're headed to the city to see *The Dr. Oz Show.*"

It hit me that I was not prepared to go nearly as far as she wanted. I had a meeting directly after stopping by the cleaners. I had imagined that she was not traveling far in the aftermath of the snowstorm.

"I'm so sorry," I began. "I thought you were going a short distance. I have a meeting in half an hour."

"No worries," she answered. "Perhaps another time."

I felt bad, but not bad enough to drive her.

A week had passed when I arrived at my temporary office in the BRC to find a sunflower plant awaiting me on my desk.

The note read, "Thank you for the offer of the ride. Glad to know that chivalry isn't dead." It was signed, "Wanda—949.518.1748." And I hadn't actually given her a ride.

Here I was, almost to be engaged, and I felt like I was being courted. I was flattered but disciplined enough to take no action save for a phone call.

"Hello?" came Wanda's voice in the form of a question from the other end of the connection.

"Good morning," I replied. "This is Max. I offered you a ride that day after the blizzard?"

"Yes, I remember," she returned with animation. "How are you?"

"I am well; thank you. And you?"

"Everything is good. Thank you for asking," Wanda answered.

"I was calling to say thank you for the plant."

"You are welcome," she replied.

"But I did not actually give you a ride."

"That's okay. It was the thought that counts."

It would be springtime before I would see or speak with Wanda again. I was on my way out of the BRC to meet a friend for lunch as she was walking in. We stopped close to one another, just before we would have bumped into each other. She wore sunglasses on this cloudless day.

"Hey, stranger," I began.

"Hello, Mister," Wanda replied.

"Long time. How have you been?"

"Better now that spring is here," she answered.

"I hear you. Winter is not my friend—more so because it's always dark. It is dark in the morning when I wake up, and it's dark at night when I go home."

"I know, right?" Wanda returned. "It can be depressing."

"Indeed. But spring is here, so let's take advantage of the daylight hours. Good to see you."

I turned to walk away, when Wanda called to me.

"Max."

I turned to face her.

"Can I ask you a question?"

"Yes," I responded with curiosity.

"Do you ever go out?" she invited me.

There it was. The invitation.

As I have grown into a man over the years, I have come to know myself. For me, it is better to avoid temptation entirely than to resist it.

"Well, I do go out," I answered. "Why do you ask?"

"I'm just asking."

"Are you asking me out?" I challenged playfully.

"No, not really. Do you want me to ask you out?"

"That depends," I started while contemplating the consequences of saying yes.

How much do I say by way of shedding light on my current relationship status?

"Let me say this," I continued. "Can we meet to talk about it?"

Wanda's brow furled enough to say that she was cautiously optimistic.

"Are you married?" she asked.

"No," I answered. "But we should talk."

"Sure, okay," she replied. "You want to stop by my house to talk?"

Here we go with the invitations again.

It was dark and raining three nights later when I went to Wanda's house. It was difficult to make out the house number, but I found the right one. I rang the bell, and after less than two minutes, the door opened.

"Hi, hi," came Wanda's pleasant voice as she pushed the screen door open.

"Good evening," I returned.

"Come in, and make yourself comfortable," Wanda offered. "Just take your shoes off."

I looked around as Wanda went to the kitchen.

"Would you like something to drink?" she asked. "A glass of wine?"

"Yes, thank you," I responded.

We moved to the couch when Wanda returned to the living room area. We saluted each other with a celebratory clink of crystal wine goblets filled with red wine.

"Cheers," she celebrated.

"Salud," I saluted her back.

"So, Mr. Man," Wanda initiated. "Tell me why we need a discussion before we go out."

"The fact of the matter," I began, "is that I am in a relationship—"

"But you're not married, correct?" Wanda interrupted.

"Correct," I answered.

However, I did not disclose my plans to get engaged to Nina. Why? Selfishness. I was flattered by and enamored with Wanda. Maybe I just wanted to fuck around a little longer until I became fully committed.

Wanda and I dated for about three months before I told her that I was getting engaged to Nina in a mere couple of months.

"Wow, Max," she stammered as we sat at the bar at Suede, the newly opened West Indian restaurant in Brooklyn. "I thought you were different. I guess I was wrong."

Wanda kissed me softly on the cheek before she walked her heavy walk that made her hips sway out the door of the restaurant.

I would go on to marry Nina, and I would not hear from Wanda for over a year. After the Mike Brown fiasco at Thanksgiving, I received a text message from Wanda.

It read "Happy Thanksgiving, Max. Thinking of you. Wishing you and your family all the best."

It is worth paying attention to the timing of the universe.

It is never in the plan for men and women to cheat after they marry, but obviously it happens all the time. Though I was about to enter that realm, it was never my intention to divorce. I was all about the "for better or worse and until death do us part" thing.

I met Wanda at a lounge near Coney Island that catered to West Indian clientele. I waited at the bar until she arrived fashionably late, about twenty minutes after I did. It gave me a chance to enjoy a cocktail alone at the bar, which was one of my favorite activities to engage in as I gathered my thoughts.

"Hey, hey," she greeted me in her singsong voice.

"Hey, stranger," I responded. We hugged politely.

We caught up on the time we had been out of touch before my curiosity could not be contained further.

"So, Ms. Wanda," I started. "I thought you were done with me after you found out I was engaged and now married."

"I was," she answered. "But I realized that I love you, and my feelings tell me that I want to be with you."

I almost staggered off of the barstool as her words came in the form of blows. I was blown away.

Wanda and I would see each other, on average, once a month. Every four months or so, we would travel out of state together as I was starting to pick up clients nationally. My feelings for Wanda grew to the point that I was having a full-fledged relationship with her. I decided that if I was going to have an affair, it would not be with a woman who was not worth the risk and consequences, and it was not going to be with women, plural. Wanda was worth it. My morality was at question, and hard decisions had to be made. It is amazing what narratives we tell ourselves in order to be able to live with ourselves and even to be able to look into our own eyes in the mirror when we brush our teeth in the morning. When was the last time you stared at yourself? I mean looking into your own eyes in the mirror for a solid minute? Try it. I dare you.

"Where do you see yourself five years from now?" Wanda asked the dreaded question.

It was such a broad question. Did she mean in terms of my professional career, my personal life, my health, where I planned to live? What?

"Are you asking where I see us?" I attempted to narrow the focus of the question.

"Yes. Sure," Wanda sounded relieved that she did not have to ask me directly.

"I really cannot say because I do not spend time trying to predict the future, let alone even plan for it at times. You know what they say about plans, don't you?"

"No," Wanda deadpanned.

"If you want to make God laugh," I started. "Tell him your plans."

"What does that mean?" Wanda asked in disbelief.

"It means if your plans are not aligned to God's plans, then you are probably wasting your time."

"So you don't plan?"

"No. I mean, yes, I plan, but I am also open to the idea that if my plans do not work out, it's not the end of the world."

"So where do you see us?"

"I can see us being together, if that's what you're asking. However, I have no plans to leave my wife."

There, I said it, and I felt good that I had put it out there so that Wanda could make an informed decision.

"I'm good with that," she began. "I think the three of us can be together. That would be cool."

In my mind, she had said the magic words. I didn't know too many guys who would not covet such a proposition—and not necessarily for the seemingly obvious reason, which was a good enough reason in itself. Another idea that welcomed such a scenario was the elimination of the lying and cheating.

I have had this conversation with so many men and women in so many bars around the country that I have exhausted the topic. The gist is that there are many paths to the same mountaintop of relationship bliss. Marital monogamy is one of them but is not the only one and may not even be the preferred path. Remember "The Road Not Taken"? I have often pondered the alternatives to monogamy because it not only has been elusive to me but apparently to roughly half the people who attempt it and especially among those of us who try it more than once. It should not be that hard. Let's not talk about the numbers. If every man were with one woman, there would be swarms of women around the world who would be single. But I digress.

I was honored and flattered that Wanda would be open to such a scenario, but I was especially amazed that she had offered it, which was totally different than if I proposed it. I stared into her eyes, stung to silence by her words. She stared back.

"What?" Wanda questioned. "What can I say except that I love you?"

"Thank you for loving me in that way," I returned.

Wanda and I would continue to date for months before Nina would find out about Wanda.

Prior to meeting Nina, I was used to going on several trips a year, either with the boys or alone. Past destinations included Vegas, Saint Thomas, and

Martha's Vineyard. So it was an easy sell to say to Nina that I was going on one of my usual vacations. Except I was not alone or with the boys.

In late August that year, Wanda and I flew to Nantucket, Massachusetts, for a three-day getaway. The first night we were there, I received a text from Nina.

"I know you're there with Wanda! You need to bring your ass home now."

"What are you talking about?" I immediately texted back. My stomach turned in knots that she knew Wanda's full name.

A few minutes passed before Nina responded with a screenshot of the flight reservation that she had found on my laptop.

I went out on the balcony of the hotel room and called Nina.

"What are you doing going through my personal shit?" I demanded to know.

"The better question is, what are you doing in Nantucket with your side bitch?"

"You have no right going through my computer, Nina!"

"And you have no right being away with another woman. You need to come home now."

I couldn't remember hanging up the phone because I could not think in the moment. It must have been an instinctive response born out of happenstance, because when I checked to see if my phone was off, it was. *What just happened?* and *What am I going to do?* were my immediate thoughts. I actually lost track of time and space in the sense that I forgot where I was for a moment until Wanda joined me on the balcony.

"Is everything okay?" she asked as she placed her hand gently in the middle of my lower back.

"No. That was Nina. She knows we're here," I replied flatly.

"Oh my God," Wanda gasped. "How did she find out?"

"She went through my laptop."

"Fuck," Wanda exclaimed.

"Fuck is right."

We were quiet for some time after that. The television was on, but I didn't remember watching it—the words the actors said sounded as if they were under water. Wanda comforted me that evening as we fell asleep without a word between us.

It would stay that way until the next morning as we caught the first flight back to New York. We said our goodbyes and hugged.

"I'll call you when I can," I offered.

"Okay. No worries," Wanda replied softly.

I hailed a taxi for her, and then I walked to my car in the short-term parking area.

As I was driving home, my cell phone rang through the car's speakers.

"Hey," I answered.

"Yeah," Wanda began. "I was thinking that maybe we should stop seeing each other so you can give your marriage a chance or until you can figure out what you want to do."

I paused in thought before answering, "No, I don't want to do that. I'm figuring it out."

"Okay, then," Wanda returned. "I love you."

"Love you too."

After parking my car at the house, the fifteen steps that it took to get to the front door were among some of the slowest and longest that I had ever taken. Putting the key in the door to unlock it was even slower. Time itself was in slow motion.

Nina was sitting at the dining room table, waiting for me. She had been crying tears through bloodshot eyes.

I set down my leather travel bag, walked meekly to the table, and sat directly across from her. Nina never took her eyes off of me.

I offered a contrite "Hey."

"Hey," she returned with sadness. "What's been going on, Maximus?"

"You know what's going on, Nina."

"Obviously," she came back immediately.

"I mean..." I started again. "Yes, I have been seeing someone."

I went on to explain that I had been seeing Wanda for months, even adding details of how we met. I offered that I had not initiated the affair and that I had avoided temptation as best I could, but in the end I could not resist. I went on to explain that the lack of discipline, restraint, and resistance was born out of our recent struggles from the micro-aggressions to the baby dilemma.

"Well, we took vows," Nina exclaimed.

"Agreed."

"So there are rules to this shit, Maximus. And being faithful is one of them. You need to stop seeing her."

"I'm not prepared to do that," I answered.

"What do mean, you are not prepared to do that?" Nina stormed.

"I mean that I have told Wanda that I am not going to leave you, and she said that she was cool with the three of us being together, so I think the three of us should sit down and figure it out somehow."

Nina gave me a wild-eyed side-look before almost stammering her words.

"You are on some real Mafia *gumar* shit, huh?" Nina exclaimed.

"I don't know what I'm on. I'm just trying to figure it out, and I want us to figure it out together."

"So let me get this straight," Nina began. "You want me to be your wife and to allow you to have a mistress?"

It sounded crazy coming out of her mouth versus the idea in my head.

"Yes..." I hesitated. "At least for now. I don't know what I'm doing, frankly, but I feel it is something I have to go through."

"Do you love her?"

"I have feelings for her."

Nina stared through me.

"You love her," she exclaimed in disbelief.

What was I going to say?

"Okay," Nina continued. "If you're going to see her, then I want to see other men."

"Of course I don't want that," I started. "But to be fair, I have to agree. Even though I don't think you really want to do that. I think you're doing it because I am."

Nina could not take any more. She grabbed the glass that was half-filled with red wine and hurled it past my head, shattering it against the wall.

"Fuck you, Maximus!" Nina stormed out of the room and up the stairs, slamming the bedroom door behind her.

We lived separately but in the same house for months, passing one another in the kitchen on occasion. We made a few attempts at reconciliation—residue sex from memories before living in a marriage set in—to no avail. Divorce was inevitable.

Wanda and I continued to see each other, but the circumstances of our union weighed heavy, and our closeness waned.

THE FIFTH DIMENSION

When my dad died from a brain aneurysm on my twenty-first birthday, I was struck by the notion of where his spirit would go in the afterlife. By virtue of the fact that I was born in a westernized Christian country, it ensured that I would most likely grow up with westernized Christian values such as "people who do not believe in Jesus go to hell." If that were true, it would mean that my father went to hell for being a Muslim. I was not then, nor am I now, ready to accept that belief.

Two experiences at his funeral have remained forever stained upon my brain. The first was that I learned that like Jews, Muslims also have a tradition of burying their dead within three days of death, and in doing so, are spared the process of defiling the body with embalming fluid.

As such, my dad's body was shrouded in white linen cloth and initially placed in a modest pinewood box. The simple beauty of it all mesmerized me.

There were no official pallbearers. It was me and other close relatives. At one point, we had to transfer his body from the wooden box to the cement vault that would be placed in the ground. It was said that this was necessary because otherwise there would be too many layers between the body and the earth to which the body would return. That meant that we had to actually lift my dad's body out of one box and place it into another.

Have you ever lifted a lifeless body? Neither had I until then. It was surreal—like, of course the body is heavy. That's where the phrase *deadweight* comes from. Now I knew what that felt like. I was holding his feet with the help of one of his brothers. Two other relatives supported his midsection and shoulder and head area. During the transfer, one of the guys supporting his shoulders lost his grip, which put pressure on the guy holding his midsection, causing him to let go. My dad's head fell to the floor. We stopped in our tracks.

Ouch, I thought. *That must hurt.*

That was when I realized my father was dead, that his body was lifeless.

Max, I said in my head. *Of course that didn't hurt. He can't feel that. Your father is dead.*

Still holding on to my dad's feet, I fell to my knees and let out an instinctual guttural wail of painful realization. I followed this with almost hysterical laughter about the fact that I had actually thought that dropping my dead father's head on the floor would hurt him. Thus began a quest to reignite the flame of spiritual journey that had begun in my youth.

"Mommy, why is it that good things happen to bad people?" I had begun asking my mother at eight years old. "And bad things happen to good people?"

"What do you mean?" my mother had replied.

"I mean, people like Aunt LouAnn who goes to church all the time are poor while some people who do not even believe in God are rich?"

"Just because people are rich doesn't mean they're going to heaven."

While that may have been true, for an eight-year-old, it did not make much sense—the whole "your reward is in heaven" thing. As I grew older—and people like Q were murdered, and Tuma was traumatized, and Roxanne sexually abused me—I began to wonder, where was God?

Through reading and research, the more I learned, the further I moved away from organized religion to a universal concept of God and spirituality. These days, I am more likely to say, "The universe conspires on our behalf," than I am to say, "God bless you."

Recently, I heard the rapper KRS-One speak about the concept of the fifth dimension—the narrative within our head, the unspoken words in our minds. Who or what is it? What is the origin? Whose voice is speaking inside your head? How do memories reside in your being? The big idea was the role of sound or the absence thereof. He talked about the four dimensions within the context of 3-D—as in our physical being is three dimensional, bound by time.

1. Up-Down
2. Right-Left
3. Front-Back
4. Time

According to KRS-One, there is a fifth dimension, which is...drumroll, please...In-Out!

KRS used the Socratic seminar method of posing questions to provoke thought. *Is there sound when you say words in your mind? Where does that sound come from? Can you see when your eyes are closed, or is that insight? When it comes to images in your mind, can you see your past and future? What sight sees beyond time?* When he talked about existence without the body, he was speaking about the fifth dimension, which is *in* and *out*.

This understanding allowed me to transcend the physical experiences I have incurred. Connecting with my being in silence and meditation, I have been, at times, able to transcend the three-dimensional world. This is why it is important to spend time alone with your inner voice—your being. You are the inner voice that writes the narrative of your physical experiences. This is the freedom that I have sought. When I think about it, I realize that this is the space I went to when Tank pushed me over the third-floor railing!

I've had dreams of this sense of being beginning from my childhood. I recall having dreams of being chased by Frankenstein, Dracula, and a werewolf through a wooded area at night. There was dense fog, and I ran until I stopped in my tracks at the edge of a cliff. Because of the elevation of the cliff, the clouds were too dense to see what lay below. With the monsters closing in, I had to make a decision. I leaped into the unknown.

This was when the outer experience occurred. As I saw myself floating through the clouds and was finally able to see the earth—and nothing but green earth—my free fall sped up until I saw myself enter my bedroom through the ceiling. My spirit-being floated back into my physical body that was lying asleep on the bed. I entered myself, and I awoke.

People will hurt as long as we are separated from one another on this physical plane. All souls will constantly ache in the spiritual plane because as long as one of us suffers, all of us do. I submit that because of the darkness in my life, I am able to appreciate sunrises and sunsets and moonlit nights. Through reading as a child and travel as an adult, I have escaped the microcosm of my world to experience a broader view of our planet and its people. Therefore I seek the feeling of being high from eating weed brownies without actually eating them. I want the freedom and clarity that happens in the presence of marijuana without the ganja. I want to sustain that essence in a natural state.

The ancestors used to say, "Get right with God!"

WE ARE OUR BODY OF WORK

We have a choice—think deeply about the *why* of life's experiences, meaning, and purpose: Why do events happen to us and not to others? What is fair, and what is not? Or just say, "Fuck it; life is random, and fuck it," and become survivalist in action—or a combination thereof?

I did not have the luxury of growing up in an environment made safe by adults. When that becomes your norm, you learn to find some measure of comfort in uncomfortable conditions, and you do the best you can with what you have. Kahlil Gibran references the dream of how I wished it to be in his book *The Prophet*: "Would that I could gather your houses into my hand, and like a sower scatter them in forest and meadow. Would the valleys were your streets, and the green paths your alleys, that you might seek one another through vineyards, and come with the fragrance of the earth in your garments."

Alas, that was not my road to travel.

—

How in the world did I get here? I often ask myself.

I never aspired to be an educator. To the contrary—it was the last career on my mind. As noted earlier, my mom was an elementary school music teacher. My dad was an educator, as was his sister and my first cousin. Teaching was the furthest career from my mind, and educational leadership was not on the radar.

After a string of two-year stints at varied jobs, I found myself unemployed after September 11, 2001. At the time, I was trading stocks for a day-trading firm on Fifty-Fourth and Lexington Avenue in Manhattan.

"Hey," Ryan yelled from across the narrow and short trading desk. "Did anyone else hear the news from our partners at the World Trade Center?" he calmly asked.

"No," came the general response, quickly followed by the company's CEO asking, "Why, what happened?"

"Guy said an airplane hit the building," Ryan deadpanned. Ryan was the youngest trader in the firm and therefore inherently the most brash and cocky of the bunch.

"Yeah, right," offered Connor, the golden-haired, blue-eyed man-child of the group.

Within minutes, all of the monitors that scanned the news every minute of the day switched to footage of a second plane hitting the second tower.

I remember the silence—pregnant with shock, denial, surprise, and fear—that suffocated the room. I remember the collective inhale of breath in the room, too, before we all exhaled.

In less than sixty seconds, every one of us moved with urgency to leave the building. Again, silence on the elevator pierced the air as we contemplated the exit strategy home to loved ones.

I made my way to the E train in hopes of getting to Queens as the fastest way out of Manhattan. Not one stop en route, the train jolted to a halt mid tunnel.

"Forty-Second Street will be our next and final stop," came the conductor's mechanical-sounding voice over the loudspeaker.

Surprisingly, all passengers politely positioned themselves to exit the train expeditiously, as orderly as could have been expected under the circumstances. No, better than could ever have been expected under any circumstances.

I broke the surface of the ground, emerging from a crowded subway. I paused to get my bearings as I headed downtown to walk across the Williamsburg Bridge to Brooklyn. After quickly pacing five blocks, I passed by a store with televisions in the window. I assumed it was a TV repair shop or a store that sold new televisions. Every screen reflected the same experience. Planes appeared to have crashed into the Pentagon and a field in Pennsylvania.

We are at war, I declared in my mind, standing temporarily paralyzed. What I meant was that for the first time in my lifetime, war had been brought to mainland United States.

Walking to the foot of the Williamsburg Bridge, I called my mom from a pay phone.

"Hello," she answered groggily, awakened from her sleep.

"Hey, Ma," I responded hurriedly. "Have you seen the news?"

My mom had retired to Albany, and her days now consisted of loneliness and church-filled nights of revivals and evangelism.

"No, sweetie," she replied. "I'm just getting up. What's going on?"

"Planes just hit the Twin Towers!" I shouted just as the second tower was imploding on its base.

Seeing it live was to see life in slow motion, moving irreversibly forward no matter how badly I wanted to reverse or unsee what I was witnessing.

"The second tower is collapsing," I was able to get out of my mouth moments before the final parts collided with the ground.

"Calm down, son," she tried to reassure me. "Surely you're exaggerating. It did not collapse."

"Ma..."

"Oh my God," she replied, having just witnessed it on the television after flipping channels on the remote control.

"Nooo!" I screamed before dropping the phone as I sobbed uncontrollably.

"Hello," my mom's voice echoed in the dangling phone receiver.

I headed for the bridge and never looked back.

Like zombies covered in the gray soot of poisonous chemicals from the now destroyed World Trade Center buildings, people marched across the bridge in shocked silence. New Yorkers became human beings that day, no longer separated by prescribed ethnic barriers and the social construct of race. On the Brooklyn side of the bridge, we were greeted by Orthodox Jews bearing cups of water filled from gallon jugs of unlimited supply. The gesture was significant because under circumstances of any other usual day, Orthodox Jews in Brooklyn moved in self-imposed isolation.

I made it home that day due to the generosity of strangers. Immediately, I staggered to my SUV and made it to my girlfriend's apartment in Sunset Park, where we watched in silence the carnage of the day before dozing off to sleep, huddled tight in each other's arms.

The next day we decided to make our way to Coney Island Beach, where we flew a kite. I remember the day clearly—it was bright and sunny without a cloud in the sky. I also distinctly remember the absence of the usual roar of airplanes taking off and landing from nearby John F. Kennedy International Airport, as the day had been declared a no-fly day across America, save for the flights evacuating Saudi Arabians, which we'd learn about later on.

I recall feeling suspended in a time before the advent of airplanes. *This is what the peaceful sky must have sounded like and looked like*, I thought. I preferred this time to the time in which I found myself living.

I spent the next year drifting, waiting on God and the universe to conspire on my behalf. Becoming an educational leader found me and called to me. I embraced the calling with a knowing that this was my verse to contribute. How else could many of my life's experiences and hauntings be made worth anything, if not to accept a role as steward and protector of unlimited possibilities for children to pursue their verses in a safe environment—one that was never afforded to me?

YOU ARE WHERE YOU ARE MEANT TO BE

In bed by ten o'clock and up by six o'clock. I grocery shop on Tuesdays or Sundays. Once a week I juice one bale of kale, one bale of spinach, two cucumbers, two apples, one pineapple, one bag of carrots, one bag of celery, three garlic cloves, a couple of turmeric and ginger roots, and lemon, all of which lasts three days.

I arrive typically at seven thirty in the morning, which gives me a chance to eat all-natural Raisin Bran cereal in a bowl filled with chocolate almond milk and begin to sip on my daily concoctions as I read the daily newspapers. This has been my daily ritual for the past decade now. I take my last bites and swallow and check my face one last time in the mirror before beginning my workday.

"Good morning, Mr. Talisman!" scream several prekindergarten students as they see me emerge from my office while they take pitter-patter footsteps, following their pied piper teachers.

"Good morning, boys and girls," I return with sincere enthusiasm.

I am the principal of PS 693 elementary school—the Nelson Mandela Institute for Leadership.

Several of the students cannot contain their impulses to embrace me, so they rush to my knees and waist, clambering over each other to exchange hugs with me. I do not fault the teachers for not being able to manage their students from breaking their assigned line spots. Secretly, I want the children to bum-rush me. I need their hugs.

This is a ritual in which I engage at least fifty times a day, 180 days a year. The inviting voices of children wishing me a good morning and me returning the same with mutual authenticity is amazing.

After ensuring that the most vulnerable among us are safe in class, I walk around the entire school, greeting all students up to the senior class of fifth graders. My presence is to say, "You are safe here," which means through a strong work ethic and rigorous instruction, you can have opportunities to explore your purpose for being so that you can make a contribution to the advancement of humanity. One of our catchphrases that embodies the school's purpose is, "What will be my verse?" The idea is for the students to begin to think about what skills and talents they have to develop in order to advance the well-being of their communities and society at large.

I found my lifework as a principal of an elementary school in my hometown, Brooklyn. I get to protect children and to influence parents over the course of one hundred and eighty days of school every year.

I have become the steward of endless possibilities, just as Ms. Miller, my fifth-grade teacher, was to me.

One day while Ms. Miller was teaching reading, I was doodling on a sheet of unlined paper, when she happened to saunter ever so nonchalantly by my desk. I never saw her coming.

"What are you doing?" Ms. Miller asked in the most inviting voice that revealed her Georgian upbringing and, with it, her southern hospitality.

I felt like I was busted doing something wrong, but her voice was so welcoming. I was thinking, *This is a trap!*

"I'm drawing my dream house," I answered her, ready to accept my fate.

"What do you want to be when you grow up, Max?" Ms. Miller asked.

I answered, "A professional football player, an architect, a lawyer, and a sports announcer."

"Wow! That's a lot of professions," she replied. "You may want to get started early so that you can accomplish all that you imagine."

Ms. Miller supported my wildest notions that I could not only grow up to do something really important in one area, but that I could do it all. Looking back on that experience, I now realize that she was one of my guardian angels sent at a specific time in my life's journey. She was a steward of my endless possibilities on my way to finding my purpose, which in and of itself could be thought of as endless.

We all have had a Ms. Miller in our lives—the guardian of the idea that we can create our world. In truth, without them, we can lose our way too early in life to even get a good head start along the long, difficult road of life. Some of our children have lost their stewards too early in their journeys.

—

All things considered, as it is for all of us, the universe continues to conspire on my behalf, as I have found a lifework that gives me purpose. I have heard its cry and given myself to it. You can find your way as well. Start with doing something that helps someone else, which contributes to the well-being of your community. Your purpose will come into view.

SAY HELLO TO THE BAD GUY

So were we the bad guys? It is all relative. Did we know that some of the things we did were wrong and that they hurt people tremendously? Absolutely. Anyone who does these things and does not admit to knowing that it is wrong and hurtful is just lying to themselves because the pain of it all is too acute to admit. Denial is the ointment that temporarily soothes open sores.

Since we knew it was wrong and hurtful, why did we do it? Rarely is it asked of us how we feel when we knowingly hurt other people. We feel shame and pain and guilt. Barely able to look ourselves in the eye when brushing our teeth in the mirror.

"So if you knew what you did was wrong and hurtful, and even though you felt bad about doing it, you still did it. You must be a selfish, egotistical, narcissistic, and coldhearted son of a bitch!"

Guilty as charged. The trigger element that is overlooked is the fact that what we did, knowing the outcomes, occurred in part due to the idea somewhere in our unconscious minds that the wrong and hurt we did was nowhere near as great as the harm inflicted upon us in our youth by our peers and the adults who were responsible to love and protect us.

Nonetheless, I have no regrets. When I reflect on some of my past relationships, I want to go back and tell the women, "Hey, I'm sorry for the pain and trauma that occurred between us. In some regard, I did not know any better, and I did the best I could with what I had and where I was at the time in my life, and the same probably holds true for you." Lying has been a survival mechanism for me in part because I never had a love where I could be honest. I did not see any of these relationships in any intimate way along my path. You know, someone who is your best friend, whom you are committed to, and to whom you can say shit and not worry about hurting their feelings because you know you are going to make it through the rough patches since it comes from a place of genuine love. At least not in a romantic way. I have that with my boys from 369. But that was where we were at the time, trying to figure it out. The experiences served a purpose. The idea was and is to identify the purpose. In many of the romantic cases, it was simply that we were not meant to be a lifetime.

For instance, if you want children, and I do not want children, that's probably a good indicator that we should not be together. And neither of us should be angry with the other. No regrets. That was the way that the universe chose to communicate with us or the way that we allowed the universe to communicate to us that it was time for us to separate in order to move into better places.

This is one of many reasons why black men in particular should not get married until late their thirties or forties—not to sow wild oats but to work on getting our minds and souls right.

And women, black women in particular, have their own shit, which in part is no fault of their own, yet they must not let these things consume them. For example, the world has told my women that they are not beautiful because of their natural hair. And our women have internalized it.

My mom has been wearing a wig for so long, probably going back to her early thirties. I thought it was the thing to do. I did not give it a second thought. It was not until I was well into my forties that I saw my mother's head uncovered for the first time in decades. I was weak in the knees from shock.

There were bald patches randomly spotted around her scalp, with thin patches of hair surrounding the empty spaces. I was devastated by the idea of my mom being reduced to this. The irony is that my maternal grandmother was a hairdresser by trade and ran her own salon.

Seeing the look of disbelief pasted on my face, my mom said, "What? I'm okay with it. This is what happens when you grow up with hot combs for straightening the hair and all of the other stuff my mother used in her salon. Sometimes she'd leave it on your scalp too long until it started to burn," she'd say matter of factly.

In that moment I saw the heads of so many church mothers going to church in their Sunday best with their best wigs on because all of them had several wigs to choose from depending on the occasion. They were made to cover their heads for the vanity of wanting to look like someone else.

When I was young, natural hair on women had a period of being hip, and I grew a love for women with natural hair. Then for most of my adult life, black women have taken hairweaving and other hair alterations to new decorative heights as only our women can. But it is a flaw nonetheless.

Now, I begin to see the cycle shifting back to sisters rocking natural hair in many more ways than just an Afro. Hopefully this is the beginning of an end to the cycle.

As my uncle used to say, "Black people will never be free until our women's hair is free!"

WE DIDN'T ALWAYS SING "GYPSY WOMAN"

My crew and I did good things that kids were supposed to do, and we had great experiences as well. So why is it that we remember the bad over the good? I say it is because the good was age appropriate for where we were developmentally. The bad constituted innocence lost way too early in our lives that forged stained memories upon our DNA forever. Some people talk of abused DNA being passed down through generations. I believe it.

Yet there were plenty of times of joy. I was the most athletic and popular boy at my predominantly all-black private elementary school, with its mostly black staff. Growing up in that culture instilled a sense of self at an early age that said I was just as good as humans from other ethnic groups. I was third in my eight-grade graduating class. I was the class master of ceremonies at the eighth-grade prom. I won a scholarship to play football at a midwestern prep school, and in my first semester of school, I earned the highest grade point average of all students in grades seventh through twelfth.

Growing up in 369, with its twenty-five floors of stacked apartments, we grew up in a ready-made village and played games in the little park such as skelly, coco livio, freeze tag, RCK (Run, Catch, and Kiss—y'all do not know nothin' about none of this!), and hide-and-go-seek. Whoever was "it" last was often left searching as everyone else secretly went home.

Even when one of us would get in trouble for staying out past the time when the streetlights came on, the rest of us would gather around the poor unknowing soul's apartment door and listen while his mom or dad wailed on his ass. Then one of us would bang on the door, and all of us would scatter to our respective apartments on different floors before the door was flung open by angry parents. Our boy would get a moment's reprieve before the ass whupping continued. In a few instances our surprise interruption saved the day.

—

So how is it decided—what we remember? For so long, the traumatic experiences remained with me longer than they otherwise should have because perhaps they are among my earliest life experiences. My psyche was impaled at a vulnerable time when I was not equipped to handle the experiences. Can these experiences be used as springboards when most of us use them as crutches?

"I can't do that because my father was murdered when I was young," one might say.

Another may offer, "Had my aunty not been diagnosed with cancer, I would've been able to go to law school."

Simultaneous to all of the trauma invading my life, there were magical experiences occurring. I still get to enjoy all that matters in the world—good company, good food, and good drink.

Most importantly, I have come to learn that the true measure of a man is not his sexual prowess, stamina, and conquests, especially if you are gifted in those areas. Gifts are a responsibility.

I realize that my idea of manhood was passed down hoochie-coochie style. Sometimes I have wondered if the Gypsy's words were a curse or a blessing in disguise. In many regards, I have lived several lifetimes in my fifty years on this earth. How does one travel between lifetimes without causing pain and suffering?

It was not until well into my forties that I heard the song from which we derived our own bastardization of the idea of "Gypsy Woman." It came from Muddy Waters's song "I'm Your Hoochie Coochie Man." In any event, I told the gypsy that I did not want to be the hoochie-coochie man any longer.

The gypsy woman told my mother
Before I was born
I got a boy-child's comin'
He's gonna be a son-of-a-gun
He's gonna make pretty women's
Jump and shout
Then the world gonna know
What this all about

I got a black cat bone
I got a mojo too
I got John the Conqueror
I'm gonna mess with you
I'm gonna make you girls
Lead me by my hand
Then the world'll know
The hoochie-coochie man

Made in the USA
Middletown, DE
21 January 2020